THE
OVERTHROW OF HAWAII

By

Tropical Tom Radakovich

To Sam, Dolores, Steve, Linda, Sara, and Julie

Thanks to:
Mike
Linda
Hawaii State Archives
Hawaiian Independence web site (www.hawaii-nation.org)

Published by
Nautical Technologies LLC
nautical.tech@yahoo.com

This book is a work of fiction based on actual historic events.

ISBN 978-0-9907286-1-0

CHAPTER 1

Twenty-six-year-old David Coe loved his job. The work was interesting, challenging and would ultimately make him a wealthy man. The early morning sun struck his face as he turned the corner onto Merchant Street in downtown Honolulu. He enjoyed the mild temperatures and refreshing trade winds, stark contrasts to the bitter cold winters in Boston. Pausing for a moment across the street from his office building at the corner of Fort and Merchant Streets, he gazed at the two-story structure known as the Powers Building.

It was one of the first stone buildings in late nineteenth-century Honolulu, built fifteen years earlier from large rectangular blocks of weathered, gray-black volcanic rock. The blocks were once molten lava flowing from one of the two volcanoes forming the island of Oahu a few million years before. Such grand concepts humbled Coe. They were the work of the Lord.

Approaching the hand-carved mahogany door at the building's entrance, he stared at the glass pane in the top half of the door. In gold letters with a black border were the names POWERS, THATCHER, and JAMES, stacked one above the other, centered on the pane, with POWERS on top; below the names, in smaller letters, Attorneys at Law. He focused on the C in THATCHER and the O and E in POWERS. His name was already there, but not in finished format. He would be fulfilled once the scattered letters were assembled to form the three-letter sequence, COE, on the pane.

Coe entered the building and bounded up the stairs to the second floor, his long legs comfortably taking two steps at a time. The large conference room on the right side at the top of the steps was unoccupied. Being thirty minutes early afforded enough time to head into the bathroom and check his appearance.

"Definitely not a matinee idol," he muttered, smiling at his reflection in the full-length mirror. "More like Ichabod." It was a name given to him by a law school classmate. Coe was glad the moniker didn't follow him to Hawaii; however, he easily recognized his general resemblance to Washington Irving's colorful description of Ichabod Crane, the forlorn schoolmaster, in *The Legend of Sleepy Hollow.*

"He was tall, but exceedingly lank, with narrow shoulders, long arms and legs, hands that dangled a mile out of his sleeves, feet that might have served for shovels, and his whole frame most loosely hung together. His head was small, and flat at top, with huge ears, large green glassy eyes, and a long snipe nose, so that it looked like a weather-cock perched upon his spindle neck to tell which way the wind blew."

"I guess I'll just have to get by on my personality," he said, grinning as he left the bathroom and returned to the conference room to find it still empty.

Like the entire second floor, the conference room was plush. Highly polished dark hardwood floors were brightened by off-white walls. Paintings of America's founding fathers, Washington, Jefferson, and Benjamin Franklin, framed in ornately carved dark wood, hung on the walls. In preparation for the upcoming meeting, the room was furnished with a small wooden podium in front and six rows of chairs, five chairs per row, facing the podium.

A single chair stood alone along the side wall, ninety degrees to the others. All the furniture was hand-crafted by skilled New England furniture makers, then shipped around the southern tip of South America to Hawaii. The outside wall featured two large windows that offered spectacular views of Honolulu Harbor and the cobalt-blue Pacific Ocean. Both windows were open, and the refreshing scent of sea air circulated.

Coe made his way to the sixth row and sat in the chair at the end of the row, farthest from the door. He leaned back, lazily placed his left arm across the back of the chair next to him, crossed his legs with his right ankle resting just above his left knee, and looked out the open window. The view of the ocean and the scent of the salty air created an aura of surfing. After a few minutes, the resonance of voices approached from outside in the hall. He returned to a more erect sitting posture as six men entered the room and sat in the first two rows.

For the next ten minutes, others entered one or two at a time and filled the first four rows. All were well-dressed, middle-aged, and Caucasian. A few offered a quick nod, but most did not. Coe recognized almost all of them as clients of the firm. They were sugar plantation owners, the wealthiest men in Hawaii, multi-millionaires. Among them were all five members of the 'big five,' the wealthiest of the wealthy. All the plantation owners were descendants of missionaries who arrived in Hawaii earlier in the century, and, therefore, collectively known as 'mission boys.'

One day, he would be like them, living where they lived and owning what they owned. But, today, he relished the opportunity to be in their presence, see how they acted, and hear what they said.

Ten minutes later, two others entered. Coe watched the first, a large muscular man, probably in his forties, with his head shaved and a robust handlebar mustache tightly waxed at the tips, stride across the front of the room and sit in the lone chair along the side wall. He sat upright, arms folded across his chest, projecting a serious, even menacing appearance. Coe had never before seen the man, who looked nothing like any other plantation owner.

Suddenly, as if prompted by Coe's stare, the man snapped his head in Coe's direction, his deep-set, steely blue eyes flashing an icy, penetrating, evil glare. At first startled, Coe returned a tight-lipped smile and a nod, then turned his attention to the front.

The crowd became silent as Jack Powers, senior partner in the law firm, strode to the podium. Powers was in his early fifties, ruggedly handsome, and impeccably dressed. His obvious confidence commanded the room. Scanning the audience and pausing to acknowledge Coe with a discreet nod, he then announced, "The young man sitting in the back of the room is David Coe, one of our promising young attorneys. He's been working closely with me, and I asked him to join us today."

A few turned around for a quick look at Coe before abruptly returning their focus to the front as Powers continued.

"As you all know, the American minister and I recently returned from Washington, D.C. One of the items on our agenda was to meet with members of the Senate Foreign Relations Committee to negotiate the extension of the Reciprocity Treaty of 1876. Let me first summarize the proceedings, then take questions.

"First of all, the committee is facing considerable pressure from United States farmers to terminate the treaty. The sugar market is very lucrative right now, and farmers from the Southern states who grew cotton during the Civil War to support the Confederacy have now switched to sugar cane. Also, beet farmers from California, Texas, and Louisiana can make a greater profit if they produce sugar from their beets. These parties are pressuring their senators to end the treaty. Their goal, of course, is to eliminate competition from Hawaii, thereby increasing their market share.

"Second, since the beginning of the treaty, the cost of sugar has greatly increased, which means the U.S. is losing more potential tax revenue from Hawaii. At the same time, the demand for imported goods, such as iron, wool, and textiles, from the United States into Hawaii has decreased significantly. This has resulted in a substantial trade deficit for the United States. Overall, there's a strong feeling among Senate committee members that the Reciprocity Treaty is no longer beneficial to the United States. Gentlemen, the situation is not favorable, to say the least."

Coe realized the problem the sugar plantation owners now faced. They all had made a fortune growing and exporting unrefined sugar, but without the treaty, which permitted tax-free export into the

United States, their business would be greatly diminished by untaxed sugar produced in the United States and by cheaper sugar from the Philippines and the Caribbean countries. They desperately needed this treaty.

Powers continued, "The good news is that the Senate committee has offered to extend the treaty on the condition that Hawaii grants the United States exclusive permission to use Pearl Harbor as a repair and coaling station for U.S. ships."

The crowd turned inward toward each other and erupted into a clamor of discussion. Then, finally, Roland Chambers, president of Chambers and Tate Industries and a member of the 'big five,' rose from the crowd and said, "Jack, you know the King of Hawaii vehemently opposes granting the use of Pearl Harbor to a foreign country. His position on this issue is on record. Can we convince him to change his mind?"

A voice from the crowd shouted, "We have to, and we will, one way or another."

Someone in the front row stood and began to speak. Coe couldn't clearly see him from his seat in the back of the room, but he'd heard that distinctive voice before, coarse and gravelly. The voice belonged to Roy Matthews, the most outspoken member of the 'big five.'

"You all know my position. If Hawaii were annexed to the United States and became a U.S. territory, we wouldn't have this damned problem every time the treaty comes up for extension. There would be no taxes, no tariffs, nothing, ever!" Matthews said.

Daniel Mitchell, president of Mitchell Sugar Company and another of the 'big five,' stood and said, "Roy, you think annexation is the solution to everything, but it's a sensitive topic to the Hawaiians."

"Just listen to me for a minute." Matthews continued, "We absolutely need one of two things; either this treaty or for the United

States to annex Hawaii as a U. S. territory. Now we can screw around with this damned treaty every year and still have it pulled out from under us. You all heard what Jack said; the Senate committee is leaning away from us. Or we can use our political influence to convince Congress to annex Hawaii."

Matthews then turned to Powers and said, "Now, Jack, you have a contact on the Senate committee, right?"

"Yes, Senator John James from Massachusetts is a partner in our law firm and a close friend."

Matthews continued, "The United States is interested in Hawaii. As Jack said, they already want Pearl Harbor. We just have to sell them on the idea of taking the rest of the country."

Chambers, still standing, responded, "Hold on there, Roy. The treaty has been good for all of us. It's made us all wealthy men. So, instead of using our influence to attempt annexation, why don't we use it to pressure the King to turn over Pearl Harbor? The King is beholding to us. We should be able to get his consent.

Besides, the Hawaiians are still irate over that new constitution. Not long ago, there was a revolution that had to be suppressed by force. Remember that? Men were killed in that revolt, and there are still public protests almost every day. If we pursue annexation, a civil war is possible. If that occurs, our business, our property, even our lives and our families' lives would be in danger. We risk losing everything."

Matthews interrupted, "Those protests are nothing. That's just Robert Alton stirring things up again. He's a real screw-up. He views himself as a champion of the Hawaiian people, and he's not even Hawaiian. Once he goes, everything will calm down."

Mitchell chimed in, "That's what you say, Matthews. I think the pot is just about to boil over, and if you turn up the heat right now by pushing annexation, we'll be in for the fight of our lives."

Matthews, the vein in his neck bulging, pointed a trembling finger at Mitchell and shot back, "What's wrong, you son-of-a-bitch? You afraid of a little fight?"

At that point, the others erupted in loud commotion. Powers banged his gavel repeatedly, finally restoring order. The meeting proceeded for another hour without further outbursts, but the situation was unanimously recognized as a serious problem without a clear solution.

Upon adjournment, Coe waited behind until the others left the room. Only Jack Powers and a sixtyish man with long flowing white hair and a finely trimmed mustache and goatee remained. Powers called to Coe, "David, come here for a moment."

"David, this is Franz Schmidt, our biggest client. As I told you a few days ago, you'll be doing contract work for him."

"Pleased to finally meet you, Davey. I've heard a lot about you. Jack tells me you're an outstanding lawyer. I 'm looking forward to working with you."

"Thank you, Mr. Schmidt. And I'm certainly looking forward to working together with you."

They shook hands again, then Coe headed to his office on Powers Alley as the associate attorneys referred to the end of the second-floor corridor where four large, plush offices were located. The firm's three partners, Jack Powers, Alexander Thatcher, and John James, occupied three of the offices. The fourth belonged to Coe.

Business was booming at the firm, and with the hiring of nine associate attorneys to handle the workload, office space was scarce. Most associates sat two per office in the smaller offices at the opposite end of the corridor. Three worked in cubicles on the first floor where the accountants and bookkeepers shared space, but Coe, although not the most senior associate attorney, was widely recognized as exceptional. He was born with extraordinary natural intelligence and was valedictorian at Harvard Law School. Coe remembered and could instantly recall almost everything he'd ever read or heard. He was a walking law library. The associate attorneys, as well as the senior partners, often consulted him on matters concerning legal precedence and case histories. His abilities enabled him to eliminate time-consuming legal research steps and quickly produce astounding volumes of high-quality work.

He'd moved into his newly furnished office on Powers Alley only a month ago. The new chair behind his desk still emitted a fresh leather scent. He relished his position among the partners and vowed to drive himself until his office also housed a partner. He viewed his assignment with Schmidt as an opportunity to advance toward his goal. Contract law was one of his strongest attributes, and he savored the chance to demonstrate his expertise to the firm's most important client.

Coe sat behind a finely crafted hardwood desk, his Harvard Law School diploma framed and hanging on the wall behind him, a view of downtown Honolulu through the large window to his right. Before he began working, the image of Roy Matthews referring to Robert Alton as a screw-up popped into his mind. He'd known Alton, 'Reb,' short for 'rebel,' to his friends, from when they were children and attended school together at the mission run by Coe's father. Reb was a likeable and intelligent guy, and they were still friends, but, in many ways, 'screw-up' was a perfect description.

Coe smiled at the recollection, then focused on the Schmidt assignment. It seemed the most satisfying periods were when he was hard at work. The Book of Psalms, chapter 128, verse 2, reminded him that it should be so. 'You shall eat the fruits of the labor of your hands; you shall be happy, and it shall be well with you.'

After he'd spent a few hours reviewing documents, a knock on the door interrupted his concentration. The door opened, and Jack Powers leaned in.

"I want to show you something." Powers held up the evening edition of the Honolulu newspaper. The emboldened headlines read, KING ANNOUNCES TRIP TO CALIFORNIA.

"Could be trouble," Powers said before closing the door on his way out.

The interruption provided an opportunity to check the clock; eight-thirty. As Coe left his office, he glanced toward Powers' office at the end of the hallway. A sign hung on the office door. The first line read, DO NOT DISTURB, in bold, black capital letters, centered on a white background. The second line, centered beneath the first read, UNDER ANY CIRCUMSTANCES in larger, black capitals.

It was the first time he'd seen the sign. He looked in the other direction. All the office doors at the opposite end of the corridor were closed. He glanced at the narrow space between the bottom of the doors and the floor to see the rooms were dark. Everyone had obviously gone for the day. He crept up to Powers' office door and leaned his head against it. Voices from inside penetrated the thick wooden door, but they were muffled so that he couldn't recognize the voices or understand what was being said.

Coe left the building, but didn't feel like going home. Living alone since the day his father was exiled, he was often haunted by loneliness and bad memories in the house. Nevertheless, he had a great day and wasn't ready for it to end, so he decided to go to a more cheerful place.

INSIDE JACK POWERS' OFFICE, Powers reclined in a plush leather chair behind his beautifully finished koa wood desk. Roy Matthews sat in a padded leather chair in front of the desk, rolling a cigarette. He lit it, propped his feet on a small table, took a drag, then exhaled a smoke ring into the air.

"Jack, I don't know what we're going to do. These other plantation owners just can't see the future. They're too damned complacent. They act as if this treaty will be renewed forever, but we'll lose it one day, and then what? We can't wait until that day, then decide what to do. We have to do something now, before it happens. Am I right?"

"You *are* right, Roy, and there's something else to consider. Right now, we control the King. We supported him in his election, and he owes us. He's a weak man, and to a large extent, we can impose our will on him, but he won't rule forever, and his sister is heir to the throne."

Matthews paused, took another drag, and blew another ring of smoke. "Yeah, and she probably won't be nearly as cooperative."

Powers pushed an ashtray across the desk. "Undoubtedly. She doesn't owe us a thing, but we'll get some insight into her level of cooperation rather soon."

He held up the newspaper he'd shown David Coe an hour ago.

Matthews glanced at the headline. "So even with the budget deficit soaring, the King is taking another damned vacation. I hadn't seen today's paper yet. How long will he be gone?"

"The paper says about two months."

"So, his sister will take his place on the throne while he's gone." Matthews lowered his head into his hands, then looked up at Powers. "Jack, how do you see this eventually working out?"

As Matthews' exhaled smoke surrounded Powers, he went to the window while he spoke. "I'll tell you. If you don't take pre-emptive action, you plantation owners face economic disaster."

Powers often used 'you' instead of 'we' when discussing a problem, reasoning that, psychologically, it isolated the plantation owners, compelling them to seek his help.

He opened the first window, then moved to the other while continuing. "It's inevitable that someday you'll lose the Reciprocity Treaty."

After opening the second window, he finished speaking as he returned to his desk. "Then, your sugar gets taxed, and you lose a major competitive advantage you now enjoy."

"Then we need to get moving with plans for annexation."

"Annexation is the eventual solution, I agree, but it's a complicated proposition, Roy. To a large degree, it's political and, therefore, not certain at any point in time. It depends on the positions of the members of Congress and the President, and even if you get a favorable, pro-annexation group, the legislative process takes time. You need something to bridge the certain time gap between the termination of the treaty and annexation. Otherwise, competitors will take market share from you during that time gap."

"Makes sense to me, but you don't think annexation is the immediate answer. So what are you suggesting we do?"

Powers had bold ideas on the topic, engendered by a terrible childhood experience and, therefore, deeply personal. They were dangerous, radical ideas. He'd shared them with only one other to this point, but he needed help implementing his visions, specifically, help from the 'big five.' Now that the very livelihood of the 'big five' was threatened, Powers figured they might be more receptive to a radical idea, and the one Powers considered most receptive currently sat alone before him.

"I'll tell you, but this is highly confidential. You can't tell anyone, not even your wife."

Matthews took his feet off the table, moved his chair close to the desk, and leaned in. "Okay. Go ahead."

"We overthrow the King and set up our own government, installing our own people to run it."

"Come on!" Matthews cried out as he leaned back and threw his hands into the air.

"Think about it for a minute, Roy. We eliminate the King, his sister, or any other Hawaiian ruler and negotiate directly with the United States government. We'd be in control until the United States agrees to annex Hawaii and the annexation process runs its course to completion. It eliminates the time gap. It's perfect for you."

"That may be true, but overthrow the King? How in the hell do you plan to do that?"

"Look, I've thought about this a great deal, and I'm certain we can achieve it. The first step is to destabilize the throne by discrediting the King. We coerce him into committing a crime or frame him somehow, and we have a big advantage there. This King is greedy and careless. He'll take the bait and commit a criminal act if money is involved."

Matthews shot back, "He's already committed a crime. Remember the scandal for the opium license? He passed a law allowing him to grant an exclusive license to sell opium in Hawaii, then took numerous bribes for that same exclusive license."

"Yes, of course, I remember, and that's exactly my point. As I said, he'll take the bait and commit a crime if there's money involved, but the crime has to be something more serious than simple bribery. It has to be something that shocks the public. Right now, his popularity is at rock bottom, and with another major setback, many will call for a change. They'll demand his dismissal. But his crime has to be so egregious that most of the people will accept a new form of government, not just a different face on the throne."

Matthews snuffed his cigarette butt into the ashtray, rolled another, and lit it. "Okay, Jack. You've got my attention. Then what?"

"We get the American minister to call in the troops from the warships in the harbor. Then, with martial law in effect, we take over Iolani Palace and install our governing officials to fill the void left by the King's departure, a provisional government, if you will. In due time, we form a republic and push for annexation."

"Just like that," Matthews said as he stared at Powers.

"No, not just like that," Powers snapped back. "The situation has to be just right. It has to look like a natural succession of events, not some planned conspiracy, and who knows when that 'right situation' might arrive. But we have to be ready when it comes, which requires planning. First, we develop a plan to discredit the King, then analyze the situation and decide how and when to proceed with the next step."

Matthews responded, "And the next step would be to get the American minister to call out the troops? Andrew Blackburn is afraid of his own shadow. He won't do it."

"He called them out in the aftermath of the King's election."

"Yeah, but after the King's election, there was rioting in the streets. American lives were truly in danger."

"We'll have to convince him American lives are again in danger with the destabilized government and that it's his responsibility to summon the troops to protect them from violence and rioting."

"But what if there is no violence and rioting?"

"I've already considered that scenario."

"Yeah?" Matthews said.

"If necessary, we create it."

After a brief pause, a sly grin formed on Matthews' face. "Jack, you're absolutely diabolical. I sure am glad we retain the services of your firm. I'd hate to have you working against us."

"Look, Roy, there's still a lot of work to do, but I need to know if the 'big five' are on board before moving this forward."

"Well, count me in. It's risky, but I see your point. It does solve our problems, and if we're careful, we can minimize the risk. Besides, I always wanted to run a country."

They both laughed.

"You know what will provide just as much pleasure as running the country, Roy?"

"Yes. I believe I do. You'd revel in the simple satisfaction of taking Hawaii from the native Hawaiians."

"You're right. There's so much opportunity here in Hawaii, and they're all just too lazy to take advantage. They're totally worthless people."

"Tell me, Jack. Why do you despise the Hawaiians so much? I mean, I don't like them. None of us do. But you have such a deep-seated hatred for them."

Powers expression hardened. His eyes glared. "You're right. I hate them. It's personal. and it goes way back."

Both men took a deep breath and leaned back in their chairs.

"Hey, Jack, you want to join me for a nightcap at the Hawaiian before heading home?"

"I never turn down a chance for a drink, Roy, but let's have the first one right here."

Powers reached into the lowest drawer on the right side of his desk and pulled out two glasses and a bottle half filled with an amber liquid.

"Glenfiddich Scotch whiskey; the best."

Powers poured three fingers into each glass, lifted his drink toward Matthews, and toasted, "To the overthrow of Hawaii."

Matthews extended his glass toward Powers. "The overthrow of Hawaii."

CHAPTER 2

Downtown Honolulu consisted of narrow earthen streets lined by one or two-story wooden or stone structures with elevated wooden walkways passing in front. During the daylight hours, the area bustled with activity from the small, family-owned businesses. At night, the recently installed electric street lights eerily illuminated a deserted Fort Street as David Coe passed through the business section. Coe preferred the warm, rich look of the old open-flame, oil street lights, but a fire a few years earlier that destroyed most of Chinatown hastened the installation of electric bulbs.

Downtown Honolulu – c. 1890 *(Hawaii State Archives)*

He turned left onto Hotel Street through the seedy part of town. As he progressed, the streets became more crowded, but it was still too early for the derelicts and prostitutes who would later abound. After a right onto Nu'uanu Avenue and about a block and a half block up Nu'uanu, he turned right into the Rialto, a saloon and billiard parlor owned and operated by his best friend, Kimo.

Coe enjoyed the Rialto with its diverse clientele. Sailors from the United States, Great Britain, Holland, Russia, and other countries frequented the establishment. They came from military and commercial ships docked in Honolulu Harbor just a few blocks away. There were also native Hawaiian and *haole* (the Hawaiian term for 'Caucasian') customers as well as former sugar plantation workers from China, Japan, and the Philippines who remained in Hawaii after completing their labor contract.

The Rialto was a long, narrow room with a bar along the left side and three pool tables in the back, beyond the bar. As he stood just inside the doorway for a few moments scanning the premises, a voice from behind the bar called out, "Hi, Davey." It was Julie, the regular bartender. Julie, a native Hawaiian, appeared to be in her forties and always flashed a wide, toothy smile.

While returning her greeting, he caught Kimo's voice bellowing from the rear of the establishment. "Hey, bruddah. Come back. Talk story," he said in a Pidgin English dialect spoken by many native Hawaiians. Kimo was Coe's age, dark in skin, hair, and eyes, short in stature but broad and powerful, all features of his Samoan ancestry. Coe made his way through the crowded, smoky room. After a warm handshake, Kimo kidded, "What gives, stranger? Jack Powers die or something?"

Coe grinned. "No, I'm sure you'll be happy to know that Jack Powers is alive and well. It's just that I've had a lot of work since he returned from Washington, D.C."

"Just don't forget your true friends. Seems like sometime you getting too much like Powers. You even start to look like him."

Coe chuckled as the left side of his pursed lips turned up, forming a devilish half-smile. "Well, you know the story, Kimo. Powers advises me not to go to places like this or spend time with people like you. He feels it projects an image that's not good for my career. But don't worry. You can't get rid of me that easily."

They both laughed.

"Davey, you so funny," Kimo said. "Hey, you just miss Reb. He say maybe he come back later."

"At the meeting of the plantation owners this morning, Reb's name came up. Roy Matthews referred to him as a screw-up."

Kimo smiled. "Yeah, Reb a screw-up, no doubt about it, but he a good kind of screw-up. He mean well."

The smile left Kimo's face. "Roy Matthews and the mission boys screw-ups, too, but they evil screw-ups. All the mission boys, your boy, Powers, too, act like they own our country. They want to push us out of the way and take over."

"Look, Kimo, I've learned a lot from working with Jack Powers. I know he's not perfect, but we all have our faults."

"You right about one thing, Davey; Powers has faults, lots of them, big ones. Powers arrogant, he greedy, and he hate all Hawaiians. He think we all lazy and worthless, and Hawaii be better off with us out of the way so the mission boys can have it all."

Kimo became more intense. "Him and all the others, they come as visitors, but they're not gracious visitors. They just take and take and take, more and more and more. They want to take everything until we have nothing left." Sensing a full-scale argument, Coe backed off and apologized, but he knew Kimo had a valid point.

About 1500 years earlier, courageous, seafaring people from Polynesia, Kimo's ancestors, migrated to Hawaii. They loaded family, food, and freshwater, as well as livestock and seeds from native plants, onto small, double-hulled sailing vessels and, guided by the stars and an intimate knowledge of ocean currents, sailed across four thousand miles of the vast Pacific Ocean to settle in Hawaii. The new Hawaiians, called Kanaka Maoli, lived and prospered in blissful isolation for several centuries until 1778, when

Captain James Cook, a British explorer, landed on the northernmost island of Kauai.

European trade ships had been sailing in the general vicinity for more than two hundred years, following trade routes between the Americas and the Orient. However, because the Pacific Ocean was so vast and the Hawaiian Islands so tiny, this was the first time anyone had stumbled upon the islands. Cook charted the territory, then left and, during his second visit, was killed during a dispute with angry natives at Kealakekua Bay on the most southern island, Hawaii. However, between his visits, Cook revealed the islands' location to the world. He emphasized that they were an ideal stopover point for merchant vessels making the long trans-Pacific journey. The word spread and, as a result, foreign ships began to visit the islands more frequently.

The effects on the Kanaka Maoli were devastating. Living in isolation for centuries, they had developed no resistance to diseases such as smallpox, tuberculosis, and syphilis. At the time of Cook's arrival, the population was estimated at around eight hundred thousand. Within a century, the census dwindled to about forty thousand.

Foreign settlers aggressively pursued land ownership. By 1888, more than half of the land was privately owned. Kanaka Maoli held less than seven percent, and there were significant encroachments into government, culminated by the Constitution of 1887, the Bayonet Constitution. In short, the arrival of foreigners had disenfranchised the majority of Kanaka Maoli, leaving them powerless and landless in their homeland. Yes, indeed, Kimo certainly had a point.

"Davey, you like a brother to me. We best friends for years. I know Powers your role model. He probably a good role model for lawyer but not for human being. All I say is to keep your eyes open.

"Kimo, I work with Powers every day, and I'm aware of his

position on annexation and his attitude toward the Hawaiian people, but that's not me. Come on, man, you've known me for twenty years. You know who I am. I'm not going to change. But, professionally, this is an excellent opportunity for me. I want to be successful. That's very important to me, and I can learn so much from Powers.

He possesses skills I want to acquire, and I'm not just talking about the law. I can learn that on my own. Powers is an expert negotiator and a shrewd businessman. Just his confidence and bravado, the way he carries himself. Those are attributes you can't pick up by reading a book. In a few years, I want to be where he is now, but personally, I'll still be the same."

"I hope so, but you be careful. Sometimes it hard to keep business and personal separate. You try to be like him in business, and you take on personal traits, too, whether you want to or not."

An old Hawaiian man, sitting at the end of the bar near the pool tables had overheard the conversation. He looked up from his seat and mumbled something in Hawaiian, then turned away and continued with his drink.

Coe looked quizzically at Kimo. "He say, '*Ua mau ke ea o ka aina i ka pono*.'"

"It mean, 'The life of the land is preserved in righteousness.'"

Kimo racked the billiard balls, and Coe broke. Their games and small talk about surfing and mutual friends continued until late into the night.

As Coe walked home, the words of the old Hawaiian man at the bar echoed in his head, *The life of the land is preserved in righteousness.*

ROY MATTHEWS HAD LEFT the lounge at the Hawaiian Hotel some time ago. Powers stayed for one more drink that turned into four or five. He had actually begun contemplating a plot for the overthrow shortly after meeting Colonel Ralph Grimes for the first time. For the last month or so, he'd been considering various plans to take the first step, discrediting the King, but none of the options seemed viable until just a few hours ago. A couple of statements Roy Matthews made earlier in the evening sparked an idea that enthused Powers.

First, Matthews said the people of Hawaii were sure to be upset with the King when they heard, even with the country's debt rising at an alarming rate, the King was taking a pleasure trip to San Francisco at taxpayer expense. Later he said even Queen's Hospital, which treated indigent native Hawaiians and had long been a pet project of Hawaiian royalty, was financially strapped.

Finishing his final drink of the evening, Powers tried to assess the overall situation through his inebriation, a feat at which he excelled. Now, with a strategy to implement the destabilization of the King and a member of the 'big five' committed to his plan, he was ready to move forward.

Powers staggered out of the lounge at closing time. Unfortunately, he was far less competent at overcoming the physical impairments of drunkenness. After making it through the open-air lobby and outside to the turnaround in front of the hotel, he stopped and took a deep breath of the refreshing night air. As he approached his carriage, he stumbled, then, in desperation, grabbed the reins to keep from falling. The horse reared his head and whinnied. After Powers steadied himself, he patted the horse gently on the side of the jaws with both hands and affectionately placed his cheek against the horse's cheek. "Aww, Titus, I'm sorry, boy."

As he turned to board the carriage, an elderly Hawaiian couple, who had stopped to observe the spectacle, stood about ten feet away.

"What the hell are you looking at?" Powers shouted.

The startled couple smiled, and the man lifted a hand as a gesture of friendship.

Powers reached behind his back with his right hand and pulled out a pistol he always carried in a secluded holster. He pointed the gun at the couple and shouted, "You think this is funny? I'll show you something funny."

He fired a shot into the air. The couple became frightened and turned to move away. Powers took a few quick steps toward them, feigning pursuit, and yelled, "Faster, faster."

The couple panicked and tried to hurry.

Powers returned the gun to its holster, snickered, muttered a profanity, then boarded the carriage to begin the trip home. Having made the trip many times, Titus seemed to know the route, which was helpful since Powers couldn't provide good direction.

The carriage pulled to a stop in front of a large, stately house in the affluent Manoa area. Corporate heads, bank presidents, and other wealthy individuals also resided in the neighborhood. The law firm of Powers, Thatcher, and James provided legal services to many of them.

When Powers first joined the firm, known simply as Thatcher and Associates at the time, it was mundane and inconsequential. The aggressive, hard-charging Powers transformed the business. First, he purchased an older building, funded a massive remodeling project, and moved the firm from its previous, drab locale into a plush, first-class facility, eventually named the Powers Building.

Then, he lured wealthy sugar plantation owners from the other firms by providing political advantages as well as first-class legal services. His magnetism and confidence made the plantation owners feel obligated to him and the firm. Other well-heeled clientele followed. He hired nine additional lawyers to keep up with the work. Powers was amply compensated both professionally and financially. At the age of thirty-two, he became the senior partner in the most powerful, influential law firm in the country of Hawaii. Less than two years later, he was a millionaire.

Powers gingerly disembarked from the carriage and staggered up the steps and into his house. As he entered, a light came on. He looked across the room at his wife, Ellen.

"Oh, I thought it might be Audrey," she said.

"Our daughter's not home yet? Where the hell is she?"

"She's out with friends."

"What friends?"

"Friends from school, I suppose."

"At three o'clock in the morning?"

"Jack, she only has a brief time before she leaves for school in Massachusetts. She just wants to spend time with them before she goes."

"It's three o'clock in the morning. She should be home," he muttered as he flopped onto the sofa.

Ellen slowly shook her head and said, "Oh, Jack, you've been drinking again. It's getting to be too much. You have to stop."

He rose from the sofa and stumbled toward her. Suddenly he straightened up and slapped her across the face, sending her flying to the floor.

"Don't you ever tell me about my drinking. I'm the head of the household. I'll do what I want. Now, I want to know where my daughter is at three o'clock in the morning."

"I already told you, I don't know," she said, slowly rising from the floor while continuing to rub her cheek.

"To hell with this. I'm going to find her," he yelled. As he turned toward the door, he tripped over the edge of the carpet and fell to the floor.

Ellen walked over to him as he lay on the floor, barely moving. Looking down, she didn't see any blood. Apparently, he wasn't injured by the fall. But, at that moment, he was vulnerable. She gritted her teeth, clenched her fists, and raised her right foot off the floor to kick him. Then, after a moment of reconsideration, she turned out the light before heading upstairs to bed.

CHAPTER 3

About two weeks later, on a rainy Saturday evening, Jack Powers entered his office, locked the office door behind him, walked over to one of the two windows in the office, and peered out. The street below was deserted. He closed the recently installed, heavy, black drapes, carefully checking the overlap in the middle to ensure no light from the office could leak through a slit and be visible from outside. After addressing the other window in a similar fashion, he turned on a dim, shaded electric lamp.

Powers then left the office through a storage room door behind his desk. He passed through another door in the rear of the storage room, descended a flight of stairs, and traversed a dark, narrow, twenty-foot-long inside passage to unlock the door to the back alley so the others could enter. He then returned to his desk and anxiously waited.

In less than an hour, the men Powers deemed necessary to overthrow the King of Hawaii would meet for the first time. Besides Powers himself, there were three other carefully chosen members of the group. Powers kept the group small because secrecy was paramount.

Roy Matthews was chosen to rally support among 'big five.' They owned Honolulu's only newspaper, and their power and influence would be a valuable ally, especially to sway public opinion once the King was discredited and again in the aftermath of the overthrow.

Andrew Blackburn, the American minister, was selected because he was the only one in Hawaii with authority to land United States troops from warships in the harbor, troops that would provide the military force to suppress any revolts following the overthrow. Powers had spent a lot of time with Blackburn during their recent trip to Washington, D.C. He felt, by using a political promise as an inducement, he'd coaxed the American minister into supporting the overthrow plot, but Blackburn was passive and timid and, therefore, Powers was still uncertain he could be trusted under pressure.

The fourth member of the group was Colonel Ralph Grimes, the commander of the Honolulu Rifles, a private paramilitary organization. Powers retained Grimes to supply miscellaneous support as needed.

One by one, they arrived, entering the building through the back-alley door and making their way to the Powers' office. Powers didn't want to risk an outsider becoming suspicious by seeing the same group of men entering through the front door after hours and on numerous occasions.

The first to arrive was Andrew Blackburn. He took a seat in front of Powers' desk. The tall, thin, silver-haired, fiftyish man appeared edgy, his face ashen and his hands shaking as he tried to roll a cigarette. Finally, he lifted his head to look at Powers and said, "Look, Jack, I'm with you on this, but I do have some reservations."

"Anything we should talk about before the others arrive?"

"No, no. I think I'll be all right. It's just the meeting at night, all the secrecy. Also, the prospect for violence concerns me."

"Andrew, your part in this is straightforward. When the time comes, you simply give the order to land the troops and do it promptly. That's it, and if you act promptly, the prospect for violence is minimal."

Powers studied Blackburn's blank expression and began thinking about the American minister's performance in the aftermath of the King's controversial election. Despite extensive rioting and violence in the streets of Honolulu, Blackburn was reluctant to give the order to land American troops. He was concerned he would be chastised if he acted too early. Therefore, the insurrection continued for two days, and only after a bullet shattered a window in his office, raining shards of glass on him, did Blackburn finally give the order.

Powers wanted to ensure there was no such delay the next time. So he emphasized the word *promptly*.

They were interrupted when Roy Matthews entered Powers' office through the storage room door.

"That's one hell of an entrance. So dark. I almost killed myself on the steps."

"Next time, bring a candle, Roy."

Blackburn chuckled. Powers hoped the momentary humor would settle him. After greeting the other two, Matthews moved to a chair in front of Powers' desk next to Blackburn. He stood for a moment and looked down at Blackburn's jittery hands fumbling to roll a cigarette.

"Jesus Christ, Andrew, relax."

Matthews rolled two cigarettes and gave one to Blackburn. After they lit up, Powers began.

"Colonel Grimes will arrive later. Let's get started."

Suddenly, the storage room door flew open, and a large muscular man with a robust handlebar mustache entered. He extended a firm handshake and a baritone "Good evening, sir. Colonel Ralph Grimes" to the other three, then sat next to Matthews. He rolled a cigarette and extended it to Powers.

"No thanks, Ralph. I'll just breathe the air."

Grimes grinned, then lit up as Powers continued, "Tonight, I want everyone to meet and discuss our general plan moving forward. But first, let me remind you all of the extreme importance of secrecy. What happens in this room must stay in this room. Not a word to anyone. Not your wife, not your girlfriend, not your mistress. Nobody."

To emphasize his point, Powers considered reminding them that if the plan failed, they could all be charged with treason, a crime punishable by death, but he didn't want to further rattle Andrew Blackburn.

"If it's necessary to refer to our group, we're The Committee of Safety."

Powers had created the name and considered it bland, unlikely to draw attention.

"Now, we all know why we're here. I've talked to each of you individually about the plan to accomplish our goal. Let me quickly review, then take questions or comments.

"Our plan is four-fold. Number one, we discredit the King so the people demand a replacement. He's already on the precipice due to his irresponsible behavior in the past. We just have to nudge him over the cliff. Number two, when the King leaves the throne, we form a provisional government to fill the vacancy. That government will be staffed by our own people. That bodes especially well for you, Andrew."

During their trip to Washington, Powers had suggested that, if Hawaii were annexed to the United States, Blackburn would most likely be appointed the first governor of the new territory of Hawaii. Powers observed that Blackburn was keenly interested in the governor position, so he mentioned it often.

"Number three, in the aftermath of the King's dismissal, the native Hawaiians who may support his removal will expect a successor to occupy the throne. There may be civil unrest when we install our provisional government instead of a successor. If rioting occurs, Andrew Blackburn will bring in the American troops to quell the uprising. Colonel Grimes and the Rifles will supply support as needed."

"Number four, our new government will strive to achieve two primary goal: to aggressively seek annexation to the United States, and, second, to maintain the Reciprocity Treaty until the very day of annexation. We'll give the United States the Pearl Lochs and whatever else is necessary to maintain the treaty until Hawaii is officially annexed."

Powers turned his attention to Matthews. "Roy, we'll need the plantation owners, especially the 'big five,' to use their influence to demand the King's dismissal after we discredit him. Do you think you'll have a problem with that?"

"Well, of course, I'm in, and I think Franz Schmidt can be convinced, but you heard Mitchell and Chambers at the meeting last week. Hell, they won't even support an annexation move, let alone a plot to overthrow the King, and John Tate will agree with his partner, Roland Chambers. They're concerned that all these protests will turn into violence. You heard them at the meeting. We have to take out Robert Alton and stop the protests before we can get those three to support our plan."

Powers responded, "Franz Schmidt is the most important to us. So let's make certain we get him on board. He owns the only daily newspaper in Honolulu, and we'll need the newspaper, especially to support the provisional government. But we'd be stronger with solidarity among the 'big five.' Those protests are insignificant, but you're right. Mitchell and Chambers are concerned."

After thinking for a moment, Powers continued, "They're both coming to the office next week. I'll talk to them. You do the same, Roy. Make it a point to see them."

"It's going to take more than talk," Matthews said.

"Look, it would be easy to kill Alton, but then the protests might escalate into violence. The Hawaiians revere Alton and might view his death as some kind of martyrdom."

"You know, Jack, I never understood why in the hell the Hawaiians follow a haole like Alton. Besides not being Hawaiian, he's such a screw-up."

"I think he's half Hawaiian, and, yes, they do follow him. In that respect, he's a factor. The option to kill him is always available. I'd prefer to take the less risky step first and simply try to persuade Chambers and Mitchell to change their view."

Andrew Blackburn interjected, "I agree with Jack. A principal rule of negotiations is to take the safest path first. If it succeeds, we avoid the violence. If not, we can explore other avenues, but killing Alton should absolutely be the last alternative, and even then, I'm not sure I support it."

Powers was delighted to see the American minister participate. He needed the man on board.

"Agreed," Ralph Grimes bellowed. "We'll have plenty of violence before we accomplish our mission. Let's not use it all up at the beginning."

Powers cringed at Grimes' remark. He immediately looked at Blackburn to see if he was visibly unsettled by the suggestion of 'plenty of violence.' Blackburn appeared calm.

"Any questions?" Powers asked.

Matthews responded, "Yeah. What about the first objective, discrediting the King?"

"I'll take care of that," Powers answered.

"How?"

"I have a plan in place and will act soon."

"What's the plan?"

Powers paused for a moment. "Your question raises an important point, Roy. First, let me say that this mission will be conducted on a need-to-know basis. Everyone won't be informed of the details of the others' activities because there's no need for it. That's critical for two reasons. Number one, it absolves each of us to some degree of complicity in the others' activities. Number two, by reducing the dissemination of information, even among those in the room, we increase security, and that's paramount. To answer your question, let's just say I'm going to call in a favor. That's all. Just call in a favor."

The others looked at each other, but nobody said anything, so Powers moved on.

"Are there any other questions?"

Andrew Blackburn responded, "Look, you all know I favor annexation. We all do. That's why we formed this secret committee. But as American minister, I answer directly to the President of the United States. My primary duty here in Hawaii is to ensure the safety of the American citizens living here."

"Now, if the King or his sister does something that, in some way, endangers Americans, I can take action. But I can't simply order American troops to take up arms and forcibly move against the ruler of a foreign country. That's an act of war. Only the President can declare war. For me to respond, there has to be a valid, highly public action that imperils the safety of Americans. Please remember that. I'd be most appreciative. Thank you."

"I promise you, Andrew, we all respect your position. Your part is simple. If rioting occurs, we expect you to promptly land the troops. That's it; nothing else. Just carry out your responsibilities as American minister. In that respect, you're insulated from everything else we're doing. You only have to do your job."

"Thank you, Jack."

"Anything else?" Powers asked.

There were no responses.

"I believe that's about all we can do at the moment. I'll take care of my part, and Roy and I will try to convince the other members of the 'big five'. I'll let everyone know when the next meeting is scheduled. Remember the importance of secrecy. I can't stress that point enough. It's vital."

Matthews and Blackburn rose and exited through the storage room. They each lit a match as they descended the dark stairwell. Powers waited at the top of the stairs until he heard the two exit through the back-alley door, then closed the storage room door, locked it, and returned to his desk.

He pulled out two glasses and a bottle of amber liquid, filled each glass, and pushed one across the desk to Colonel Ralph Grimes. They clicked glasses and drank.

"Glenfiddich Scotch whiskey; the best. They don't have this at Tiger Lilly's," Powers said with a smile.

"No, they sure don't." Grimes laughed. "Hey, Jack, if you want me to take care of Alton, just give me the word."

"Not at the moment, Ralph. I may have something else for you."

"Need a little help calling in that favor, huh?"

"Maybe."

CHAPTER 4

Two days later, on a sunny Monday morning, Jack Powers entered the First Hawaiian National Bank at the corner of Merchant and Bishop Streets and gazed around the lobby. Marble and highly polished brass surrounded him. Marble wasn't naturally present on any of the Hawaiian Islands. Every piece of marble and all the brass had been shipped in.

He ascended the stairs to the second floor and approached the desk outside the office of bank president, George Kingston. Seated at the desk was an attractive blonde woman in her mid-twenties. She returned his full smile as he introduced himself. Powers leered at her as the woman rose from her chair and walked into Kingston's office to inform him. He fondly remembered when his firm employed an attractive young woman. A few years ago, he replaced her with an older, ordinary-looking one to convince his wife of his faithfulness.

Returning, she announced, "Mr. Kingston will see you now."

Powers again flashed his smile as he passed close by her on the way into Kingston's office, then closed the door behind him and latched it.

Like Powers, Kingston was one of the mission boys. Powers had known him for several years, though not well, and remembered him as timid. He was tall, thin, and in his sixties. His deeply wrinkled face made him look older. His wife was about twenty years younger than he. They had adopted two orphaned young Hawaiian children a few years ago after trying unsuccessfully to have their own.

"Jack, it's been a while since I last saw you. How have you been?" Kingston asked as they shook hands.

"I've been fine, George. How are you?"

"Fine, thank you."

Powers immediately observed Kingston was apprehensive. He had come without notice so Kingston was unsure of his purpose. Powers took some time to let his eyes scan the office. He was deliberate. He wanted Kingston to notice. Everything inside the office was plush, like the lobby and the vestibule outside the office.

"Yes, George, I can see that everything is fine; actually, better than fine. So that little favor I did for you a few years back has really helped?"

Kingston shifted nervously in his seat and began fumbling with his hands. He cleared his throat before speaking. "Yes, yes, it did."

"You enjoy your lucrative salary?"

"Ah, yes."

"And your beautiful house in the Manoa Valley?'

"Yes."

Powers paused and again surveyed the office.

Kingston blurted out, "Jack, what can I do for you?"

"I need a favor."

"What kind of favor?"

"Do you remember a few years ago, when I convinced the sugar plantation owners to deposit their millions into your bank, convinced them to do all their banking business with your bank, I told you that someday I might need a favor from you?" Powers asked.

"Yes, yes, of course, and I'm most appreciative of your help. What kind of favor do you need?"

"If I'm not mistaken, you're the trustee for the Queen's Hospital trust fund, right?"

"Ah, yes." Kingston swallowed nervously.

"So only you and the King have access to the trust fund, and the King also has his personal account here, right?"

"Yes." Again, Kingston gulped hard.

Powers then blatantly laid it out on the table. "I want you to withdraw a hundred thousand dollars from the Queen's Hospital trust fund and deposit it into the King's personal account."

The statement staggered Kingston. He became flustered and in total panic.

"What? Jack, you can't be serious. Why, I mean, why do you want me to do that?"

Powers ignored Kingston's remarks and calmly continued, "Wait until after the King departs for San Francisco before making the transactions, then backdate them so it appears the King made the withdrawal. Have the transactions completed before the King returns to Hawaii."

"Please don't misunderstand me. I want to return the favor. I really do, but it can't be this. I don't even know if I could transfer money like that. It's not that simple."

"I know you can figure out a way. You're quite resourceful. That's why I chose your bank in the first place."

"Jack, I appreciate what you did for me, and I'm more than willing to do a favor for you, but I can't break the law and ruin my reputation."

"George, when you accepted my favor, you also accepted that you'd return a favor for something I need. Now is the time to repay that favor. That's the way it works."

"Please, try to understand my position. You're asking me to commit a felony offense. I'd go to jail. Think of my family."

"I understand your position, but there are powerful people behind this, and they may not be as understanding as I am if they find out you refused to return a favor you promised. And they probably won't have much regard for your family either."

He sat calmly and stared back at Kingston.

Kingston said, "I could go to the police. I could have you arrested."

Powers laughed. "It would be a big mistake for you to involve the police; a big mistake. Besides, it's all just hearsay. You couldn't prove anything."

Powers stood. "You'd be wise to repay the favor. I can't be responsible if you refuse."

He headed toward the door without saying another word.

As he exited the office, Kingston called out, "I won't do it, Jack. I won't do it."

The secretary, hearing Kingston through the open door, contorted her face into a puzzled expression as Powers passed by her desk.

Powers stopped, turned to her, and smiled. "He turned down my loan application."

POWERS LEFT THE BANK and returned to his office, thinking about the meeting with George Kingston. Queen's Hospital provided free medical care to the native Hawaiian people. A benevolent queen formed the trust fund several years earlier to sustain the services in perpetuity. It had been supported by all subsequent royalty and was one of the most popular programs among the native Hawaiians.

Powers was sure if the general populous could be convinced the King had embezzled money from the trust fund, they would demand his dismissal. With his popularity at an all-time low, embezzlement charges, especially from the popular Queen's Hospital trust fund, would seal his fate. Even many native Hawaiians would turn on him, and the timing was perfect.

Accusations against the King would be raised while he was in San Francisco and unable to defend himself. The Honolulu city newspaper would repeatedly pound the story to the public. By the time the King returned, the public would already be convinced of his guilt. But, to be most effective, the transaction had to be completed shortly after the King's departure. That would allow four to six weeks for the discovery of the embezzlement to be announced and for public outrage to grow uncontested.

Powers was certain Kingston wouldn't follow through on his threat to call the police, but wasn't sure he would promptly act on the favor. Powers couldn't afford a delay. He decided to wait a couple of days and, if there was no progress, send Kingston a powerful, unforgettable reminder.

A knock on the door interrupted his flow of thought. Sara, his fifty-ish, plain-looking office assistant, entered to deliver an envelope. Powers briefly thought of the gorgeous office assistant working at Kingston's bank. Sara was the woman who replaced the eye candy in his law firm to appease his wife. He just shook his head and returned his focus to the envelope addressed to 'Mr. Powers.' Powers recognized the handwriting. The envelope contained a note that simply read, *7 Tonight.*

AT ABOUT SIX-THIRTY that evening, Powers left the office and hurried up Fort Street, anxious for news about his daughter. She was the most precious thing in his life, and he was concerned she was out late every night and evasive when he asked her whereabouts.

Arriving at the stables at the corner of Union and Hotel Streets, where he kept his horse and carriage while at work, Powers entered the long, narrow building. There were ten stalls on each side of a center aisle. He walked down the aisle between the stalls, the smell of hay and horses meeting him as he looked over each stall gate to make sure only the horse was inside. Soon, a young Filipino approached him.

"Good evening, Mr. Powers," he said.

"Good evening, Danny."

Danny looked up and down the aisle before continuing. "Mr. Powers, I follow your daughter for one week like you ask."

"Yeah, and where did she go?"

"Four nights, she go to bar on Fid Street. Same bar every time. Bar called Tiger Lilly's."

Powers was struck by the coincidence. He'd been there before.

"She meet same man every time, Mr. Powers. Man they call 'Reb'."

"Who's Reb?"

"Reb, you know. Robert Alton. Everyone call him 'Reb'."

Recognizing the name, Powers first felt a kick in the gut, then mounting anger.

"They have couple of drinks, then leave Tiger Lilly's. They go to his room. He live in Chinatown. They always stop at this place on Hotel Street before they go to his room. This place sell opium. Then they go to his room."

Filled with rage, Powers lifted his expensive leather briefcase above his head and slammed it to the floor.

"God damn it," he yelled, then kicked the briefcase into the air. It smacked against the gate of one of the stalls. The horse inside the stall jerked back from the gate, reared up, and whinnied.

As Danny jumped back, Powers glared at him.

"So sorry, Mr. Powers."

"What's the address of Alton's room?" Powers shouted.

"Here, I write it down for you." Danny's hand shook as he wrote, then extended the small square of paper. Powers grabbed it from Danny's hand and jammed it into his pocket without looking at it. He then stood silently for a few moments, staring at the floor, trying to calm himself.

"Go on."

"The man who own the building is Mr. Chong. All Chinese in the hotel except Reb. Mr. Chong like Reb. Everyone in Chinatown like Reb."

"Do you like him?"

"I'm not Chinese, Mr. Powers. I'm Filipino."

"Yes, I know. But do you like Alton?"

"I don't know him, Mr. Powers. I just follow him because he with your daughter. You ask me to do that, Mr. Powers."

"Anything else?"

"One more thing, Mr. Powers. One night, Reb take your daughter to a Chinese junk boat in small lagoon near Honolulu Harbor. Junk boat owned by man they call Doc. Doc own tailor shop in Chinatown."

"Thanks." He slipped Danny a folded bill as they shook hands.

"Thank you, Mr. Powers. I have your carriage ready in twenty minutes, Mr. Powers."

CHAPTER 5

Elizabeth Kingston's auburn hair glistened in the afternoon sunshine that beamed through the window above the kitchen sink. She stood at the sink washing vegetables, freshly picked from the garden she nurtured in the backyard. Squash, tomatoes, and onions would be part of the family dinner that evening. Her two young children would be home from school soon. Her husband would arrive from the bank in about an hour. As a deer ran through the backyard, she lifted her petite, five-foot three-inch frame onto tiptoes to watch it bound across the yard and into the woods.

Suddenly, her serenity was shattered by a sharp blow to the side of her head. She stumbled backward, stunned and dazed, and instinctively grabbed the back of a chair to steady herself. The chair couldn't hold her, and she pulled it over as she fell. Pots on the chair clanged to the floor around her. Hazy but still conscious, she rolled over as a large man wearing a black hood over his head pounced on top of her. Straddling her chest, he pinned her arms beneath his knees. She tried to throw him off by bucking wildly, but he was strong and too heavy.

With his left hand, he grabbed her neck and pinned it to the floor. With the other hand, he pulled a knife from a scabbard on his right calf and pressed the flat portion of the blade firmly across her face, the pointed tip an inch above her right eye. Horrified, she stared close up at the eight-inch long, razor-sharp blade, the polished finish of the shiny steel reflecting the terrified look in her eyes.

"I'll kill you if you scream," the baritone voice shouted.

Her heart raced with fear as she tried to calm herself. "What do you want? I'll give you whatever you want. Just please don't kill me."

"Tell your husband to return the favor."

Confused, she began to lose composure. "Favor? What favor? I don't understand."

"Just tell him to return the favor, and no police or I'll do your whole family." The deep voice was louder and angrier. He moved the knife to her throat. She felt the tip of the blade piercing her skin and a warm stream of blood trickling down the side of her neck.

Panicked, she began to weep, then cried out, "Okay. Okay. I'll tell him. I'll tell him. I promise he'll return the favor. Please don't kill me. My children need me. I beg of you. Please."

Then she heard the front door opening two rooms away and joyful shouts of "Mommy! Mommy!" echoing through the first floor. As she began to let out a warning scream, the assailant quickly removed his left hand from her neck and covered her mouth, muffling her shriek while pushing the back of her head into the floor. She looked up at him with unimaginable terror as she struggled to somehow alert her children, then barely felt the punch to her face that knocked her unconscious.

GEORGE KINGSTON DROVE his horse-drawn carriage to his beautiful home feeling unusually upbeat. He'd just approved a sizable loan for a large San Francisco-based shipping company that would soon begin serving Hawaii. The shipping company would also conduct its banking transactions through Kingston's bank. Business was good.

Also, he noticed, with each passing day, he thought less and less about Jack Powers' visit five days earlier. He anxiously awaited the day when those thoughts would leave him entirely, like a horrible nightmare that fades with time, then one day is gone.

Kingston walked up the steps to his house and stared at the front door. It wasn't like his wife to leave the door open, and he became apprehensive. He rushed to the door and threw it wide open. The sight shocked him. The living room was in shambles.

The sofa had been thrown through a large window on one side of the room. Part of the sofa was still inside the house. The other part protruded through the smashed window pane to the outside. He imagined the strength it took to do that. The delicate porcelain vases that once adorned the fireplace mantle had been flung around the room and now lay in broken pieces strewn all about. He briefly focused on fragments from priceless vases dating back to the Ming Dynasty in China. The hand-crafted, wooden-cased grandfather clock, shipped from New England, had been toppled, then violently smashed. The fine crystal cabinet from Austria was now just pieces of broken glass on the floor.

"Elizabeth! Elizabeth!" he cried out as he ran from the living room to the dining room, which had been similarly ransacked, furniture broken and strewn about, pieces of glass and wood everywhere, but his wife and children weren't there. He continued into the kitchen, where the horrific scene halted him. He could barely breathe, and his heart seemed to stop beating.

His wife and both children, lying on the kitchen floor, bound and gagged. Each had their legs bent back at the knee with the right foot tied to the left hand and the left foot tied to the right hand behind their back. The children were barely conscious and moaning. His wife, more alert than the children, was writhing wildly, trying to free herself from the ropes.

All three were completely naked. Shreds of clothing strewn about the kitchen, along with pots and pans and other kitchenware, indicated their clothes were cut off after being tied up. They all had been slit across the neck from ear to ear. Dried and partially coagulated blood covered their necks and the floor near them. The cuts apparently weren't deep enough to kill them but drew a lot of blood. All three also showed dried and semi-coagulated blood around the nose and mouth.

George sunk to his knees, stunned and in disbelief. When his wife spotted him, she let out a muffled yell through the gag. He couldn't understand the words, but the sound of her voice empowered him. Instantly he rose, pulled a knife from a cabinet drawer, and cut the ropes bounding his wife. The skin on both wrists and ankles had been abraded to bloody. He snatched the tablecloth from the kitchen table and threw it to her to cover herself.

As George cut the ropes from the oldest child, Charles, Elizabeth wrapped the table cloth around her, grabbed a knife, and began to cut the bindings from Jonathan, her youngest. She was now fully conscious, aided by an adrenaline rush. Both children started screaming when their gags were removed. Each parent hugged one of the children. Finally, after several minutes of hugging and words of comfort, they all settled down. Both children continued crying, but not loudly.

The parents used wet towels to wipe the blood from the children. As George wiped the blood from Charles' neck, he saw the incision close-up for the first time. It wasn't very deep, but had been made with surgeon-like precision. That indicated two things to George. First, the attacker didn't intend to kill his family. He could have easily done it but chose not to. Second, this wasn't an act of random madness. They were dealing with an experienced professional who came to deliver a message. Immediately he thought about the visit from Jack Powers.

They continued to clean the children, then carried them upstairs. The intruder hadn't disturbed anything on the second floor. Both children were thoroughly exhausted by the ordeal and quickly fell asleep.

George then turned to his wife. "My God, what happened, Elizabeth?"

She looked at him, face drawn and tired. "I was getting ready to make dinner when a big, burly man came out of nowhere and knocked me to the floor. He held a knife to my throat and threatened to kill me. When we heard the children come in, he punched me in the face. That's the last thing I remember, that big fist with the black glove coming down at my face."

That explained the blood around the nose and mouth of his wife and kids. George assumed the attacker first punched them in the face to subdue them, then bound and gagged them. He sympathetically thought of his wife and especially his children. They would be bruised, swollen, and sore for days, but at least they were all alive.

"Did you get a look at him, Elizabeth?"

"No, he wore a black hood over his head, but he had blue eyes. I could see them through the eye holes in the hood."

Blue eyes eliminated all Hawaiians and those of Asian descent. "Anything else?"

"Yes, he had a deep, resonating voice."

"Did he say anything?"

"Yes. He said to tell you to return the favor. He said it a couple of times. 'Tell your husband to return the favor.' What does that mean, George? What favor?"

"Elizabeth, we have to call the police."

She abruptly rose and shouted, "No police. The man said no police, or he'd come back and kill us all."

Her statement frightened George. He trembled at the thought of his family being murdered. Today's ordeal was extremely traumatizing, but they were all still alive. He loved them and couldn't bear losing them.

Elizabeth, clearly irritated, said, "How are you involved with these kinds of people? What kind of favor do you owe them?"

"I can't tell you, Elizabeth. It's better if you don't know; safer for you and the children. Trust me on this."

She lowered her head into her hands and wept. "Just return the favor. Please, George, just return the favor. Whatever it is, just do it. You have no choice. Don't put us through this again."

He hugged his wife to console her. He felt sorry and guilty for having subjected his family to such cruelty by associating with a man like Jack Powers. Yet, he knew what he must do. His wife had perfectly summed up the situation. He had no choice.

EARLY IN THE EVENING that same day, Jack Powers entered a bar on lower Nu'uanu Avenue. Tiger Lilly's was one of several saloons in the area known as Fid Street, 'fid' being the sailors' term for spirits. Located a few blocks from Honolulu Harbor, the fid street establishments were the favorite haunts of blue-collar workers living in Honolulu and sailors from the four hundred ships docking in the harbor each year.

Tiger Lilly's wasn't Powers' kind of place. Small, dark, and musty, it was patronized by the lowest class of clientele and reeked of stale cigars, cheap rancid beer, and sweat, and the scotch wasn't the smooth, aged drink he craved. Instead, it was harsh and biting, like paint thinner that had been distilled just yesterday in the back room.

The bar was about half-filled. He had arrived a couple hours before the throngs of sailors packing the place almost every night. Danny, the young Filipino from the stables, had told him his daughter, Audrey, came here with that deadbeat, Robert Alton. He looked around. They weren't here tonight. He ordered the paint thinner scotch, took the first bitter sip, and, while he waited, recalled his first visit to Tiger Lilly's.

It was a rainy evening about ten months earlier. He was on his way back from Franz Schmidt's estate when his carriage hit a large pothole on Nu'uanu Avenue and broke a wheel, right in front of Tiger Lilly's. After tying his horse and hustling inside to escape the weather, Jack Powers met Colonel Ralph Grimes for the first time. Grimes was sitting at the bar, drinking heavily. The only empty seat was the one next to him. Powers took the open seat, and they began a casual conversation.

The two men were different in most respects. Powers was educated, articulate, and suave. Grimes hadn't finished the third grade and was direct and gruff. Powers lived in a beautiful house in an exclusive area and enjoyed fine liquor at the upscale Hawaiian Hotel lounge. Grimes rented a room in a flophouse near the harbor and drank bottom-shelf liquor at Tiger Lilly's, but they did have a few things in common, a love of alcohol and guns; and one powerful feeling that would bond them tightly--an intense, burning hatred of the native Hawaiian people.

Powers recalled Grimes telling of his abhorrence of the American Negro, especially after the slaves were freed when President Lincoln enacted the Emancipation Proclamation on January 1, 1863. As a twenty-year-old, he joined the Confederate army to somehow right the 'injustice.' Quickly rising to lieutenant colonel through battlefield bravery and natural leadership skills, he became further enraged when General Robert E. Lee surrendered at Appomattox Court House on April 9, 1865, ending the Civil War.

Realizing the slaves would remain free, he became a vocal leader in the newly formed white supremacist organization, the Ku Klux Klan, and led groups of like-minded racist soldiers on killing raids against the freed slaves and their families across the South. He fled to Hawaii to avoid imprisonment for his crimes, but when he arrived in Hawaii, he found 'island niggers,' as he called the dark-skinned Hawaiian people, running the country.

At first, Powers considered Grimes' younger days interesting, but as Grimes babbled on, he became just a typical bar room drunk venting his frustrations with life. Powers had spent a lot of time in bars and was well aware of how drunkards could blather away for hours, so after listening to Grimes ramble on for a few more minutes, Powers had heard enough and got up to leave.

He was putting on his coat, still wet from the earlier downpour, when Grimes suggested the Hawaiian government should be overthrown and put into the hands of the intellectually superior Caucasians. Powers paused and listened more keenly as Grimes continued, saying the overthrow wouldn't be difficult because Hawaii maintained no standing army and that the only national defense was the Honolulu Rifles, a volunteer militia. When Grimes said he was the officer-in-charge of the Honolulu Rifles, Powers removed his coat, returned to his seat, ordered another scotch, and began plotting.

A firm hand on his shoulder and the deep baritone voice above him interrupted his thoughts. "It's done, Jack."

Ralph Grimes sat next to Powers and ordered the paint thinner scotch. He downed the drink in one shot, slammed the glass onto the bar, and ordered another.

"Ooooo. That was so good," he joked, knowing Powers hated the stuff.

"So, everything went well, Ralph?"

"Like clockwork."

"Do you think Kingston will be scared enough to return the favor?"

"You said he was a timid man. If this doesn't break him, he's not as timid as you thought. I got his kids, too."

"And they're all still alive?"

"Yep. If he doesn't come around, I'll go back with a more serious approach."

Powers hoped it wouldn't come to that. Recalling Grimes' stories of his 'killing raids' in the South, he knew Grimes could kill repeatedly without remorse. He even seemed to enjoy it. The slaughter of a prominent banker and his family would trigger an intense murder investigation that would not only destroy his plans, but could lead back to him.

"Let's just sit quietly for a day or two and see what happens. I'll let you know."

"I'll be ready."

TWO DAYS AFTER THE ATTACK on his family, George Kingston approached the Powers Building. He had a nine o'clock appointment with Jack Powers. It was eight-forty-five. He entered the building with a growing sense of ambivalence. On one hand, he feared for the lives of his family and knew what he had to do to protect them. Still, he was hesitant to do it. His association with Jack Powers was just business. Sure, he owed Powers a favor, but it had to be something reasonable, not this. He became angry thinking that although he had done nothing wrong, his family had been terrorized, and he was being forced to commit a felony. It wasn't fair. He realized as he paused halfway up the stairs that, after spending the previous two days trying to come up with a viable alternative, this was his last chance to think of one.

POWERS' OFFICE ASSISTANT announced Kingston's arrival, and he entered the office. Powers latched the office door, walked behind his desk, and sat. Kingston sat in a chair in front of the desk. There were no 'Good mornings,' no handshakes.

"What's your decision?" Powers asked.

"You left me no choice."

"Fine. The King departs in two weeks. Wait until he leaves, then make the transactions. Backdate them. You've got two weeks after the King leaves to do it. That should be plenty of time. Let me know when you've completed everything. I want to see verification."

Kingston exhaled slowly. "Jack, I don't know exactly why you're doing this, but I assume eventually you'll want it to get out that the King has embezzled from the Queen's Hospital trust fund."

Both men sat silently for a moment, trying to read the other's reaction. Powers broke the ice, "Your point?"

"Our bank is independently audited once a year. The audit occurs at the end of July. The auditor will discover the transaction and since it's illegal, he'll reveal it. That might be helpful for you if you want to make this public. The auditor will do it for you. It'll be a smooth sequence. You won't have to get involved, potentially exposing yourself."

There weren't many times when Powers was caught off guard, but this was one of them. Kingston appeared to be right. Having an auditor announce the illegal transfer was perfect. However, the audit was scheduled just before the King's return. Powers wanted the transfer to be revealed shortly after the King's departure so public furor could grow during the several weeks the King was away and unable to defend himself. He stared at Kingston while he thought it through. Kingston gazed back expressionless.

Powers was the first to speak. "Let's move the audit forward a month, to the end of June."

"We don't schedule it; the auditors do. We never know the exact date, just sometime at the end of July. We don't have any say in it."

"Who does the audit?"

"It changes. I don't remember who did it last year, but I can get that information for you. However, I'm sure it will raise suspicion if you try to tamper with their schedule. We tried unsuccessfully to do it a few years back for legitimate reasons, and there were problems. They became leery. They wouldn't bend."

Everything Kingston said made sense, but Powers remained suspicious, and he still wasn't sure if it was worth the delay in revealing the illegal transfer. He considered it a significant advantage for public discontent to grow in the King's absence.

Powers leaned back in his chair, took a deep breath, then slowly let it out. "Why would you want to help, George?"

"Actually, it would help me. It would give me more time. Making the actual transfers isn't complicated, but it would be less risky if done at the right time, and I can't predict when that will be. My neck is out there, and I want to be as safe as possible."

"Just remember, the whole process has to be completed sometime before the King returns, regardless of where your neck is."

"Of course. It just gives me a bigger window, and it also helps you by reducing the risk I'll get caught. If I get caught, your plan is down the chutes."

Again, Powers privately agreed with Kingston's statements. Even the delay in publicizing the illegal transfers probably wouldn't be a problem. He recalled some of the King's previous pleasure trips. The King always returned later than initially scheduled. If he came back late again, there would be a couple of weeks after the auditor discovered the illegal transfers for public outrage to grow; sufficient time. All the bases seemed to be covered.

"Okay. You've got until the audit. But as soon as you know the exact date for the audit, I want to know. I want you to tell me that same day."

"I promise I will. Anything else?"

"No, you can leave now."

Kingston nodded, rose from his seat, and headed for the door. He had won something--time. The pressure was lifted, at least for a while. It was a small victory.

Powers observed Kingston's contented look and became infuriated. He gritted his teeth and pounded his fist on the desk, then yelled, "If you screw me on this, I swear, you'll suffer more than you can imagine. First, you'll watch your whole family, one by one, die a gory, excruciatingly painful death, then you'll be killed the same way."

The color drained from Kingston's face, and his hands trembled as he opened the door and left.

Powers sat at his desk and thought about the meeting. The illegal transfers had been delayed to accommodate the audit, but he considered it an improvement to the plan. Also, he felt confident Kingston would do his part when the time came. To be certain, he vowed to deliver a periodic reminder, a strong one if necessary. In about six weeks, the first step in the plan to overthrow the King of Hawaii would be complete. Powers was satisfied for the most part. Still, he had a gnawing suspicion Kingston harbored an ulterior motive.

CHAPTER 6

On a beautiful Hawaii morning, David Coe stood outside the Powers Building, gazing up Fort Street, awaiting Jack Powers' arrival. Soon Powers, in his horse-drawn carriage, rolled down the street and stopped at the curb.

"Good morning, David. Hop aboard."

All the wealthy people in Hawaii owned a horse-drawn carriage, and almost all preferred a model with an enclosed cab for comfort and privacy and a driver outside and forward of the cab steering a two-horse team, but Jack Powers loved to drive. His carriage was a smaller, lighter, two-seat model with a retractable canopy pulled by a single horse. Coe jumped into the front seat next to Powers. Powers snapped the reins, and they were off to Franz Schmidt's estate to meet the wealthiest man in Hawaii.

Schmidt owned expansive sugar plantations on Oahu as well as on Maui and Kauai, but the cornerstone of his empire was the monopolization of sugar refineries in California. Since the Reciprocity Treaty allowed only unrefined sugar to be exported duty-free to the United States, there were no large refineries in Hawaii. All unrefined Hawaiian sugar, brown and coarse in appearance, passed through Schmidt's California refineries for processing into the white crystalline sugar the American public craved.

Coe looked forward to the trip. He and Powers met in Powers' office every Monday morning for a mentor-protégé session, but those sessions were often interrupted, frequently shortened, and even occasionally canceled due to Powers' busy schedule. Coe coveted the rare opportunity to have Powers' undivided attention for the ninety-minute excursion.

"How is everything going, David? Any problems?"

"Not really. I'm still getting used to Sara, though."

Powers laughed. "Yeah, she's a hard worker and very efficient, but she can be cantankerous at times."

"Yeah, I noticed."

"After a while, she'll grow on you. She's an important member of the firm. One piece of advice."

"What's that?"

"As you know, the firm purchased a typewriter not long ago. It's a recent invention, and Sara insisted we get one. And she loves it; uses it for everything. She thinks it will revolutionize the business office."

"And I agree with her, Jack."

"Interesting. Anyhow, I'm sure she'll use it for the Schmidt contract you're preparing. When you review the typed copy of the contract, do not, I repeat, do not mark up the typed copy. Just note the corrections on a separate sheet of paper and give it to her."

"Thanks for the advice, but why not mark the typed copy?"

"To reduce the time to re-type, Sara tries to save as much of the original typed copy as possible. She's quite resourceful at it, and it gets the work out faster. She claims mark-ups on the typed copy create more work for her and slow her down."

"I can see her point."

"Yeah, but she didn't warn me, and when I marked up the typed copy, she jumped all over me. That was the first and only time I did it. I don't ever want to go through that again."

"So even the partners aren't safe."

"David, no man escapes the wrath of Sara scorned."

They both laughed. As they left the busy streets of downtown Honolulu and entered the open road, Powers snapped the reins, and the horse moved into a quick trot.

"Titus loves the open road," Powers said.

With the cover fully retracted, the sun caressed their faces, and a warm breeze blew pleasantly past them. The road turned toward the water, and Coe enjoyed the expansive view of the deep blue Pacific Ocean framed by stands of coconut trees with the clear blue sky above. The fresh scent of sea air was invigorating. Seeing several surfers in the water, Coe was reminded that he hadn't been out in a while. Long hours at the office had reduced his leisure time. He was willing to make the sacrifice to further his career, but, for the moment, he wished he were out with the surfers.

"Well, David, what did you think of the meeting with the sugar plantation owners?"

"Pretty intense."

"Yes, it certainly was intense, and I'm afraid things won't get much better until we get a permanent solution for the Reciprocity Treaty. If this situation doesn't get resolved the right way, our lifestyle, everything will drastically change, your future as well. We must make certain the United States continues to buy Hawaiian sugar. I'm sure you understand."

Coe turned his head from the scenery to look at Powers, then asked, "Yeah, I understand, but, in your opinion, what *is* the permanent solution? I mean, at the meeting, there seemed to be no agreement on how to resolve the issue."

Powers kept his focus on the road ahead and replied, "The only permanent solution is the annexation of Hawaii as a United States territory. That's a certainty."

It was the response Coe expected. "You know, Jack, the Book of James, chapter 3, verse 18, states, 'And the harvest of righteousness is sown in peace by those who make peace.'"

Powers snickered. "I know many think a move toward annexation will result in a civil war, but, in my opinion, the process can be peacefully negotiated and, in the long run, be better for everyone, including the native Hawaiian people."

"How can it possibly be better for the native Hawaiian people?"

"Look, Hawaii won't continue to be the isolated, independent country it was when your great-grandfather and my grandfather came as missionaries. It was paradise back then, but the situation has changed. Several countries are exploring the world and colonizing areas that are economically advantageous to them.

At this moment, British, Russian, and Dutch ships are moored in Honolulu Harbor. British admiralty dines with the King twice a week. Hawaii is the most crucial location in the Pacific Ocean, and all these countries want to take it for themselves. And it will happen; somebody will take it. The native Hawaiians will lose control of Hawaii. That's inevitable."

"The best scenario for the Hawaiian people is for the United States to assume control. Things would remain pretty much as they are now. If another country comes into power, the fate of the Hawaiian people is much less certain. In the worst case, imagine the Russians, with their totalitarian czar, taking Hawaii. The native Hawaiians would be forced into slave labor."

Coe recognized Powers' attempt to persuade him, but he'd heard it all before. It was the party line the mission boys used to justify their intentions. To Coe, the party line actually meant-- Hawaii might lose its independence someday, so it's best if we take it now. The logic disgusted him.

He knew the probability of the Russians colonizing Hawaii was low, and Powers only mentioned it for shock value, but he also knew the Dutch and British were aggressive colonizers, and they exploited their colonies for profit.

In Indonesia, the Dutch confiscated all the fertile land and converted it into Dutch plantations. As a result, natives didn't have enough land for subsistence farming and suffered through poverty and famine. While Coe certainly didn't want a similar situation in Hawaii, he felt it was morally wrong for any country to forcibly take Hawaii from the native Hawaiian people.

"You're an intelligent man, David. Please consider my arguments. I think you'll conclude I'm right."

Coe nodded in agreement, but only to avoid a heated discussion.

THE CARRIAGE TURNED onto a long straight road flanked on both sides by beautiful, evenly spaced Norfolk pine trees, all at a uniform height of about twenty feet. The road was divided into two lanes by a narrow, grassy center strip adorned with lush, well-trimmed leafy green bushes. As they rode down the quarter-mile-long road, a large white wooden mansion with two columns supporting a portico drew near.

The road ended in a circle passing in front of the mansion and onto the outbound lane. In the center of the circle was an ornate water fountain surrounded by purple azaleas and yellow hibiscus in full bloom, complemented by a small white picket fence. A finely manicured lawn covered several acres of land surrounding the mansion. Coe was awed by the overall beauty and opulence.

Even before the carriage came to a halt in front of the mansion, Schmidt strode out of the front door and down the steps. Coe began to move to the back seat of the carriage, but Schmidt stopped him.

"No, no, Davey boy, you stay put. I'll hop into the back."

Schmidt greeted the other two with a handshake. "Let's get going. I want to show you something. You boys have a lot of business with us sugar producers, so I think you should know a little something about the sugar industry."

They departed down the long straight road, turned toward the cane fields, and about ten minutes later arrived at a large two-story wooden building.

"Your visit came at a good time. This is our processing plant. Usually, the place is hot, noisy, and busy, but we're doing a burn now. You probably noticed the smoke from the cane fields on your way out. So right now, the building is empty," Schmidt said.

All three disembarked from the carriage. Schmidt held open the door to the building for the other two to enter. Inside the building was an assembly of heavy machinery used for processing the sugar cane.

Schmidt first described the massive cylindrical granite stones used for crushing the cane stalks to release the juice. The stones were specially made in China, he said. The juice, comprised of sugar and molasses, was then transferred to large copper kettles to allow particulates to settle, then to boil off the molasses. The kettles were salvaged from the once-booming whaling industry.

Schmidt moved to a piece of equipment resembling a large hollow cylinder with perforations in the cylinder wall. The cylinder was connected to a steam engine that rotated it at a high speed.

"Now, according to the Reciprocity Treaty, we're allowed to ship only unrefined sugar to the United States, but we do some refining here to satisfy the demand in the islands. And this . . ." Schmidt said proudly, pointing at the cylinder, ". . . is the future of sugar refining. It's the first one anywhere in the world.

Instead of boiling the cane juice in those kettles to boil off the molasses, we can load it into the centrifugal separator, that's what it's called, and spin the molasses out using centrifugal force. That process . . ." Schmidt said, pointing to the kettles, ". . . takes two weeks or more. This process takes a couple of minutes, and it produces a higher quality sugar we can sell at a higher price."

Schmidt beamed with every word.

"Pretty interesting, Davey. Don't you think so?"

"Absolutely, Mr. Schmidt. I'm interested in industrial machinery. In fact, I considered a career in engineering before finally deciding on law, and I'm somewhat familiar with the centrifugal separator. It was invented by a machinist from Boston,

David Weston. I read about him and his invention while I was in Boston, studying at Harvard."

"Yes, that's right. I'm impressed, and, by the way, I'm glad you decided on law. Otherwise, I would never have met you."

"Thank you, Mr. Schmidt."

"Franz, Davey; call me Franz. 'Mr. Schmidt' makes me feel old."

Coe winced at the thought of using Franz. His strict Calvinist upbringing had seared his brain with the ultimate respect for elders. He spent his entire life addressing everyone at least ten years older as Mister, Missus, or Miss, followed by the family name. It took him a month to call his mentor 'Jack', even though Powers corrected him every time he said Mr. Powers.

"Okay, Franz," Coe said. "I have a thought."

"By all means, let's hear it."

"Since this separator is the only one in the world, and it's so efficient, I was thinking that maybe you should process some of your exported sugar here and mix in a few bags here and there with the bags of unprocessed sugar you ship to the United States. Save some cost on the other end."

"That's a brilliant idea!" Schmidt exclaimed. "And . . ." lowering his voice to a near whisper, he said, ". . . that's exactly what we do."

Schmidt placed his right index finger vertically across his pursed lips and smiled. "Shhhh. We do cheat a bit. Now that's our little secret. Besides, it's only temporary, just until we get the new equipment installed in my refineries in California."

Schmidt turned to Powers. Jack, you were right. This is an extremely sharp individual we have here. He already thinks like a company executive. He'll fit right in with us."

"That's right. I see him as a senior partner someday."

"Someday? You should make him a senior partner next week."

He looked at Coe and winked.

Coe was silently bursting with joy over all the compliments. He enjoyed Schmidt's laid-back, easygoing demeanor and sense of humor.

As the three stood and talked, Coe spotted a stack of wooden boxes at the far end of the long building, each box about five feet long and one or two feet high. A canvas tarp partially covered the stack.

"What's that back there?" Coe pointed toward the stack.

Schmidt looked back toward the stack, immediately became flustered, and fumbled for words. "Oh, nothing really. Just spare parts and so forth. Wait here."

He hastened back to the boxes. A plantation worker who happened to be in the building rushed back and helped Schmidt pull the tarp over the boxes so they were completely covered. Then Schmidt angrily shook his finger at the worker and reprimanded him, pointing to the boxes. Coe couldn't hear what Schmidt said and didn't know what was in the boxes, but he was sure it wasn't something as mundane as spare parts.

AFTER TOURING the plantation and processing plant, they returned to the Schmidt mansion to discuss the contract. The island of Oahu consisted of two parallel mountain ranges, the Ko'olau and Waianae ranges. Rain that fell in the mountains filtered through the porous volcanic rock and collected in large aquifers beneath the mountains. The sugar plantations were located between the two mountain ranges. To irrigate Schmidt's expanding cane fields, more water was needed. The aquifers had to be tapped, and the water transported across Crown Lands, land owned by Hawaiian royalty since Kamehameha I, Hawaii's first king. Schmidt needed a long-term, iron-clad contract signed by the King to grant permission to construct water transport systems across the Crown Lands. Neither

Powers nor Schmidt anticipated a problem getting the King's signature on the contract if they offered monetary consideration.

The three sat at a large table in the dining room, and Powers looked at Coe. "You're on, David."

Schmidt then also turned his attention to Coe. "Okay, Davey, what do you have for me?"

"Well, Mr. Schmidt, sorry, Franz, I've nearly completed the contract, but before I finalize it, I want to present an idea that may be to your advantage."

"What's that?"

"There's a large tract of Crown Lands immediately adjacent to your sugar plantation. Instead of simply creating an easement to build water transport systems across those lands, we could add the acreage to your plantation."

Schmidt's face brightened. "Really. How many acres?"

"About three thousand. You'd more than double the size of your current plantation."

"My gosh! And you have a way for me to use that land."

"Yes, we can do it through a long-term lease. We'll make the lease for one hundred years so your company can continue using it well into the future. The lease will convey until its expiration date regardless of who occupies the throne. We'll put it in your company's name so those who follow you can use it. Jack feels getting the King's signature won't be a problem since the land isn't in use."

Powers interjected, "Yeah, we'll just add a little extra to the fee."

Schmidt chuckled. "Then I could simply expand my cane fields into the Crown Land, make it a bigger plantation just as if I owned the land."

"That's right."

"Good work, Davey. Let's do it."

"There is a drawback. The Crown Lands will require a professional survey before I can properly prepare the lease. I searched the public records and discovered that many of the boundaries are described by non-permanent landmarks like rocks and trees."

"Rock and trees?"

"Yeah, let me give you an example." Coe opened his briefcase, removed a document, and turned a few pages.

"Here, 'From the large volcanic rock near the koa tree, step off two hundred paces to the large opia tree.' It goes on and on like this. In twenty years, neither the rock, the koa tree, nor the opia tree may be there, and you'll still have eighty years to go on the lease. To protect you and your company, we need a professional survey to identify accurate, permanent boundaries."

"I talked to a team of professional surveyors, and they said it'll take a couple of months to do the work. That means the survey won't be completed before the King departs. You'll have to wait until he returns to get his signature."

"No problem. I can wait. I'll be in California checking on my refineries while the King is gone, so I won't get started here until I get back anyhow. The survey will be completed by the time the King returns, won't it?"

"Yes. It will."

Schmidt turned to Powers. "Jack, if I'm not back before the King returns, get his signature on both the contract and the lease. Pay him what he wants, and I'll reimburse you when I get back. And, Davey, thanks for your creative suggestion regarding the leased land. Planting that extra acreage will make millions for me. You'll be rewarded."

"Thank you, Franz."

After wrapping up the contract talk, the three men exited the house onto the portico.

"Oh, by the way, Jack, I think we should meet with the King's sister prior to his departure. You know, an informal get-together, us two, him, and his sister, just to get acquainted."

"I've already taken care of it. The four of us are going to meet at the Kapiolani Park race track on Race Day."

"Good idea. The race track always works for me."

As Coe descended the steps from the portico, he glanced to his left, and about fifty feet away was the most captivating woman he'd ever seen. She appeared to be in her early twenties, obviously of Asian descent, with long, straight black hair that grew down past her waist and shimmered in the sunlight. Her almond-shaped eyes were less pronounced, possibly from Caucasian blood in her lineage. She wore a long white dress off her shoulders extending to her ankles and no shoes. Their eyes met, and they stared for several moments, then she flashed a broad glowing smile. He was entranced.

The aura was broken by Schmidt's voice. "Well, I see Davey has an eye for Malia."

Coe turned and looked up the five steps to see both men still standing on the portico, looking down at him. Schmidt was grinning. Powers was not.

"Davey, that was some smile Malia flashed. Will you still be able to concentrate on those contracts?"

Coe's face flushed as a sheepish expression emerged. Before he could utter a response, Powers interjected, "David is an attorney. He's not interested in a housekeeper."

"I don't know. If I were a young man, I think I'd be interested," Schmidt returned as he turned to Coe and winked.

On the return trip, Powers warned about associating with laborers or housekeepers like Malia. It could ruin your professional image, he said, but Coe didn't hear a word. Although he was a successful attorney and well-respected among friends and colleagues, thus far in his life, he hadn't had much luck with women, especially beautiful women. They didn't find his unappealing physical appearance to their liking.

His only prior tryst was with Mary Ellen Higgenbothen. She was a student at Radcliffe College, a prestigious women's institution, while he was studying law at Harvard. She was pleasant, and he learned a lot from her, but, physically, she was the female version of him; tall and lanky with a prominent, angular nose. They often joked that if they ever had children, the children might resemble flamingos, but with gray feathers.

Coe always desired to be with a beautiful woman, but they currently seemed beyond his reach. He expected the situation to change when he became a wealthy and influential attorney, and even though he assumed he would never see Malia again, she opened a window into his future. That, along with the favorable impression he made on Franz Schmidt, made for a relaxing return trip.

His mind at ease, he viewed with admiration the ancient, man-made fish ponds on the *makai* (the Hawaiian word for 'toward the ocean') side of the carriage.

Fish ponds (note walls with openings for makaha) *(Hawaii State Archives)*

For centuries, Hawaiians had systematically raised fish for food. They used natural lagoons as the fish ponds and constructed a wall at the mouth of the lagoon to separate it from the open ocean. The wall was built of volcanic lava rocks and contained several openings about five feet wide. In the openings, they mounted a gate called a makaha. The makaha resembled a jail cell door with vertical bars made of bamboo. The bars were critically spaced to allow small fish from the ocean to enter the lagoon, but to prohibit larger fish that had grown after feeding in the lagoon to escape back to the ocean. The large fish trapped in the lagoon were easily harvested.

CHAPTER 7

Kamehameha Day, a Hawaiian holiday paying tribute to Hawaii's first king occurred on June 11. The holiday festivities included Race Day, the most celebrated horse racing day of the year at the mile-long, oval Kapiolani Park race track in the shadows of spectacular Diamond Head mountain.

Kapiolani Park race track *(Hawaii State Archives)*

Franz Schmidt and Jack Powers stood alone outside the royal box awaiting the arrival of the King and his entourage, including the King's sister. The royal box, located at ground level right at the finish line, consisted of a bamboo frame and a roof of coconut palm fronds. The four hundred square foot area, reserved for the King and his invited guests, contained about ten chairs and a bar. A young Hawaiian man stood behind the bar, also awaiting the King.

"It's a beautiful day," Schmidt said. "It should put the sister in a favorable mood. Maybe she'll win a couple of races and we'll all go home happy."

"She doesn't gamble," Powers returned.

"Not at all like her brother, huh? Then I guess we'll have to use our charm to win her over."

"Let's hope so, Franz. I view this as a critical period, and not just for the next two months while the King is gone. She's the successor to the throne, so we'll get some insight into the political environment after the King's reign is over."

A roar of cheers in the distance alerted them to the King's arrival, but the mass of people obscured their view of the King's carriage as it rolled down a path leading onto the race track. The path, bordered on both sides by a column of ironwood trees, was lined with patrons who cheered as the King passed. Schmidt and Powers spotted the horse-drawn carriage when it reached the race track. In addition to the driver, only the King and his sister were in the carriage.

The carriage rolled down the race track and stopped in front of the royal box, where the King and his sister disembarked. The King showed dark brown skin, black wavy hair, and a neatly trimmed beard and mustache. He wore a white suit and a wide-brimmed, white Panama hat. Known as the Merry King, he was about forty pounds overweight from all the merriment.

The King swiveled back and forth, smiling and waving to the cheering crowd as he made his way from the carriage to his seat in the royal box. His sister also was dark-skinned, her black hair streaked with gray and worn in a stack on top of her head. She wore a long, neck-to-ankles Mother Hubbard dress and a weak smile as she walked behind her brother.

Approaching Schmidt and Powers, the King smiled and extended his hand. "Good afternoon, Franz. Good afternoon, Jack. It's a beautiful day for horse racing."

"It is indeed," Schmidt returned. Powers smiled and nodded.

They all moved into the shade, and the King announced, "Let me introduce my sister, Lydia."

Schmidt stepped forward. "Pleased to meet you, Your Majesty."

The sister returned a weak handshake and a slight smile but didn't say a word. Powers followed.

"I'm looking forward to working with you, Your Majesty," he said, extending his hand.

"Don't be so sure, Mr. Powers," the sister said without returning the handshake, leaving Powers' hand dangling in mid-air.

"I, unlike my brother, won't be easy to manipulate. This may be a more difficult period than you anticipated."

Powers, Schmidt, and the King were stunned. A chilling silence fell over the box. The King emitted a weak laugh, attempting to melt the ice, but was unsuccessful.

"Drinks. We need drinks." The King nervously motioned to the nearby attendant. The King and Powers ordered scotch; Schmidt and the sister, a cup of water. After the drinks arrived, they all sat and sipped in uncomfortable silence for several minutes.

Finally, the King stood. "Why don't we all go down to the stables? I want to show Franz a horse running in the third race. I think he has a great chance to win today. I'm going to bet on him."

"Okay. Let's go. I'm always interested in meeting a winner, especially an equine," Schmidt said as he chuckled.

The sister spoke from her seat. "I have no interest in gambling. I'll stay here."

Powers turned to the King and Schmidt. "I'll stay behind as well. You two go ahead without us."

The King and Schmidt glanced at each other, eyebrows furrowed in bewilderment, then the King said, "Yes, perhaps it's good for you two to get better acquainted."

After the other two had gone, Powers turned to the sister and smiled. "Your Majesty, I want to clarify any misunderstandings and put your mind at ease so we can work productively during your reign."

The sister glared at Powers. "Rest assured, Mr. Powers, my mind *is* at ease, and there *is* no misunderstanding between us. You and your mission boy cohorts have already taken much of the land from the Hawaiian people as well as much of our ability to govern ourselves in our own country. Your next step is to take our country from us and annex it to the United States. So you see, Mr. Powers, I understand you very well and despise your actions and intentions."

Powers was set back by the frankness but maintained eye contact while his mind raced to come up with an appropriate response. The sister's statement was accurate, and there was nothing he could say to dissuade her from her position. He also knew there was no point in denying; it would only start an argument he couldn't win. He decided to simply remain calm and exercise diplomacy to diffuse the situation.

"Your Majesty, I hope you'll approach the coming months with an open mind. I look forward to working with you in that light."

The sister offered no response. After a few moments, they both turned their attention away from each other and sat in uneasy silence, observing the people in the grandstand, the horses entering the track before the first race, and beautiful Diamond Head mountain in the background. Powers ordered another scotch, then another as he waited impatiently for the other two men.

Schmidt and the King returned just prior to the first race. Shortly after that, the King's sister said she felt light-headed, probably from the afternoon heat, excused herself, and departed.

"So, Jack, did you and my sister have a good conversation?"

Powers whipped his head around to face the King, holding his glare momentarily before speaking. "It was revealing. That's all I can say. It was revealing."

Powers seethed as he recalled the sister's rejection of his offer to work together but soon realized her attitude may have worked to his advantage. Franz Schmidt heard the sister's initial blast; harsh words Powers could use to rally the 'big five' behind his plans.

The rest of the afternoon's conversation encompassed only events on the track. There was no further discussion of politics. Happiness returned to the royal box, especially after they all won a substantial bet in the third race by following the King's advice.

AFTER THE FINAL RACE, the King left in his carriage, and the other two departed for Powers' office. Schmidt insisted on knowing about the conversation between Powers and the sister, and Powers was eager to enlighten him.

They arrived at Powers' office and sat after Powers latched the office door.

"What did you and the sister discuss?" Schmidt asked.

"It was a continuation of what you heard, Franz. In no uncertain terms, she told me she despises us and vehemently opposes everything we're trying to accomplish."

"She certainly is direct, isn't she?"

"Yes, she is. And when the King departs in five days, we'll have to deal with that directness for a couple of months. You know, in the time she's on the throne, she doesn't have to be our most ardent supporter, just not a radical opponent who will take action against us."

Schmidt looked squarely at Powers. "That's right, Jack. So let's not do anything to antagonize her in the brief period she's on the throne."

The tone of Schmidt's comment surprised Powers.

"What do you mean?"

"I'm talking about the Committee of Safety. Roy Matthews talked to me about it. Look, I'll support whatever action we need to ensure the United States continues to buy our sugar, but right now, we don't want to provoke the sister. We just want her to sit quietly on the throne until the King returns. I suggest the Committee not even meet while she's the Queen. Annexation is a sensitive issue; even rumors of a meeting could prompt her to act. Just put everything on hold. It's only a couple of months."

"No problem, but let's not lose sight of the big picture. At some point, the sister will be a major problem."

"Maybe, but right now, the King is on the throne, and we have him in our pocket. He's a relatively young man and will probably be around for years. Let's just enjoy our current situation and tone down the talk about annexation for a while. As long as we control the King, we'll get what we need, and we'll get it without the possible consequences of annexation, like a civil war. We may not be in a perfect situation, but we're all making lots of money. Let's not rock the boat."

"Franz, I'm a lawyer, and I'm paid to consider contingencies. The King is in his fifties. He's not that young, and he certainly doesn't lead a healthy lifestyle. What if he's not around for years, and it's the sister we have to deal with in the long term?"

"Then we'll deal with the sister. My biggest concern right now is getting the King's signature on the contract and the lease Davey is working on."

Schmidt exhaled slowly, then asked, "By the way, how is Davey? I really like that kid."

"He's fine."

"You know, Jack, I'm impressed with him; his creative idea to lease the Crown Lands, his knowledge of the centrifugal separator; just an intelligent individual. If he had chosen engineering instead of law, I'd bet he would be an outstanding engineer."

"Franz, if David Coe had chosen to study engineering, he'd be another Sir Isaac Newton. He's supremely gifted with natural intelligence, probably one of the most intelligent human beings on the planet. He understands advanced concepts instantly. His encyclopedic knowledge of case histories and legal precedence astounds me. He's already a brilliant lawyer and will get even better. We're extremely fortunate to have him on our side."

"That's extraordinary, Jack, just extraordinary. You're right. We are fortunate to have him on our side. Be sure to reward him accordingly so we don't lose him."

"Sure thing. By the way, I wouldn't repeat these compliments to David. I don't want him to get complacent."

"I understand, but please pass along my regards to him."

"Will do."

Schmidt looked at Powers for a few moments, then began in a slow, deliberate tone. "Jack, there's something I want to ask you."

"What is it?"

"I know Blackburn wants annexation because he covets the governorship, and I know Matthews wants it because he's convinced the Reciprocity Treaty is going away and all us sugar growers are doomed. And the colonel, well, who knows what he wants. I think he just enjoys the fight. But you're a lawyer, highly successful, lots of clients, lots of money. It seems to me that maintaining the status quo would be most beneficial to you. So, tell me, why are you so passionate about annexation?"

"Because, in the long run, it's the only way we can guarantee our future prosperity. If the United States doesn't annex Hawaii, the

British, the Dutch, or some other country will colonize it, and we'll lose control."

"I know that. You're right. Some country will probably take Hawaii someday, and that may have an effect on us plantation owners, but your law firm would benefit from all the new foreign businesses needing counsel to establish themselves here. Same question, Jack; why are you so passionate about annexation? And, please, tell me the true reason. Level with me."

Powers thought for a few moments. He reached into the bottom drawer on the right side of his desk, removed two glasses and a bottle, and placed them on his desk. After filling one of the glasses, he turned to Schmidt.

"Join me? Glenfiddich Scotch whiskey; the best."

"Never touch the stuff, Jack."

"Yeah, I know. Maybe another time."

"Maybe."

Powers leaned back in his chair, put his feet up on the desk, and took a sip. "Franz, we've had a mutually beneficial attorney-client relationship for several years, but I also consider you a friend. What I'm going to tell you is in strict confidence, one friend to another. Agreed?"

"Certainly."

"My great-grandfather arrived in Hawaii in 1821 with the first wave of American missionaries on the brig, Thaddeus. He was sent to Maui to begin his work. My grandfather succeeded him, then my father. My sister and I attended missionary school with native Hawaiian kids, just us two white kids and twenty or more Hawaiian savages. They teased and harassed us mercilessly. My sister was in tears every day. I tried to defend her. Got in lots of fights but was always outnumbered, so I took a lot of beatings."

"Couldn't your father do anything to help?"

"Oh yeah, he was a big help," Powers said sarcastically. "He forgave them and prayed for them."

Powers took another sip and cleared his throat. He removed his feet from the desk, leaned toward Schmidt, and glared. "Then, one day, we found my sister at home sitting in a squatting position facing the wall. She was frozen in a catatonic state. I was too young to understand what happened back then, but my father put her on the next ship out of Hawaii. My father never talked about the incident, but when I became older, I realized those damned savages most likely had sexually molested her. She was only twelve years old."

"Twelve years old!" he yelled with bloodthirsty anger.

Powers' face flushed red, then he slammed his drinking glass onto the desk, shattering it. Schmidt recoiled as shards of glass flew. His jaw dropped as he focused on the blood flowing from the cut on Powers' right index finger.

Powers took a big gulp from the bottle, then addressed the cut by wrapping a handkerchief around the base of his four fingers and holding it in place with his thumb.

"My God, I'm sorry, Jack. Has your sister recovered? Is she alright today?"

"No, she never recovered. She went back to Massachusetts, was raised by an aunt, and never married. I saw her once about ten years ago when I went to Washington, D.C. She was still sullen and distant."

"Again, I'm sorry."

"Since that time, I've wanted to get revenge. I deserve it; my sister deserves it. And taking their country is the ultimate revenge. It's even better than killing. This way, they all have to suffer, and so will their future generations."

Schmidt exhaled a deep breath and paused while Powers calmed down. "Jack, I want to apologize in advance if I sound insensitive, but that was a long time ago. You have to move on. I understand a traumatizing event like that might be with you for a lifetime. Who knows, if it happened in my family, I might feel the same way, but please don't let it cloud your judgment going forward."

"My mind is clear, Franz, but we still have major problems with the Hawaiians. Since I've been practicing law, we've had to deal with the Hawaiian government on issues involving contracts, legislation, and other legal matters, and let me tell you, the Hawaiian people, their bureaucracy; it's totally incompetent. They impede progress, squelch innovation, and make it nearly impossible to move forward. They're all lazy and just don't care. You work in that environment on a daily basis, and you get frustrated beyond belief. You learn to despise the Hawaiian people. The faces in the bureaucracy change, but the new faces are all Hawaiian, and they're all the same—totally worthless. It's time to move forward."

"I agree with you to some extent, Jack, but let me get right to the point. I need to get this contract through. If I don't get it, I can't get water to my cane fields. That's millions of dollars lost. And if somehow I don't get it because of all this annexation talk, I'm going to blame you. Just remember that."

Powers clenched the bottle of scotch as his blood pressure rose and anger again welled inside. He wanted to blast out at Schmidt. This fight was personal, and he didn't care if Schmidt lost money he didn't need. Powers struggled to control his fury. He took a deep breath as he gazed at the firm's biggest client. After a sip of Glenfiddich, Powers calmly said, "Don't worry, Franz. I'll take care of it."

"I know you will, Jack." Schmidt smiled as he rose and extended his hand. After they shook, Schmidt departed, and Powers returned to his seat. He took another sip and vowed not to allow even the firm's biggest client to impede progress toward a goal that consumed him.

CHAPTER 8

It had been over five weeks since the King departed, and harmony existed between the mission boys and the Queen. The mission boys facilitated the tranquility by putting everything on hold. The Committee of Safety didn't meet, and the law firm of Powers, Thatcher, and James avoided any business requiring input or approval from the throne.

On a Wednesday morning, David Coe was working in his office when Jack Powers entered, carrying a large manila envelope and whistling. He closed the door behind him, smiled, and handed the envelope to Coe. "David, the survey of the Crown Lands is complete. After you've inserted the survey information into the documents for Franz Schmidt, please let me know."

"Sure, Jack," Coe said. "You seem quite jovial today. What's up?"

"Life is good, David. Life is good."

Powers continued, "Schmidt came back early from California. As soon as you're finished, we'll go out to his plantation. You can brief him about the specifics and get his signature on the documents."

The mention of a trip to Schmidt's estate instantly brought to mind the image of Malia. He resolved to complete the work as soon as possible so he might see her again.

"When the King returns, we'll get his signature to finalize both documents."

"I guess Mr. Schmidt doesn't need the contracts so urgently that he wants to present them to the Queen for signature," Coe joked.

"No, indeed he doesn't. We've been fortunate during the Queen's reign. No incidents at all. We don't want to do anything to change that. The King will return soon. We can wait."

"And you think these documents would set her off?"

"Without a doubt. A contract allowing a sugar plantation owner to build canals across the sacred Crown Lands, then a long-term lease to grow sugar on those same hallowed Crown Lands. Heaven forbid we have progress," Powers said. "She would explode."

As soon as Powers finished the word *explode*, both he and Coe were shaken by the sound of a cannon firing in the distance. After a few minutes, they heard another boom; a few minutes later, another. The sounds were coming from the direction of Punchbowl. As the booms repeated every few minutes, Powers' expression became blank.

"Oh, my God, it can't be," he said, then scurried from the office.

Coe, unaware of the reason for the cannons, became alerted by crowd noise from his open office window. He crossed the office and looked from the window to the street below. A stream of people hastened, some even running, toward Honolulu Harbor. When he stepped out of his office, he saw no one remaining on his floor. Assuming they all left the building to follow the crowd, he descended the stairs and exited the building to join what seemed like the entire population of Honolulu.

Following the throng *ewa* (the Hawaiian word for 'away from Diamond Head') on Merchant Street, then turning *makai* at the police station, everyone continued down Nu'uanu Avenue to Honolulu Harbor, cannons still booming intermittently in the background. He reached the harbor to find the piers already jammed with people. Still with no understanding of what happened, he tried to stop one of the passers-by.

"The King. It's the King," the man yelled as he continued running toward the waterfront.

Coe presumed the King had returned early from his trip to California. His first thought was he would have to work late to insert the survey data into Schmidt's documents so they would be ready for signatures. He didn't want to be responsible for any delays, recalling the additional revenue created by the expansion of Schmidt's plantations. Millions, Schmidt said.

He approached the pier where *USS Boston* was berthed on the Diamond Head side of the pier. As he tried to navigate through the crowd, past the ship, to the head of the pier to get a clear view back toward Diamond Head, a voice from above called, "Davey, Davey."

Coe looked up to the main deck of *Boston*.

"It's me, Brian. Brian Hall. Remember me from the Rialto?"

He thought for a moment before the memory of Brian Hall returned, a vivid memory. Hall was the best billiard player he'd ever seen. One night, while hanging out with Kimo at the Rialto, Coe saw him win game after game, often running the table, against overconfident British sailors. Then, after winning a substantial sum from the Brits, Hall set up the bar, buying a drink for everyone in the house. Coe had never seen such a gesture before or since, and it made quite an impression. He considered it a classy move. Before leaving, Hall came over to say goodbye to Kimo, who introduced them.

"Come aboard," Hall yelled down.

Coe climbed the ladder to the main deck, and the two shook hands.

"So, the King cut his trip short, huh?" Coe said.

Hall wrinkled his eyebrows in puzzlement. "I guess that's one way to say it."

"What do you mean?"

"Davey, haven't you heard? The King died in California, and his ship is bringing his body back to Hawaii. Here, take a look."

Hall extended a telescope to Coe. Coe accepted the telescope but didn't raise it to look. He was stunned at the news and considered the ramifications. Everything had changed in an instant.

The Queen was on the throne for good. The livelihood of the plantation owners was threatened, and the stability of Hawaii in jeopardy. The color drained from his face as his expression went blank.

"Yeah, that's why they're firing the cannons. Apparently, it's Hawaiian tradition to signify the death of *ali'i* (the Hawaiian word for 'royalty'). His ship is coming around Diamond Head right now. Look."

Hall pointed in the direction of Diamond Head.

Coe looked out, his view from the main deck of *Boston* unobstructed by the mass of people on the pier below. His mind still in a daze, he raised the telescope to his eye and scanned the horizon. Then he saw it, the King's ship, black banners flowing from the masts and draped over the bulwarks around the main deck. He followed the vessel for several minutes, still in disbelief, then a buzz of conversation began on the pier below as the ship became visible to the naked eye. As the ship drew nearer, the voices escalated amid overtones of weeping.

Coe and Hall moved to the starboard side as the King's ship moored on the opposite side of the pier from *Boston*. Down on the pier, police dispersed the crowd to create a path for a horse-drawn carriage to travel down to the ship and receive the King's body. Two beautiful white stallions led the carriage, which was draped in black fabric. The casket, also draped in black, was loaded onto the carriage, which then moved off the pier to the wailing sounds of the bereaved crowd.

Coe turned to Hall. "Things are going to change. Of that, I'm certain."

"You know, Captain Wolfe briefed the crew a couple of months ago. He reminded us of our duty to protect American citizens here in Hawaii. Then he said we should be on a higher readiness that while the Queen was on the throne. It was like he expected trouble. Well, now she's there for good. I wonder what it all means."

"Exactly. I wonder, too."

Coe turned to leave.

"If anything happens, Davey, I'll let you know."

Coe turned back to Hall and extended his hand. "Thanks, Brian. I'd be appreciative if you could do that."

They shook and Coe descended the ladder into the mass of people, their fate now hanging in the balance.

JACK POWERS SAT ALONE in his office, feet up on the desk. He emptied the bottle into his glass, then reached back into the drawer for his spare bottle of Glenfiddich. The door was latched and the DO NOT DISTURB sign hung outside. There was no need to rush down to the pier. He was well aware of what had occurred and had no desire to witness the ceremony.

Earlier that morning, Powers was elated when George Kingston visited and told him the audit was scheduled for the following week, that he would make the transfers tomorrow, and that Powers was welcome to visit on Friday if he wanted to see verification. Now, Powers' first thought, ironically, was of Kingston, one day removed from committing a serious crime. With the King dead, he was off the hook. No point in framing a dead man. Powers lifted his glass to the ceiling and muttered to no one, "George Kingston, you lucky son-of-a-bitch."

He downed the scotch from his glass in one gulp as his thoughts turned to his daughter, Audrey. They had argued bitterly the night before when he confronted her about the secret meetings with Robert Alton. She said she hated him for spying on her and would continue seeing Alton. He was distracted from the incident when Kingston stopped by, but with the excitement from Kingston's morning visit now obliterated, the distress from his daughter returned.

"Kids," he grunted as he raised the bottle to his lips and took a couple of gulps. His daughter would soon leave Hawaii to attend college in Massachusetts and be gone for a couple of years. He hoped to repair their relationship before her departure, but, he reasoned, even if he failed, at least Alton would be out of her life.

After another swig from the bottle, he turned his attention to the future. The Queen, unlike her brother, owed no favors to the mission boys, and she was committed to returning Hawaii to the Hawaiians. Also, unlike her brother, her reputation was impeccable, and she was popular with not only the native Hawaiians but with the growing number of former plantation workers from Asia who decided to remain in Hawaii, as well as with a fair number of Caucasians who felt it morally wrong for anyone to forcibly take control of Hawaii.

On the positive side, he would now have full support from the plantation owners. Their livelihood was threatened, and they would soon be desperate if they didn't react. Franz Schmidt's plans to expand his plantation into Crown Lands died with the King. He would now be more than willing to use his newspaper to back the plantation owners and to oppose the Queen's actions, but first, the Committee of Safety needed a new plan to get rid of the Queen, and nothing was readily apparent.

CHAPTER 9

After lying in state for two days in the throne room in Iolani Palace, the King was laid to rest in Mauna Royal Mausoleum in the Nu'uanu Valley, and his sister was proclaimed Queen of the Hawaiian Islands. The day of her coronation was a grand occasion. Government offices and most businesses were closed for the day. It seemed the entire population of Hawaii turned out for the celebration.

The main event was a parade down King Street to Iolani Palace, followed by the official coronation ceremony on the palace grounds. King Street was lined on both sides by large crowds of the Queen's adoring subjects. Leading the parade, the Royal Guard in bright red dress uniforms marched in formation. The Queen's carriage followed, adorned with brightly colored leis and covered by a blanket of flowers, red, yellow, orange, and purple azaleas, hibiscus, and orchids. The Queen wore colorful leis around her neck and a genuine ear-to-ear smile while waving to her fellow countrymen.

Six men, three on each side of the carriage, carried kahilis, poles about six feet long held vertically with colorful feather plumes adorning the tops of the poles. As her carriage slowly proceeded down King Street, individual well-wishers occasionally ran up to the carriage and threw a lei or bouquet of flowers into the carriage. Smartly dressed Royal Guardsmen, marching in formation, followed.

Jack Powers, Franz Schmidt, and Roy Matthews stood at a large window on the second floor of Ali'iolani Hale, the government building directly across King Street from Iolani Palace. Looking down at the festivities, Schmidt remarked, "Beautiful day for a parade."

"Yeah, and it might be one of the last beautiful days unless we do something," Matthews said.

Suddenly, Matthews extended his neck toward the window, focusing on something below. "I'll be damned. Look at that. It's Robert Alton. I guess the champion of the Hawaiian people is happy today. Nothing for him to protest now. He's with that other troublemaker, the big Hawaiian. And the haole boy with them; I've seen him before."

Schmidt also spotted the trio in question. "Isn't that Davey down there with the other two? What's going on, Jack?"

"It's nothing."

But both Schmidt and Matthews stared at Powers, expecting further explanation.

"Look, I often advise David that poor choices of friends could hurt his career, but he's known those guys since grade school, so he still sees them occasionally. I don't like it, but it's no big deal."

"The haole boy is a lawyer?" Matthews asked.

"He is, and a damn good one."

"In your firm?"

"Yes, in my firm."

"Well, that's a problem, Jack." Matthews continued, "We're in a critical period now with the Queen a permanent fixture on the throne. It's imperative our plans remain secret, and you've got a guy who's chummy with the opposition roaming around your offices. Hell, the kid may have been planted in your firm just to channel information to the enemy."

"You're paranoid, Roy. I grew up with his father and have known David since he was a young boy. He's like the son I never had. He's an outstanding attorney and totally trustworthy."

"Well," Matthews began, looking out the window to see the Queen's carriage turn off King Street into the Iolani Palace grounds, "I'm going over to see the coronation, then I've got some business to take care of. Let's just not take anything for granted. In times like these, we all need a little paranoia. Good day, gentlemen."

Matthews shook hands with the others, then departed down the stairs.

Powers and Schmidt remained on the second floor and watched below as Matthews exited the building and walked away toward the palace grounds. Schmidt turned to Powers. "You know, Jack, I like Davey, but Roy has a point. Maybe you should keep an eye on him just to be sure."

"You may be right. I'll look into it."

They left the building for the coronation stand.

IOLANI PALACE was the most magnificent structure in Hawaii. The cornerstone for the palace was laid in 1879 and construction completed in 1882. Built in an American Florentine style, the building featured four corner towers and a veranda on all four sides of both the first and second floors. The interior was highlighted by a central main staircase of highly polished dark wood and was decorated using native woods such as koa and opia, as well as American walnut and Oregon white cedar. The palace had running water and was equipped with electric lights about ten years before the White House in Washington, D.C.

Iolani Palace – c. 1890 (*Hawaii State Archives*)

As the Queen's carriage pulled up to the coronation stand next to the palace, the crowd of people on the palace grounds cheered. The Queen stepped from the carriage onto the stand and acknowledged the applause with a broad smile and an exuberant wave. The cheers quieted as she began to speak.

"First of all, I want to thank all of you for your kind reception. I'm most appreciative. I look forward to serving you, and I will begin by returning Hawaii to you, the Hawaiian people, the rightful owners of this beautiful country."

After a brief pause, she enthusiastically added, "*Ua mau ke ea o ka aina i ka pono.*"

The crowd responded with deafening cheers, which continued as the Queen left the coronation stand, moved across the lawn to Iolani Palace, and up the steps to the front door. She turned to the crowd, waved to even louder cheers, then repeated, "*Ua mau ke ea o ka aina i ka pono.*" Again, the crowd roared as she entered the palace, and the applause continued for several minutes after the palace door had closed behind the new Queen.

DAVID COE FELT SHIVERS OF PATRIOTISM from the crowd's electricity, sparked by the Queen's Hawaiian language statement. It was the same sentence the old Hawaiian man uttered in Kimo's bar, and one of the few Coe would recognize. He turned to Kimo. "The life of the land is preserved in righteousness."

"You got it, bruddah. I always knew you Hawaiian inside." They both laughed.

Kimo turned to Reb. "Reb, you Hawaiian inside, too."

Reb looked puzzled, then smiled.

As the crowd began to disperse, suddenly, Reb sprinted off. Coe and Kimo looked at each other, then at Reb. Kimo took off after him when they realized Reb had spotted Powers, Schmidt, and Matthews across the lawn.

Coe froze in his tracks and ducked behind a nearby tree. He peeked around the trunk to see Reb stop just short of Matthews. Kimo had stopped behind Reb, prepared to restrain him if necessary. Coe heard Reb address the mission boys, "Roy Matthews, you old, skinny son-of-a-bitch. I should kick your ass right here in front of everyone just to punctuate the celebration, but I feel so good today that I just can't bring myself to do it. It's the beginning of the end for all you mission boys."

SCHMIDT AND MATTHEWS STOOD without responding, but Powers became livid at the sight of Robert Alton, the one violating his precious daughter, Audrey. He immediately understood the reason for her attraction to him--rugged handsomeness, coal black hair combed straight back, exotic hazel-green eyes, square jaw, and tan skin. Audrey, herself physically attractive, was drawn to men like Alton. It was the reason she repeatedly refused her father's insistent offers to introduce David Coe. Powers was oblivious to everything else as he stared intensely at Alton.

Kimo grabbed Alton by the arm. "Okay, Reb. That's it. We go now."

They started to walk away when Alton suddenly spun around as if prompted by the burn of Powers' glare. "What the hell are you looking at, Powers?"

Powers maintained his look but said nothing.

"You know, it's been almost as enjoyable screwing you mission boys as it has been screwing your daughter," Alton said. As he broke into a condescending laugh, Powers became furious. He reached behind his back, pulled his gun from its holster, and charged toward Alton.

"My God, Jack, think about what you're doing," Schmidt said as he and Matthews tried to block Powers' path. The two older men weren't strong enough to constrain him, but Powers quickly realized, with so many witnesses present, this wasn't the time or place to deal with Alton. He was still fuming as Kimo yanked Alton away from further confrontation.

COE HAD OBSERVED the entire scene hidden from view. When it ended, he felt relieved to have avoided a situation where he was forced to choose between Jack Powers and the Hawaiian side, with both parties present for the decision. Coe hustled away in the opposite direction from the mission boys while keeping an eye on his departing friends. He circled and met up with them a few blocks away, expecting criticism of his disappearance, especially from Reb.

Reb didn't disappoint. "Well, if it isn't the little chicken. Where the hell were you?"

Coe smiled and shook his head as he looked to Kimo. He turned back to Reb. "Sometimes you just don't get it. I work for those guys. I can't be cavalier about this. Unlike you, I've got a lot to lose."

"Yeah, well, Kimo and I are beginning to wonder if we can trust you."

Kimo whipped around and grabbed Reb by the shirt with both hands, ripping off two buttons in the process. He quickly extended his arms, throwing Reb backward to the ground, and said, "I trust Davey. I never say otherwise. Don't you ever lie like that again or I make you silent for a long time."

"Okay. Okay. I'm sorry," Reb said from the ground.

"Now apologize to Davey and shake hands."

After amends, Kimo announced, "All good now. Let's go to my place. Beer on me."

THE THREE MEN passed through downtown Honolulu on the way to the Rialto. The bars on Hotel Street were overflowing. Men and women were drinking, laughing, and cheering in the streets. Coe observed that many men wore the wide-brimmed straw skimmers and said to Kimo, "I think I'll get one of those."

"Just what you need, bruddah."

"Yeah, Davey. You can start a trend among the lawyers, and don't forget to get one for Jack Powers," Reb added.

All three laughed.

Celebration in downtown – c. 1890 (*Hawaii State Archives*)

They arrived at the Rialto and worked through the crowd to enter. The room was loud and thick with smoke. Like all the other bars, it was packed. Even the billiard tables were being used as seats. They found a tight spot at the end of the bar, and Kimo went behind the bar and got drinks for the three. Kimo raised his glass and said, "To Hawaii."

Reb responded, "May she ever be free."

"Amen," Coe added as they clinked their glasses together.

After a few beers and many stories about good times in the past, Kimo looked at Reb. "So, you seeing Jack Powers' daughter, huh?"

"Yeah, for now, but she's leaving next week for Massachusetts to go to college. She'll be gone for a couple of years."

"She ever take you home to meet Dad?"

Kimo barely finished the statement before breaking into a hearty laugh. The other two joined him.

"Yeah, Kimo. I go to the Powers house every Sunday for dinner. Mom prepares a delicious meal for the four of us. Dad wants me to work in his law firm after Audrey and I are married."

They all roared, then paused for a breath before Reb continued.

"I want to name our first-born son Jack, but he insists on Reb."

More raucous laughter followed.

When the laughter subsided, Coe asked, "Do you love her?"

"I love screwing her; as a bonus, it infuriates Jack Powers. Did you see him today? He was out of control. I loved it."

"If I was you, I be extra careful. Powers a vengeful man. He not going to forget you," Kimo warned.

"I'm not worried. Besides, it's all over for the mission boys."

"She's really beautiful," Coe offered.

"What?" Reb said.

"Audrey Powers. She's beautiful."

"Yeah, I bet you wish you could get a woman like that, Davey."

Reb moved his head closer to Coe and pointed to their reflections in the large mirror behind the bar. "Look, there's the reason you can't."

Coe looked at the reflection of his homely face next to Reb's, then grinned and shook his head. "Let me tell you something, Reb. In a few years, I'll be wealthy and powerful. Beautiful women love wealth and power. Think about what you'll be in a few years, old and broke."

When Coe saw Reb's expression sink, he said, "I'm sorry, Reb. I didn't mean anything by it."

"No. No, Davey. You have a point."

Reb's face beamed as he continued, "But right now, I'm doing quite well with Audrey Powers."

All three laughed.

"No doubt there," Coe responded with a smile.

Kimo and Reb returned their attention to the festivities, but Coe dwelled on the previous conversation for a moment. He realized, while he may side with the Hawaiians on the fate of the country, he needed to maintain his connection with Jack Powers to achieve his career goals in Hawaii.

CHAPTER 10

The Queen had been on the throne for almost a year. Most of Hawaii had comfortably settled into her reign, and progress continued in many areas. The entrance of Honolulu Harbor was deepened as international commerce increased. Modern coal-handling machinery was constructed for Oahu Railway and Land Company to handle the growing fuel demand for visiting steamships. The Hawaiian Electric Company was formed as the availability of electricity in businesses and homes continued to spread. Electric streetlights proliferated. The Foster Building at the corner of Nu'uanu and Marine Streets was completed. Modern equipment to record the tides in Honolulu Harbor was installed. Macadamia nut trees were successfully planted on Mount Tantalus as part of a reforestation program. Admiralty from foreign navies readily renewed friendly relations with the new ruler. The country was at peace.

The mission boys, however, were in a state of flux. They had grown accustomed to having the King's backing in every venture. That support had vanished with the Queen on the throne. Communication between them and the Queen was strained. Cooperation was nonexistent. In fact, it seemed to them that, from the very beginning of her reign, the Queen had consciously acted to oppose their ambitions. Six months into her reign, they were sure of it.

Just before to the King's ill-fated trip, the mission boys had pressured him to grant the United States exclusive use of the Pearl Lochs as a naval facility, a condition the United States demanded for extending the Reciprocity Treaty. The King signed the treaty, extending it for five years, but either party retained the option to cancel the treaty by notifying the other party one year in advance. Six months into her reign, the Queen notified the United States that Hawaii was exercising its option to cancel the treaty. She resolutely refused to turn over a beautiful recreation area like the Pearl Lochs to a foreign navy. The area belonged to the Hawaiian people, she said. Her decision put the sugar plantation owners on the clock. They had one year to resolve the problem. Failure to settle the issue would result in economic disaster. Now, with six months to go, they were more deeply concerned.

The plantation owners depended on Jack Powers for a solution. He had their full support and continually reassured them, but thus far, all his attempts at resolution had failed. With Franz Schmidt and his newspaper fully on board, Powers first tried a media blitz. The Honolulu daily newspaper ran stories for about two months to garner public support. The stories covered a variety of angles.

First, the articles detailed the economic catastrophe Hawaii would face if the Reciprocity Treaty were canceled. The Hawaiian government, they said, would lose much-needed tax dollars due to the reduced revenue from sugar export and, therefore, be unable to continue many projects benefiting native Hawaiians. Other editorials said the contract laborers who worked the plantations would lose their jobs and, as a result, both they and their families would face financial hardship.

Without access to newspaper publicity, the Queen published and hand-distributed flyers with her rebuttal. She essentially said revenue lost by the reduction in sugar export would be covered by increased proceeds from international commerce and from a new industry, tourism, which had been burgeoning with advancements in steamship technology. Her position on contract labor was that it was a form of slavery and, therefore, a barbaric practice she intended to outlaw.

Another commentary in the paper said, since the King signed a five-year extension to the Reciprocity Treaty, it was the duty of subsequent rulers to honor the commitment. Failure to honor it would create a precarious distrust from other nations. The Queen countered by stating the sole reason the mission boys wanted to extend the treaty was to further line their own pockets.

When the public failed to respond strongly to either position, Jack Powers tried a different approach. Knowing the Queen despised him, he briefed David Coe and sent him to discuss the situation with the Queen. The tactic didn't help Powers but provided an unexpected opportunity for Coe.

The Queen graciously received Coe and openly discussed renewal of the treaty with him, even proposing alternative concessions to the ceding of Pearl Lochs. After the discussions, the Queen offered tea and, during casual conversation, said she was well aware of his rising reputation as a brilliant young attorney and offered him a position on her legal staff. He thanked her profoundly but said he was content with his current position. Before he departed, the Queen assured him the offer was standing.

Powers thoroughly debriefed Coe after the meeting. He received detailed information regarding the alternatives proposed by the Queen, none of which were accepted by the Senate Committee on Foreign Relations. There was no mention of the Queen's job offer.

DURING THE SIX MONTHS after the Queen announced she was exercising the option to cancel, Powers maintained frequent communication with Senator John James from Massachusetts, his contact on the Senate committee. James was a classmate at Harvard Law School, and after graduation, the two remained close friends and became business associates. Despite never having been to Hawaii, James was conferred a senior partnership in the law firm in Hawaii and received a healthy salary. In return, he vigorously represented the sugar plantation owners as chairman of the powerful Senate Committee on Foreign Relations. He had been invaluable in the past in supporting favorable legislation, but for the previous six months, had been unable to convince his colleagues to approve the treaty without Hawaii's ceding of Pearl Harbor.

Powers sat at his desk and stared at the telegram he'd received from James, RECIPROCITY TREATY DEAD. TAKE ACTION.

One week from today, all five members of the 'big five' were coming to the law offices. They insisted on the meeting. Powers was frustrated he couldn't offer progress toward a solution. During a similar meeting four months earlier, he simply reassured them he would handle the situation. The 'big five,' supremely confident in Powers, based on his past record, were satisfied. However, with no solutions to offer, he had no choice but to employ the same strategy at next week's meeting.

Powers wasn't in a strong position, and he knew it. With the clock ticking and no progress toward a solution, the 'big five' would undoubtedly be less patient. He again considered a desperate option, one he'd rejected after every previous consideration.

It came from Colonel Ralph Grimes; assassination, in fact, multiple assassinations. Grimes' plan was to kill the Queen, then her successor, who was her niece, and any following successors until there was no one left to govern. It was a plan similar to the one hatched by John Wilkes Booth and his associates to throw the United States government into chaos by killing Lincoln and both of his successors to the Presidency.

Again, he dismissed the plan. The American minister would never support such a violent undertaking, and the entire population of Hawaii would turn on the mission boys when word got out that they initiated the action. But, on the other hand, it would rid them of the vindictive Queen.

A knock on the door interrupted his train of thought. David Coe cracked open the door and glanced in. He had come for their regular mentor-protégé meeting held every Monday morning. During each session, they talked for an hour or more about the work for the upcoming week and Coe's career path. Powers shared his experiences as a successful lawyer and businessman, providing career guidance and 'fatherly' advice.

Powers welcomed the interruption. "Good morning, David. Please, come in."

During the previous few months, in addition to the mentor-protégé relationship, Powers and Coe had also developed a personal connection as well. It began when, at Powers' invitation, Coe started to join him on Saturday mornings at the armory firing range. Powers was a serious marksman, owned an extensive gun collection, and fired all the guns expertly. Coe was initially reluctant but quickly discovered that he, too, enjoyed shooting. It seemed to come naturally to him and, in a brief time, he became proficient.

Jack Powers closed the office door and sat at the conference table across from Coe. The first ten minutes of their session almost always covered the previous Saturday's experiences at the range. The conversation had just begun when, after a brief knock on the door, a short, middle-aged man burst in. He was out of breath and flustered.

"I'm sorry for barging in," he said, looking first at Powers, then at Coe.

He turned his attention back to Powers. "Jack, this morning, the cabinet met with the Queen, and the first thing out of her mouth was, 'I've written a new constitution and plan to introduce it next week.' All of us cabinet members were shocked. We tried to dissuade her, but she seems set on this. During a break, I excused myself, then ran down here to tell you. I thought you should know, but I've got to get back."

"Thank you, Paul. Try to delay her as long as possible."

After the man left, Powers leaned forward toward Coe and exhaled a deep breath.

"David, that was Paul Evans, a member of the Queen's cabinet. You heard what he said. This is serious. Don't tell anyone else. It'll get out soon enough."

Powers was sure that a new constitution, especially one written by the Queen, would further harm the sugar plantation owners. However, he was also confident that the situation with the Reciprocity Treaty, an agreement between two nations, wouldn't be affected by a constitutional change. They would still have six months.

Coe then said, "You know, Jack, I was just thinking. When the Queen took her oath of office, she promised to uphold the constitution of Hawaii. So, technically, she'll violate her oath of office when she signs this new constitution."

The statement hit Powers like a bolt of lightning. His entire attitude abruptly changed. A glow of contentment crossed his face.

"Thank you, David. Your insights were most helpful. Now, if you don't mind, I'd like to postpone our meeting until another time. I have some urgent work to finish."

Powers quickly ushered Coe from the office and closed the door behind him. Once alone in the office, he leaned back in his chair, put his hands behind his head, looked upwards, and smiled.

AT ABOUT EIGHT O'CLOCK, David Coe left his office. He looked toward Jack Powers' office on the way out. The door was closed and the DO NOT DISTURB sign was hanging. That morning, he had heard first-hand from one of the Queen's cabinet members of her plan to introduce a new constitution, written by the Queen herself, which restored sovereign power to the throne and rights to the native Hawaiian people. The Queen's constitution would be unacceptable to the mission boys, and they would vigorously fight it. He didn't know who, besides Powers, was in the office but was certain plans for action were in the making.

Filled with guilt, he descended the stairs. Having figured out Powers' strategy to use the Queen's signing a new constitution as a premise to demand her abdication, he wanted to kick himself for providing the stimulus for the plan. Why did he have to offer an opinion? His father always taught him that silence was golden, but he failed to heed the advice this time. He tried to assuage his guilty conscience by telling himself that, even without his input, the mission boys would have eventually discovered a means to continue their run toward annexation, and it was true. The mission boys wouldn't have given up. In time they would have found an alternative, but it didn't happen that way. His words alone provided the spark which re-ignited the fire for overthrow.

JACK POWERS STOOD BEHIND HIS DESK addressing the hastily assembled members of the Committee of Safety. As usual, the window shades were drawn, and a dim, shaded electric bulb provided the only lighting. Despite the short notice, the other three members were all present. They were comfortably seated, had rolled their cigarettes, and lit them.

Powers had already informed the trio of the Queen's intention to introduce a new constitution, then said, "I've been thinking about this situation all day and have come to the conclusion that this is a great opportunity for us to permanently remove Hawaiian royalty from power, form our own government, and begin the process of annexation."

Andrew Blackburn took a quick, nervous drag, blew a puff of smoke, then said, "Come on, Jack. I told you before, as the American minister, I just can't support overthrowing a foreign government."

"I can," Ralph Grimes interjected as he smiled. "Just give me the word, and I'll have my men ready."

"Listen to me," Powers responded. "The Queen has no legal authority to introduce a new constitution. Legally, she's committing an act of treason by attempting to overthrow the present government with the introduction of a new constitution. That's an impeachable offense."

Matthews and Blackburn shuffled in their seats and leaned forward.

Blackburn asked, "How can it be that the Queen doesn't have the legal authority to introduce a new constitution when her brother, the King before her, announced the Bayonet Constitution, and that was legal?"

Powers said, "When the King signed the Bayonet Constitution, he was acting under the previous constitution, which granted autonomous power to the King. So, legally, it was within his power to implement a new constitution. However, once the Bayonet Constitution was signed into effect, the autonomous power of the King and all future rulers was relinquished."

"It seems like just a technicality to me."

"It's the law, Andrew. She violated her oath of office to obey the constitution. By attempting to expunge the existing constitution and replace it with a new one, she committed an act of treason."

Roy Matthews stood and clapped. "Brilliant, Jack. Just brilliant. So the King had the legal authority to sign into effect a new constitution, and that new constitution prohibited him and future royalty from legally signing into effect any future constitutions."

"Exactly," Powers said.

Blackburn asked, "So this can be construed as an act of treason?"

"It *is* an act of treason, attempting to overthrow the government, and it imperils the safety of American citizens living in Hawaii by introducing the threat of violence."

"I'm not sure that's enough for me to authorize the troops to come ashore. If, as you say, violence broke out, well, then absolutely, but her just illegally signing a document, I don't know."

"Andrew, I agree with you. Let's first draft a proclamation stating the Queen violated her oath of office to obey the constitution and demand she vacate the throne. If she agrees and abdicates, we establish a provisional government, then apply for annexation."

"And what if the Queen refuses to vacate the throne?" Blackburn asked.

"That's when you come in. You order the American troops ashore to maintain order and protect American lives. Meanwhile, Colonel Grimes and the Rifles will physically remove the Queen, entering Iolani Palace if necessary."

Powers watched as the American minister fumbled to roll a cigarette. "You'll just be doing your job, Andrew, protecting the safety of Americans. You will have become aware of the potential for violence between the Rifles and the Queen's Royal Guard and called out the troops before the violence escalates. You're covered."

"I believe there has to be an outbreak of violence *before* I call out the troops, Jack. "

"Do you remember what happened when you delayed in the aftermath of the King's election? Rioting quickly got out of control. Wouldn't it have been better if you had called out the troops promptly to prevent the rioting in the first place? Wouldn't it have been safer for the American citizens?"

Blackburn didn't answer and kept his head down as he completed the rolling process. Powers pursed his lips, shook his head slowly, then exhaled and said, "Do you remember when we were in Washington D.C. to discuss the Reciprocity Treaty? We met with President Benjamin Harrison, and he told us he was receptive to annexation."

"Yes, of course, I remember."

"Well, since Harrison lost his bid for re-election in November, he'll only be in office until March, when Grover Cleveland, the incoming president, is inaugurated. We have to get an annexation treaty passed before March. Cleveland most likely won't support it. That means we won't have another opportunity for at least four more years. You want to be governor of Hawaii, don't you? This is your only chance. It's now or never, Andrew."

Blackburn lit his cigarette and sat silently, then tilted his head toward the ceiling and blew a big puff of smoke. After a few moments, he snapped his head down to look Powers in the eye, slapped his hand on the table, and said, "You're right, Jack, we have to maintain order, and the best way to accomplish that is to prevent chaos in the first place. So if the Queen refuses to yield the throne, I'll order the troops ashore to prevent violence threatening the safety of American citizens."

"Great. I'll begin drafting the proclamation. I should be finished tomorrow. We'll deliver it to the Queen as soon as she introduces the new constitution," Powers said.

Grimes bellowed, "I'll have my men ready to support the American troops if necessary. The presence of the Rifles will provide additional numbers which may deter the Queen's Royal Guard from fighting at all."

"Good idea, Colonel," Powers replied. "Have them ready, and, as you say, maybe we can pull this off without a shot being fired."

"Anything else?" Powers asked. There were no responses.

"Let's do it," Powers said, pounding his fist on the desk.

CHAPTER 11

The signing of the new constitution was a well-publicized event eagerly anticipated by many. On a beautiful Honolulu morning, a large crowd of mostly native Hawaiians, but also including diplomats, legislators, and invited guests, gathered on the Iolani Palace lawn to witness the historic occasion. After presiding over the closing ceremonies of a legislative session at Ali'iolani Hale, the government building across King Street from the palace, the Queen crossed the street to proclaim the new constitution. The Royal Hawaiian Band began to play as she entered the palace grounds. The crowd cheered as the Queen passed through to enter the palace. The Queen returned the adulation, smiling and waving to the adoring guests.

David Coe stood among the crowd, but unlike the others in attendance, he wasn't in a joyous mood. He was wary. Coe felt a hand on his shoulder, then heard a familiar voice. "Davey, what a great day."

He shook hands with Reb, then scanned the crowd, hoping none of the mission boys were there to see them together.

"Well, right about now, the Queen is signing the new constitution, and in about ten minutes, she'll come out to the veranda and proclaim it law," Reb said as he pointed to a spot on the second-story veranda. "It'll be the end of the mission boys, and a new beginning for the Hawaiian people."

When the Queen didn't appear after thirty minutes, Coe became more suspicious even though the crowd seemed to dismiss the delay as a political expectation. Smiles and lively conversation still abounded, and the band continued to play. After another thirty minutes, the crowd became uneasy. Thirty minutes later, there was genuine concern. The smiles had been replaced by worried looks, and the Royal Hawaiian Band had stopped playing.

A well-dressed woman on Coe's left turned to him and said, "I wonder what's going on."

"Yeah, she should have been out by now," Reb added.

After two hours, the Queen emerged on the second-story veranda. She appeared disheveled, her expression somber. The crowd below didn't cheer; instead, they became eerily silent.

"Ladies and gentlemen, the declaration of the new constitution has been delayed. I have been served a proclamation charging that I violated my oath of office by writing the constitution. I issued a rebuttal proclamation stating that I will seek to implement the new constitution through legal channels. Following the advice of my cabinet, I am announcing the postponement. Thank you for your understanding."

As the Queen disappeared inside the palace, the audience erupted into a rumbling of uncertainty.

The well-dressed woman placed an open hand on each cheek, her expression blank, her head slowly moving from side to side, and said, "My God, this is terrible."

"This is the work of the mission boys. I know it is," Reb said before he ran to the gazebo where the Royal Hawaiian Band was seated, leaped onto the stage, and yelled to the crowd, "Can I have your attention? Everyone, can I have your attention? We've witnessed an attempt by the mission boys to derail efforts to return Hawaii to the Hawaiian people. We must not let them succeed."

The dazed crowd, initially facing the palace to see the Queen, turned around to the gazebo. As Reb continued, many dignitaries began to leave, but most of the crowd, comprised of native Hawaiians, moved closer to the gazebo to listen. Dejected by the turn of events, Coe left the palace grounds and returned to his office.

FOR THE FIRST TIME since joining the firm, Coe could not ignore outside distractions and concentrate on his work. By three o'clock in the afternoon, he decided to leave the office for the day and take his work home. Maybe a change of scenery would help re-establish focus. Outside the building, the weather had changed since the morning. Dark clouds obscured the sun, and the wind had picked up. He leaned into the gusts and headed up Fort Street, leaves and paper blowing around him, then boarded one of the horse-drawn trolleys that rolled down King Street several times daily, bringing riders to and from downtown Honolulu.

Horse-drawn trolley – c. 1890 *(Hawaii State Archives)*

The rectangular trolley car featured a center aisle running front to back and a wooden bench, similar to a church pew, along each side facing the center aisle. There were five other passengers on board. He moved to the rear of the trolley and sat on the left side.

A riotous crowd noise surged through the trolley as they approached Iolani Palace. The sound intensified as they got closer. Coe, his back to the palace, twisted around in his seat to see the action. The sight astonished him. The crowd had grown tenfold since that morning and was no longer a quiet, passive gathering.

Reb stood alone on the coronation stand in front of the palace. His inflammatory words and gestures often incited the rowdy crowd into a wild, cheering frenzy.

Suddenly, a shot rang out, then another, then several more. The shots seemed to come from beyond the coronation stand, possibly from the palace guardhouse behind it. One of the shots strayed through the area and struck a woman seated near the front of the trolley. She cried out and grabbed her injured arm. Others on the trolley screamed. As the shots continued, Coe ducked down, his heart racing. After a few seconds, the shooting ceased, and he cautiously sat up and looked toward the coronation stand but didn't see Reb. He didn't know if Reb had left the stand, if he'd been shot, or if he simply dropped below the paneling surrounding the stand to protect himself. Initially he thought the shots were aimed at Reb but he couldn't be sure. The crowd on the lawn scattered in a panic, yelling and screaming. The trolley driver snapped the reins, and the trolley sped from the area.

REB LAY ON HIS SIDE on the floor of the coronation stand, a sharp pain in his lower left abdomen. Reaching across with his right hand, he felt wetness through his shirt. Looking down at the bloody area, he realized he'd been hit by one of the bullets. He paused for a moment to gather his thoughts and assess the situation. Loud screams from all directions surrounded the stand. His first thought was to lie in place and conserve his energy. He was sure someone from the crowd would come to his aid or at least send help.

On second thought, the shooter could simply come to the stand, lean over the paneling, and finish him off with a pistol. Reb decided to leave the stand and try to escape using the dispersing crowd as cover. He rose cautiously, keeping a low profile, and flopped over the paneling onto the lawn. When he stood, he felt strong enough to at least begin the walk into Chinatown, where help was available.

He started out quickly holding his right hand firmly over the wound, looking around for anyone brandishing a gun. By the time he'd completed the half-mile trip into Chinatown, he felt weaker, and his pace had slowed considerably. He continued, nearly doubled over with pain. Blood dripped from the wound down onto his pants and shoes. When he occasionally looked up, the ghastly expressions on the faces of oncoming pedestrians met him. A few stopped to offer help, but he ignored them and kept plugging forward.

Finally, he reached an alley between two wooden buildings, stumbled down the alley, and entered the back door of one of the buildings. "Doc, Doc, Doc!" he yelled. A middle-aged Chinese man came through a curtained doorway from the front of the building. Doc was a tailor by trade, but knew about herbal medicine, seemed to have other rudimentary medical experience, and had previously treated Reb. "My God, Reb, what happened? Here, lie down over here on the couch."

He yelled something in Mandarin, and in a few moments, an elderly Chinese woman arrived. She gasped when she saw Reb, left immediately, and quickly returned carrying a large pan of hot water and a couple of clean towels draped over her shoulders.

"We going to have tea, so we have hot water ready," Doc said, half smiling.

Using scissors, he cut off Reb's shirt and examined the wound. "This going to hurt a little."

As Doc probed the area around the wound with his fingers, Reb winced. Then, finally, Doc said, "You know, I think I feel the bullet. It not very deep. You lucky. I think the bullet first hit something else, then bounce into you. Otherwise, it would be much deeper, and you would have more bleeding. I think you going to be okay, but I have to get the bullet out so no infection."

The elderly lady put a rolled towel across Reb's open mouth so he could bite down when he felt pain. Then, utilizing forceps sterilized in boiling water, Doc used one hand to work the bullet toward the forceps he'd inserted into the wound. Reb's muffled screams through his clenched jaws didn't rattle Doc as he worked quickly to grab the bullet and extract it from the wound.

As he examined the bullet, still clenched in the forceps, Doc marveled, "I never see a bullet like this before."

Reb turned his attention to the bullet. It wasn't round like all other bullets the men had seen. Instead, this bullet was shaped like a hexagon, having six flat sides. Doc dropped the bullet into an empty cup on a nearby table. After applying an antiseptic compress on the wound, Doc said, "Reb, you going to be fine, but now you must rest."

Doc raised his head, turned toward the doorway, and yelled, "Chan du. Chan du."

The elderly woman reappeared with two small, round, dark-colored opium pills, a thin needle piercing one of them. Doc opened a cabinet door and pulled out a hookah. He gave Alton the pipe and the pills and lit a candle on the table then he and the elderly woman left the room. They knew Reb could take it from there.

The hookah consisted of a broad bamboo tube about ten inches long and two inches in diameter. About two-thirds of the way down the bamboo tube, a smaller metal tube protruded at a ninety-degree angle. At the end of the metal tube was a small hollow bowl about one inch in diameter. A tiny hole opened through the roof of the bowl.

Reb held the hookah in his left hand and, with his right hand, impaled one of the opium pills with the needle. After inserting the needle into the tiny hole in the pipe bowl, he gently removed the needle, leaving the opium pill on top of the bowl. Using his index and middle finger to hold the opium in place, he inverted the pipe over the candle flame until the opium started to melt and vaporize. Quickly, he exhaled all the air out of his lungs, held the bamboo tube to his lips, and took the deepest possible breath, inhaling the vaporized opium. He held his breath for as long as he could, then exhaled slowly through his nose. He repeated the process with the second pill. First-time users often felt nauseated after inhaling, but Reb wasn't a rookie when it came to opium. He immediately felt a calmness and serenity about him. The pain from the wound had subsided. He lay back and fell into a deep sleep.

CHAPTER 12

David Coe got off the trolley a block from his house, a small, single-story, four-room, wooden structure in the missionary community. There were several houses like his in the neighborhood. All were built in New England then taken apart board-by-board, loaded onto ships carrying missionaries bound for Hawaii, and re-assembled once they arrived.

Like many Americans living in Hawaii, Coe was a descendant of Calvinist missionaries from New England. His early ancestors worked on Maui. His parents were transferred from Maui to Oahu in 1863, and he was born a year later. His mother died during childbirth. He had no siblings. His father was a Calvin minister, who once taught at the mission school, but no longer lived in the community.

Coe picked up the evening edition of the Honolulu daily newspaper, then opened the front door. The hot, muggy air slammed into him as he entered. The house, with its small rooms and low ceilings, was designed for New England winters by offering less space to heat. But, in Hawaii, the confined interior concentrated the heat and humidity, and with only a few undersized windows, the rooms were deprived of fresh air circulation.

As he stood in the clammy darkness, his spirits sank. He usually didn't mind living alone, but the loneliness haunted him during stressful periods. He thought about his father and how he missed him, then lit one of the oil lamps and plopped down into a rocking chair. As he glanced at the newspaper, QUEEN CHARGED WITH TREASON, captured his attention. He read the scathing front-page story accusing the Queen of attempting to overthrow the government by introducing the new constitution, then dropped the paper to the floor and leaned back in the rocker.

Public protests were common these days, but this was the first time gunshots were fired since the ill-fated revolution two years earlier. After completing law school in Boston, Coe arrived in Honolulu two weeks before that violent revolt protesting the Bayonet Constitution. He vividly remembered the troops from the United States and British warships in Honolulu Harbor being landed to suppress the uprising. Several protesters were killed, some of them he knew well. Reb, the leader of the revolt, was arrested and imprisoned. Coe feared the violence would once again escalate.

Since being hired into the firm, he'd dedicated himself to a successful career. It was the most important thing in his life, and he despised the chaos and disorder as distractions, even threats, to his career ambitions. He drifted back to his earlier years when he grew up and attended school with native Hawaiian children and Caucasian children from other missionary families. Back then, they were all friends. Such wonderful times. He yearned for those peaceful days from the past.

A knock on the door interrupted his thoughts.

When he opened the door, Brian Hall, out of breath and perspiring heavily, said, "Davey, I told you I'd let you know if anything came up. Well, the American minister ordered the troops from *Boston* to come ashore. Captain Wolfe wants me to canvas the area in civilian clothes and get back to him. So I ran to your house to see if you wanted to come with me."

"Sure," Coe responded. "Why are the troops landing? I mean, what happened?"

The two continued their conversation as they walked out into the street. It was about four-thirty.

"The way I understand it, the mission boys accused the Queen of treason for writing a new constitution and demanded she abdicate the throne. Since she hasn't done it, Jack Powers pressed the American minister to call out the troops."

"But Brian, I was at the palace this morning when she announced to the whole crowd she would seek to implement the new constitution through legal channels. A lot of witnesses were there to hear it."

"Yeah, but those mission boys can be persistent."

"Man, this is serious."

"You bet it is. Captain Wolfe told us to be ready for combat."

Coe and Hall first walked up to Iolani Palace. The gates to the main entrance off King Street were closed and locked, but they peered through the vertical iron bars of the gate to observe the palace guarded by about a hundred armed men from the Royal Guard. Two cannons had been moved to the front of the palace.

"I don't like the looks of those cannons. I think we're going to set up right over there," Hall said, pointing to a grassy area across King Street, the exact location where one of the cannons was aimed.

"Yeah. I see what you mean. This whole situation looks ominous to me."

"Let's go. Captain Wolfe wants me to go down Bethel Street past the police station on the way back to the ship."

As they passed by the police station on the opposite side of the street, at least twenty police officers were engaged in idle conversation in front of the building. Two Gatling guns were mounted on the stoops on either side of the entrance. Both Gatling guns were unattended. Coe and Hall passed without drawing attention.

The two men continued down to the pier where *Boston* was berthed. Coe turned to Hall. "I hope nothing serious happens here, but the possibility exists. Be careful and best of luck. I'll pray for you."

"Thanks, Davey."

The two shook hands, then Hall turned and boarded the ship. As Coe stood on the pier, a crowd gradually assembled. At six-thirty, the troops began to disembark from the *USS Boston*. After all troops had come ashore, they fell into formation on the pier. There was one company of U.S. Marines and two companies of sailors, all heavily armed. Coe looked among the sailors to identify Brian Hall, but, in uniform, they all looked alike.

Troops coming shore *(Hawaii State Archives)*

When Captain Wolfe barked his orders, the troops began a march from the pier up Bishop en route to Iolani Palace. The crowd on the pier, Coe among them, followed the troops. Coe wondered if Captain Wolfe chose Bishop Street instead of Bethel to avoid the policemen and the Gatling guns Brian Hall surely reported to him. The march up Bishop Street seemed like a parade. A crowd had gathered on both sides of the street, and many were cheering as the troops passed before them, but Coe knew it wasn't a festive occasion.

As the troops crossed Merchant Street, Coe left the crowd, turning right on Merchant and taking the more direct route to Iolani Palace. He waited across King Street from the palace in the grassy area where Hall said the troops would set up. In about ten minutes, Coe observed the troops marching down King Street toward him. He moved farther down King, crossing Punchbowl Street to stand on the grounds of Kawaiahao Church.

The troops approached their destination across from Iolani Palace and settled onto the grassy area. After an hour, with no shots fired and nightfall approaching, the troops began to set up camp for the night. Coe, feeling confident peace would prevail through the night, turned to walk away. To his right, a short distance from Kawaiahao Church, stood the tomb of King Lunalilo.

The present-day turmoil actually began with Lunalilo's death. In 1874, with the Kingdom of Hawaii existing in peace, King Lunalilo died after a brief period on the throne. He wanted his wife, Queen Emma, to succeed him, but died before legally designating her. With no legal heir to the throne, an election followed. The native Hawaiian people wanted Queen Emma, partly because her husband was a member of the Kamehameha dynasty, but also because her bloodlines were closer to Hawaii's first ruler, Kamehameha I, than her opponent's.

The mission boys supported a young police court attorney who reportedly had been discharged from other government positions for corruption and incompetence. When the young attorney won the highly charged, bitterly fought election, riots broke out in the streets of Honolulu. Under orders from the American minister in Hawaii, American marines and sailors, heavily armed, disembarked from United States warships in the harbor and restored peace.

Coe was too young to clearly remember the situation in 1874 but wondered if people felt then as he did now, apprehensive and uncertain.

THE NEXT MORNING, after spending a couple of hours at his desk, Coe left the office and headed to Iolani Palace. All his office mates had already departed. As he walked down King Street toward the palace, his progress was stopped by a gathering crowd at the intersection of Bishop Street and King. He worked his way through to the front of the crowd. The next block of King Street, which ran between Iolani Palace and Ali'iolani Hale, looked like an impending battle zone. On one side of King, the soldiers from the Royal Guard were positioned in front of Iolani Palace, cannons loaded and ready to fire at the United States troops. On the other side of King Street, in front of Ali'iolani Hale, the U.S. troops from the *Boston* were positioned, rifles locked and loaded, awaiting orders for battle. At some point during the night, the U.S. troops added a cannon and a Gatling gun to their arsenal.

JACK POWERS STOOD before a large window on the second floor of Ali'iolani Hale, gazing out at King Street and Iolani Palace. He turned to Colonel Ralph Grimes and said, "You know, Ralph. I've waited a long time for this opportunity."

"Yeah, I know, Jack."

"It's only the first step. There's still a lot of work, but this first step is big, and now is the time to take it." Powers said as he looked around. "Where's Blackburn?"

"Right here, Jack," the American minister called from down the hall. "Just a quick bathroom stop."

"Let's go," Powers said as he picked up a roll of documents and strutted down the stairs, the American minister close behind.

COE HAD BEEN WAITING about an hour when he saw Jack Powers and the American minister emerge from Ali'iolani Hale and cross a deserted King Street. Powers carried documents. The gates in front of Iolani Palace opened, and the two men entered the palace. After about thirty minutes, they exited the palace grounds and returned to Ali'iolani Hale. Powers was empty-handed.

After a few minutes of stillness, Colonel Ralph Grimes burst through the front door of Ali'iolani Hale and began to blow a whistle in short bursts. With the shrill blasts piercing his eardrums, Coe looked up to see several members of the Honolulu Rifles standing on the roof of the building, raising and cocking their rifles. Other members of the Rifles, who were stationed on the tops of nearby buildings, followed suit. They were all ready to fire at the soldiers of the Royal Guard inside the palace grounds.

About a hundred members of the Rifles then ran out from Ali'iolani Hale, crossed King Street, and positioned themselves behind the wall surrounding the palace. The United States troops pulled their Gatling gun across King Street to the perimeter of the palace grounds and aimed it at the Royal Guard. They then loaded the cannon, which was pointed toward the palace.

Inside the palace grounds, the Royal Guard, which was vastly outnumbered, at first seemed alarmed by all the movement outside, then took aim and prepared to fire their rifles.

With both sides ready to unload, a death-like silence gripped the crowd. Coe stood among them in high anxiety.

After about ten long minutes, the Queen appeared on the second-story veranda of Iolani Palace, her head low. She appeared choked up and struggled to speak. Finally, after pausing to gather herself, she cleared her throat and said, "After careful consideration and to avoid bloodshed, I am ordering my forces to surrender to the superior forces of the United States government. I request that the native people of Hawaii wait peacefully as I appeal to the President of the United States to reinstate me in the authority which I claim as the constitutional sovereign of the Hawaiian Islands."

After the brief statement, the Queen hurried inside. The soldiers of the Royal Guard lowered their weapons, then the members of the Honolulu Rifles stormed through the palace gates and disarmed them.

JACK POWERS OBSERVED the sequence of events from the Ali'iolani Hale window, then turned to Andrew Blackburn, smiled, and said, "It couldn't have worked out any better."

"You're right, Jack. Not a single shot fired."

"Now, it's time for me to make the announcement. I'll cherish this moment."

A force of United States marines escorted Jack Powers and Andrew Blackburn from Ali'iolani Hale across King Street to the steps of Iolani Palace.

"What a beautiful day," Powers said as he scanned the throngs of stunned people a half block away.

They reached the front of Iolani Palace. Powers then strode up the palace steps to the front door, turned, and proclaimed, "First, the Hawaiian monarchial system of government is hereby abolished. Second, a provisional government for the control and management of public affairs and the protection of public peace is hereby established to exist until terms of union with the United States of America have been negotiated and agreed upon."

Powers nodded to Andrew Blackburn, who then ordered one of the marines to lower the Hawaiian flag and raise the American flag in its place.

When Powers and Blackburn returned to Ali'iolani Hale, Ralph Grimes met them in front of the building. All three wore broad smiles.

"We did it." Powers exclaimed. "We're almost there. The next step—annexation."

The three shook hands, then entered the building.

COE AND THE REST OF THE CROWD had heard Powers' booming voice announce the end of the Hawaiian system of government. The Queen no longer ruled; the mission boys did. The people, mostly native Hawaiians and others loyal to the Queen, were devastated. Some began to weep, but most simply looked at one another in disbelief. Coe lowered his head and started a slow walk back to his office.

Later in the day, after preparing a written statement, the Queen moved from Iolani Palace to Washington Place, her private residence about a block away from the palace. The provisional government then occupied the palace and declared martial law. American minister Blackburn immediately recognized the provisional government by proclaiming Hawaii a temporary protectorate and ordering the American flag to be raised over all government buildings. Though startled by the abrupt change, other countries also recognized the new government.

CHAPTER 13

Two days later, David Coe and Kimo hiked through the heavily wooded area along an overgrown path lit only by the intermittent appearance of the moon. Overhanging branches frequently brushed the two men. It was too dark for Coe to visually recognize the trees, but the scent was distinctly pine. The men didn't speak. An occasional hoot from an owl somewhere above provided the only sound. After about thirty minutes, they emerged from the woods onto the beach of a small, natural harbor.

Aside from the soft swishing sound of the ocean lightly lapping the sand, it was silent. The full moon appeared between the clouds, illuminating three boats in the shallow water near the shore. They scanned the area for people but saw none.

Two boats in the harbor were catamarans, and their exposed decks readily showed both were unoccupied. The third boat was a small Chinese junk with its distinctive rectangular sails, each with several battens extending the entire width of the sails. The sails fluttered gently in the night breeze. Kimo pointed to the junk and said, "There, that's Doc's boat."

They proceeded around the shoreline and waded into the water to board the boat at the stern. The main deck was cluttered with wooden boxes, wicker baskets, and potted plants. It was sheltered by a large canopy consisting of a bamboo frame covered by several sections of fabric. The canopy and stacks of clutter produced a nearly pitch-black environment on the deck. A dim glow at the opposite end of the boat provided the only light. As they moved forward, cautiously feeling their way past all the obstacles, they realized the glow was coming from a lower deck. Kimo led the way down the ladder to the deck below. The unmistakable smell of burning opium met them as they descended.

Kimo turned to look up at Coe and smiled. "I think Reb here."

They reached the lower deck, where a small oil lamp sat on a box at the base of the ladder. Looking back through the ladder rungs toward the dark stern, they could make out the shadow of a human figure lying on what appeared to be a stack of blankets. As they moved back toward the stern, Kimo called out in a firm voice, "Reb."

The two men watched as a startled Reb leaped up, bumping into the smoldering hookah on the deck beside him. The lamp from the bow illuminated Reb's face enough for Coe and Kimo to see the terror in his expression, but since the light was coming from behind them, the faces of Kimo and Coe received no light, and they appeared only as unrecognizable black shadows. Then, as Reb began to scurry around for a makeshift weapon, Kimo yelled, "Reb, Reb. It's Kimo and Davey."

Coe chimed in with another familiar voice. "Yeah, Reb. It's us. Relax."

Reb stopped his movement and studied the shadows, then he smiled.

"Man, you guys scared the hell out of me."

He strode over and embraced each of them. "It's great to see you guys."

He offered the pipe to each, and they both declined. Reb then sat on the stack of blankets, and the other two pulled up chairs from a nearby table.

"So, Reb, how is your recovery progressing?" Coe began.

"I'm doing fine, guys. The wound is looking much better. Here, look."

Reb lifted his shirt, revealing his lower abdomen, but a white dressing covered the wound. Reb looked up and smiled. "Trust me. The wound is healing nicely. I should be out of here in a day or so. Doc says I was lucky the bullet hit something before it deflected into me. Otherwise, I'd probably be dead."

"Speaking of the bullet." Reb reached into his pocket, pulled something out, and extended his open palm to Kimo and Coe. "Look."

He turned to Coe. "Davey, I know you shoot at the armory with Jack Powers and some of the mission boys. You ever see a bullet like this?"

Coe took the bullet from Alton's hand and examined it. "It's hexagonal. A hexagonal bullet."

"What?" Kimo asked.

"It's not round like other bullets. It has six flat sides."

Coe passed the bullet to Kimo.

Reb said, "Yeah, that's the bullet Doc pulled out of me. It's quite unique. You ever see one like it at the armory, Davey?"

"Never. In fact, I'm sure it requires a special gun with a hex barrel to fire it."

"Yeah, that's what I was thinking, and I hear Jack Powers owns a big gun collection. Maybe he has one of these special guns. You ever see one, Davey?"

"No, never, Reb."

"You're not just saying that to protect your boy, Powers, are you?"

"No, I'm not."

"You're absolutely sure."

Coe's face tightened as he pointed his right index finger at Reb and raised his voice. "Look, I just came by to see how you were doing, not to be interrogated. Now, I already told you I never saw a bullet like that. I can rattle off the make and model of every gun Jack Powers has ever brought to the armory. I remember them all, but none had a hex barrel."

"Well, I know Jack Powers had a hand in this. Since the revolt, he's been after me, and then me screwing his daughter probably pushed him over the edge."

"You're delusional, Reb. I think it's the drugs. Jack Powers isn't after you. He's a busy man with more important things to do."

"Screw you, Davey. You're turning out just like him."

"Reb, you know the Queen give up the throne," Kimo interjected.

"What do you mean she gave up the throne?"

"The mission boys land the troops and force the Queen to surrender."

"Then who's ruling?"

"The mission boys form a provisional government. They in charge now."

"My God, what are we going to do? We have to get her back on the throne."

"We do nothing now, Reb. We wait."

Reb became agitated. "Well, you can wait if you want, but no way I'm going to wait. I know mission boys tried to kill me, and I'm going to get my revenge. First, I'm going to kill Powers."

"No, Reb. That the wrong thing to do right now. The Queen ask us to wait until she come back from Washington, D.C. If you shoot Powers now, the Queen be angry with you."

Kimo's statement seemed to placate Reb. He looked at Coe. "So the Queen is traveling to Washington, D.C. What do you think Jack Powers and the mission boys will do, Davey?"

"I think they'll draft a treaty of annexation and take it to Washington to rally support to pass it into law, and the Queen and her entourage will appeal to the President of the United States to restore her to the throne. They'll both be there at the same time, traveling in the same circles. It should be interesting."

Reb turned to Kimo. "But right now, we have to sit back and be patient, huh?"

"Yeah. Especially you. You start up those protests again or anything like that, and they gonna kill you. That's for sure. I tell you, Reb, I hate the mission boys as much as you, and if the Queen come back with bad news, then we do something about it, but until then, we wait. The Queen ask us to wait, so we wait."

Reb took a deep breath. "Yeah. I see your point. Just lay low for a while."

"That's right. We wait and surf."

Reb and Coe both smiled at Kimo's comment. The remainder of the visit turned to casual conversation, fun, and laughter.

KIMO AND COE LEFT AROUND MIDNIGHT. Once alone, Reb lit the hookah, took a hit, then returned to the one thought that consumed him during his solitude on Doc's boat, killing Jack Powers. Maybe Powers didn't pull the trigger, but he was the man who gave the order to kill him. Reb was sure of that. All of the mission boys, with their aggressive, capitalist ambitions, contributed to the decline of the native Hawaiians, but Powers was the ringmaster. All the others looked to him for direction.

Reb considered the dilemma facing him. He wanted to help the Queen, but she had asked her subjects to wait peacefully while she tried to resolve the issue in Washington. He took another hit on the hookah. In a few minutes, an idea emerged.

Davey Coe said Powers would go to Washington to promote the annexation treaty. If he killed Jack Powers the night before his ship left for the United States, the mission boys would be in complete disarray. They would have no one to lead them. The Queen would have a major advantage when both parties arrived in Washington. Surely, she would not only forgive him for ignoring her request to wait peacefully but also appreciate his help. He was desperate to do something she could appreciate.

Reb's father was the descendant of missionary parents, and his mother was Hawaiian. Both parents died before he turned twelve. The Queen, then merely a caring native Hawaiian citizen with no children of her own, took in the half-Hawaiian orphan. She sent him to an exclusive boarding school where he rebelled against the discipline, earning the nickname "Reb," short for "rebel," and was expelled. After finally graduating from a public school, she sent him to Italy to study engineering and military science. He dropped out of the program after only a couple of months and returned to Hawaii; then, after the signing of the Bayonet Constitution, he led the ill-fated armed revolt that was forcibly defeated, resulting in several native Hawaiian men being killed and him being imprisoned. He'd failed at every turn. Now his life consisted of odd jobs and personal problems.

He became enthused about his plan to kill Powers. It would redeem him. Furthermore, killing Powers would give him renewed respect among the native Hawaiians, who despised Powers as he despised them. He would slay the evil dragon and be exalted as the savior of the Hawaiian people. Finally, the opium overcame him, and he drifted off into a pleasant sleep.

When he awakened, the vision of himself as a hero still fresh in his memory, he decided to get a rifle for the job. He dressed and ascended to the boat's main deck. It was still dark. The cool night air felt refreshing. With no sense of time, he left the boat and made his way toward Chinatown.

CHAPTER 14

Three days after the Queen's abdication, a grand celebration, complete with champagne and hors d'oeuvres, took place at the Powers Building. Sugar plantation owners, the firm's lawyers, and numerous supporters of the annexation movement all gathered to rejoice. Jack Powers received many words of praise and congratulatory handshakes for spearheading the movement. When the crowd began to chant, 'Speech! Speech!' Powers moved to the podium in the front of the large conference room, waved his hands to calm the clamor, then addressed the crowd.

"Thank you all. We have taken the first step, but still have a great distance to travel before completing the journey. We've drafted a treaty of annexation. Our next step is to deliver it to the President of the United States, Benjamin Harrison, so he can introduce it as legislation. The American minister and I will travel to Washington, D.C., in two weeks to deliver the treaty. When we return, we hope to report that Hawaii is a territory of the United States."

The crowd broke into a raucous cheer lasting for several minutes. Everyone in the room was euphoric except David Coe. Coe stood in the back of the room in a surreal state of mind. The country of Hawaii had just been stolen from the Hawaiian people. He knew it, but somehow it didn't seem real. Coe tried to suppress his emotions. He was sure no one else in the room shared them. Jack Powers, reading Coe's facial expression and body language from across the room, approached him with champagne glass in hand. "David, why the long face? What's wrong?"

"Nothing, Jack. I'm fine."

"I can see something is bothering you. What is it?"

Coe uttered, "It's not right. It's just not right." The moment he completed his statement, he regretted speaking.

Powers clenched his jaws as he glared at Coe. He snapped his head left, then right to see if anyone was within earshot. "Let's talk in my office."

They went to Powers' office, closed the door, and sat at the conference table.

"Now, what did you say?" Powers repeated, his eyes burning at Coe.

"I said, this isn't right. We stole the country from the Hawaiian people."

"Listen, David, I like you. In many ways, you're like the son I never had. So let me give you some fatherly advice. Just forget about it. This annexation movement is bigger than either of us. It's driven by powerful, influential men, and it's critical to them that the movement be completed. They'll stop at nothing to obliterate obstacles in their path. Do you understand me?"

"Yes, I do." Coe leaned back and breathed deeply. "Jack, did you ever feel that something is just morally wrong? No matter who's involved or what the consequences may be, it's just morally wrong."

Powers continued his glare but didn't respond.

"Well, that's how I feel about the overthrow. In addition to being illegal, it's just morally wrong."

Powers snapped back, "I said to forget about it."

"I can't just forget about it."

"David, some plantation owners already question your loyalties, and I'm beginning to wonder myself," Powers returned.

"The plantation owners question my loyalty? What have I ever done to make them think that?"

"During the Queen's coronation, Franz Schmidt, Roy Matthews, and I were watching from the second floor of the government building, and we all saw you with that big Hawaiian friend of yours and Robert Alton. Both Matthews and Schmidt, especially Matthews, expressed concern that you're working here and fraternizing with those two. Matthews suggested I fire you."

"I've known them both since I was a young kid. We all went to my father's school together. They're friends, especially Kimo. He's probably my closest friend. I'm close with his entire family. They're all good people. Besides, I don't understand why it's a concern."

"I'll tell you why it's a concern. Right now, we're in a crisis situation. The Queen and her supporters aren't going to just stand by and let the annexation happen. We expect them to take action, action that, if successful, will adversely affect the sugar plantation owners, our biggest client. Our clients expect us to fight for them, and they want to be sure that everyone in our firm is on their side. Your two friends, especially Alton, are enemies of the sugar plantation owners.

"For heaven's sake, David, Robert Alton led the armed revolt after the signing of the Bayonet Constitution. Even today, he's leading protests on the Iolani Palace grounds. Those friends of yours are enemies of the plantation owners. That means, in many ways, they're also enemies of this law firm. So when Matthews and Schmidt see you fraternizing with Alton and the Hawaiian, they wonder if they can trust you."

"Of course, they can trust me. I've worked on several jobs for them, including the recent contract for Franz Schmidt, and I've always done my best and produced a high-quality product."

"Yes, David, yes, you've always done an excellent job. You're an outstanding lawyer, but this fight with the Queen extends beyond the courtroom and the walls of these offices. Therefore, our loyalty must also extend beyond these office walls. Do you understand what I mean?"

Coe looked down at the koa table before him. He put his fingertips on the wood and, for a few moments, allowed them to follow the pattern of dark and light shades in the grain, then turned to Powers and said, "Yes, I do understand, but I'm a lawyer, and I fight in the courtroom. I'm not interested in joining an outside fight. When I'm here, I give the firm one hundred and ten percent. I work nights and weekends and produce high-quality output. I'm loyal to the firm's clients and to the firm, but when I'm not here, my life is my own. I don't question who Matthews' friends are, or Schmidt's or yours for that matter, and I resent being questioned about my friends. That's part of our private lives."

After a few moments of uneasy silence, Coe asked, "Where are you going with this?"

Powers answered, "At some point, you may have to decide if you're with us or with them. Our clients need to know. I need to know. Are you with us?"

"I'm with you. As I said, when I'm here, I do whatever it takes to get the job done to the highest possible standard, but those guys are friends of mine. They may have different political views than I have or you have, but that's what freedom of choice is all about. You want the United States to annex Hawaii as a territory, and you're entitled to that opinion, but everyone else is entitled to their opinion too. I'm sure you have friends with different opinions than yours, and so do I."

"But *are* your opinions different than those of your friends? Or do you agree with them?"

Coe shrugged. "We agree on some things and differ on others, just like you and your friends."

An awkward moment followed as they both stared at each other. Coe recognized that Powers was becoming impatient.

"David, are you *with* us?" Powers asked, his eyes glaring.

Coe had enough. "Yeah, I'm with you," he snapped.

"Thank you. You may go now. Close the door on your way out."

As Coe approached the door, Powers said, "David, the course of our future is determined by the choices we make today. Choose wisely."

AFTER THE DOOR CLOSED, Powers leaned back in his chair, concerned about David Coe, his hand-picked successor to the reins of the firm. He knew Coe was an outstanding young attorney and, based solely on attorney competence, an ideal selection to eventually head the firm, but for the first time, he seriously questioned whether he could trust Coe. He needed to be sure.

WHEN COE ARRIVED HOME that night, he plopped down in his rocking chair in the evening darkness and considered Jack Powers' final statement. It had been on his mind most of the day.

The course of our future is determined by the choices we make today. Choose wisely. That's what Powers said to him, but what did it really mean?

Powers obviously disapproved of his choice of friends, but he had no intention of dropping Kimo or Reb; maybe just try harder to avoid situations where Powers might see them together.

The 'course of our future' part of the statement bothered him because he placed such high importance on his career and, at least in Hawaii, Jack Powers controlled his career.

In the past, he had the Queen's standing offer in his back pocket in case working with Powers became intolerable, but that offer vanished with the overthrow, and there were no other law firms in Hawaii large enough to provide the growth potential he sought. At the moment, he saw two paths to his career goals; work for Powers or leave Hawaii. He recalled the lucrative job offers from prestigious law firms in New York and Boston, but he didn't want to leave.

He then decided it was too early to burden himself with such heavy thoughts. Powers would soon travel to Washington D.C. and be away from Hawaii for two months. He resolved to enjoy the two months of clean air and, when Powers returned, if nothing changed, to address the issue then.

He stood, stretched his arms above his head, smiled, and muttered, "Good to get that out of the way."

Acting on Powers' final piece of advice, *choose wisely*, he chose to go to the Rialto.

CHAPTER 15

Coe entered the Rialto, and Julie yelled from behind the bar, "Hi, Davey. How are you? If you're looking for Kimo, he left about an hour ago."

The news disappointed him. Kimo's company always lifted his spirits. He returned Julie's greeting, then walked back to the other end of the bar near the pool tables, sat down, and ordered a beer. It wasn't a busy night. Two young guys shot pool at the table farthest away from him. He didn't recognize either one. The two nearest tables were empty. He turned around, placed both elbows on the bar, and began to sip his first beer.

His mind wandered into his past, to the period just before his leaving Hawaii for college and law school in New England. Those were such enjoyable times, just hanging out with Kimo, Reb, and the other guys from school. Sometimes they would surf from sun up to sun down, then sit on the beach under the moonlight and enjoy each other's company. He beamed as he enjoyed the memories.

A hand on his right shoulder snapped him out of the reminiscences. He turned around and was astounded.

"Davey, right?" she said. "Remember me? Malia. We met, well sort of, at Mr. Schmidt's plantation a while back."

Remember her? He was entranced by their brief meeting at the plantation and thought of her often but never imagined they would meet again, especially in a purely social environment. Standing close, she looked even more exotic and beautiful.

"Yes, it's Davey, you're right, and, of course, I remember you. It's great to see you again. I'm just surprised to see you here."

"I came in a few minutes ago, and when I looked around, I saw you sitting here, so I came over to say hello."

"Well, I'm glad you did. It's good to see you again. Please sit down."

Malia occupied the stool next to him, then he asked, "Is this your first time here?"

"No, I've been here before, but I can only come when Mr. Schmidt is away. You see, Davey, I'm not supposed to leave the plantation. But when Mr. Schmidt travels off the island, sometimes I sneak into town if I can get a ride."

She put her right index finger vertically across her lips, moved her face closer to his, and whispered, "Shhhhh. That's our little secret."

She giggled, then smiled. They both laughed.

"Okay, it's our secret," he said, pinching his thumb and index finger together and moving them across his pursed lips, pretending to zipper them. She smiled, then laughed again.

"How did you find out about the Rialto?"

"Well, as I'm sure you know, many contract laborers working the cane fields stay in Hawaii after completing their contract. They discovered the Rialto and told their friends who are still at the plantation. Word gets around. This is a good place."

Malia looked around, then continued, "But tonight, I don't see anyone here that I recognize."

"Do you know Kimo?" Coe asked.

"No, I don't."

"He's the owner. He and I have been close friends since we were young kids and went to school together. He left early tonight."

His statement was followed by a few moments of silence as he glowed with happiness.

"So, Malia, where are you from?"

"China."

"Is your family here with you?"

"No."

"You came from China by yourself?"

"Yes."

He observed that her answers were brief, and her smile was gone.

"What's wrong?" he asked.

"I don't like to talk about my family."

"I'm sorry. I don't mean to be offensive. I just want to know more about you."

Malia lowered her head and paused, then rose up and looked into his eyes, her face expressionless.

"My father was a British naval officer stationed in Shanghai. After six years, his tour was up, and he left. My mother told me he would come back for us. She prayed every day for his return. Finally, after two years, he came back. She was so happy her prayers were answered. He stayed for another six years, then left again. Again, my mother prayed for his return, but he never came back. She eventually realized he had abandoned us and then ... and then ..."

Malia began to tremble. Her eyes filled with tears, then she started to cry. "And then she killed herself."

Coe sensed her deep heartache and embraced her tenderly. Even though he had only known her a short time, he already felt a part of her life. He shared her sorrow and felt responsible to console her.

"I'm sorry. I never would have pressed you about your family if I had known. Don't worry. I won't tell anyone."

He paused for a moment, then said, "You know, we've only known each other for a few minutes, and already we have two secrets."

Malia removed her head from his shoulder, leaned away, and smiled through her tears. They both laughed while still holding each other. Malia then moved closer, angled her head, and kissed him on the cheek.

"Thank you for caring."

They sat on bar stools, faced each other, and exhaled.

"Now, what were we talking about?" he said.

They both laughed again.

Their conversation continued. He told her his life story, then unloaded his current problems on her. She seemed genuinely interested in everything he said, smiled often, and laughed every time he interjected a humorous remark. Time flew by until the bartender announced the place was closing for the night.

"I guess we have to go, but it was great seeing you. I hope we can do it again soon," Coe said.

"Yeah, it was great. I enjoyed it."

They got up from the bar stools and, along with the other remaining patrons, filed out the door into the night.

Once outside, he asked, "Are you alright now? How will you get back?"

"Well, I had such a good time that I stayed much later than I expected. I'm sure my ride has gone back long ago. I'll probably just go into Chinatown and find a place to lay my head for a few hours, then catch a ride back in the morning. Don't worry. I'll be alright. I've done it before."

Coe considered the situation. She was Chinese, so maybe she knew some people there who would help her. On the other hand, if she fabricated the story just to put his mind at ease, she could be in real danger. Chinatown was known for opium dens and brothels. Crime was rampant there, especially in the late hours of the night after the bars had closed and the drug addicts and drunkards were out on the streets. He considered walking with her until she got settled, but knew Chinatown was particularly dangerous for Caucasians.

"Look, Malia, I'm uncomfortable with you going into Chinatown alone, especially at this hour. I hope I'm not out of line here, but why don't you come home with me? I've got plenty of room. You'll be safe, and don't worry, I'll sleep on the couch, and you can have the bedroom."

"Thanks, Davey, that's a kind offer, but I don't want to impose on you."

"No imposition at all. In fact, you'd be doing me a favor by putting my mind at ease knowing you're safe."

A wide smile appeared before she spoke. He knew from her expression that a humorous remark was coming. "Yeah, I'll be safe, but how do you know you'll be safe? I might be one of those psychotic ax murderers," she said, maintaining her smile.

"I'll sleep with my rifle loaded and cocked, and besides, I don't have an ax."

They both laughed and started toward his house.

COE OPENED THE DOOR and allowed her to enter first. She stood in the darkness inside the door while he turned right into the sitting room and lit a couple of oil lamps. The oak floors creaked as she followed him.

"Oh, my, it's so nice and cozy. Thank you for bringing me here."

He enjoyed her apparent contentment as her eyes moved in all directions surveying the small room furnished with a couch, a rocking chair, and two small tables for the oil lamps. She picked up a framed photograph from one of the tables, then dropped onto the couch. "Who's this?"

"That's my father. He doesn't live here anymore," he said as he lowered himself into the rocker.

"What happened, if you don't mind my asking?"

"My father contracted leprosy and was taken to Kalaupapa on the island of Molokai."

"I'm sorry, Davey. Do you see him anymore?"

"About once a year, the mission sends supplies, you know, clothing, blankets, things like that, over to Molokai. I help load the boat, then ride over. He's not well. It's a sad situation."

They sat in silence and gazed at each other for a few awkward moments.

"Well, the bedroom is over there," Coe said as he stood and pointed.

"Thank you. Good night," she said as she walked away.

"Good night." He began to ready the couch for sleeping.

"Davey, if your rifle is in here, you should get it now," she shouted from the bedroom.

He laughed and crossed the hall to the bedroom. As he stood in the doorway about to speak, she turned to face him and smiled, then pulled her dress over her head and laid it on a chair. She was wearing nothing else. Stricken by her physical beauty, every feature so much more appealing than Mary Ellen Higgenbothen, he was paralyzed with both awe and fear.

She moved over to him, threw her arms around his neck, and kissed him on the lips. He barely responded. She opened her mouth and licked his lips. He pulled her close and matched her actions with equal gusto. She pulled away from their embrace to unbutton his shirt. He enthusiastically helped finish the job. She pushed him back onto the bed and removed his shoes, socks, and pants. Both now completely naked, she lay on top of him in the bed.

The fragrance from her hair was intoxicating. The feel of her soft, warm breasts against his chest was pure ecstasy. As they continued to kiss, he ran his hands up and down her back and onto her buttocks, caressing her smooth, supple skin. As their passion continued through the night, she led him through a variety of erotic sexual positions he'd never before imagined, let alone experienced. When it was all over, they fell asleep in each other's arms.

When Coe awoke the next morning, he rolled over only to find Malia wasn't in the bed. He called her name, but there was no answer. He got up, dressed, and walked through the house and outside into the yard. She wasn't there. Returning to the house, he found a note on the kitchen table. *Had a great time. Will see you soon.*

He carried the note into the living room, sat in the rocking chair, and reflected on the previous twelve hours, possibly the most enjoyable twelve hours of his life.

When he first saw Malia at Schmidt's plantation, he remembered thinking she likely had Caucasian blood in her lineage because of her less pronounced almond-shaped eyes, then she said her father was a British naval officer. That also explained why she spoke English fluently. It likely had something to do with her overall worldliness as well. She seemed knowledgeable about everything. He thoroughly enjoyed talking to her, but then, he enjoyed everything about Malia; her intelligence, her sense of humor, her easy-going attitude, her smile, and most of all, her exotic physical beauty. He couldn't wait to see her again.

As he reminisced, a strange thought came to him. When they first met at the Rialto, she already knew his name. Initially, he was puzzled but concluded she must have overheard Schmidt reference him at some point while she was working in his house. For the most part, he didn't care.

CHAPTER 16

Two days after the overthrow, at about seven o'clock in the evening, Jack Powers, in high spirits, stepped into Tiger Lilly's. Colonel Ralph Grimes had not yet arrived. Grimes was quite punctual, but Powers got there a half hour early. He ordered the paint thinner scotch and took the first sip. This evening, it was quite palatable. In fact, for the past few days, everything seemed quite palatable. Even when he scanned the premises, wondering where his daughter and that derelict, Robert Alton, would sit when they were in Tiger Lilly's, he wasn't upset. His daughter was at college in Massachusetts, and it was all past history. Instead, refocusing on the blissful present, he downed the rest of his drink, coughed, held the glass up in the air, looked at it, and smiled, then ordered another.

Grimes showed up at seven forty-five. "Jack, you're early. I think this place is growing on you."

Powers smiled. "Yeah, Ralph, I'm going to become a regular. I just love the scotch."

They both laughed, then Grimes turned serious. "I missed Alton. I mean, I hit him but didn't kill him. He's still alive."

"I know. What happened? I thought it would be an easy shot for a sharpshooter like you."

"It should have been an easy shot, but from where I was perched, Alton was standing right behind one of the posts that support the gazebo roof, and it was windy that day. I waited for a clear shot and used the Whitworth. But just as I fired, a strong gust of wind came up. I hit him, but I saw that the bullet first hit the wood post, then deflected into Alton.

He dropped below this paneling around the gazebo, and I couldn't see him. I didn't know if I killed him or not, so I grabbed the Winchester and emptied it at the gazebo. Then I went down, you know, to finish him off with my pistol, if necessary, but he was gone when I got there. I looked around, and there were screaming people everywhere, but I didn't see Alton."

Grimes downed the rest of his scotch, ordered another, and downed it in one gulp.

"Don't worry, Jack. I'll get him. Ralph Grimes always gets his man."

"No, Ralph. It doesn't matter now. We got what we want. So just forget about Alton."

"Can't just forget about him, Jack. I have to finish the job."

"Listen to me, Ralph. We got what we wanted. We now run the country. The process isn't complete, but next month, the American minister and I are traveling to Washington, D.C., to introduce an annexation agreement. We're in a good position, but the Hawaiians are on edge right now. If you kill Alton, they might revolt. We don't want to deal with that possibility, so just forget about it."

"I don't care. It's a matter of personal pride. I have to kill him."

Powers hesitated, took a deep breath, then a sip of scotch. "Look, Ralph, after Hawaii is annexed to the United States, then you can kill him if you want. At that point, I won't care, but right now, please hold off."

"I can't wait until then. As soon as Hawaii is annexed, I'm on the next steamer to Australia with the ten thousand dollars you're going to pay me."

Powers was temporarily distracted. "Australia?"

"Yeah, Australia. The Brits own it. It's all white, not like here."

"Look, Ralph, I agreed to pay you that money for supporting the plan. If you kill Alton now, and that screws up our plans for annexation, you won't get a dime. You'll be stuck here in Hawaii forever."

Suddenly, with the quickness of a rattlesnake strike, Powers felt the butt of a Colt Army Model 1860 barrel beneath his chin, lifting his head. He discreetly slipped his right hand behind his back to retrieve his pistol from its holster.

While still holding the seven-inch barrel to Powers' throat with his right hand, Grimes swiftly reached his left behind Powers' back and clamped onto his right wrist, halting Powers' movement toward the gun. Powers felt Grimes' superior strength.

"Hands on the bar, Jack. I know you got a little pea shooter back there."

Powers froze for a second.

"Hands on the bar right now, or you're dead," Grimes said as he cocked the .44 caliber revolver.

Knowing Grimes wasn't bluffing, Powers abandoned thoughts of pulling his Derringer pistol and placed both hands on the bar.

While continuing to hold the Colt taut under Powers' chin, Grimes used his left hand, which was still behind Powers' back, to remove the pistol from its holster and place it in his right jacket pocket, away from Powers.

"Look, Jack. I know you're a lawyer, and you lawyers make money by screwin' people, but you better not screw me, or I'll kill you, your family, too. Understand?"

"Yes, I understand."

"You damn well better."

Grimes removed his gun from the underside of Powers' chin, then rose from his stool and glared at the other bar patrons staring at the commotion.

"What the hell are you all looking at? Get back to your drinks and mind your own business," the deep voice bellowed.

Powers observed that everyone immediately obeyed Grimes' order, hustling back to their bar stools, looking away, and returning to their earlier conversations. Grimes obviously commanded respect in Tiger Lilly's. Powers figured he probably had bashed in a few heads or even killed someone to earn it.

Grimes returned to his seat, looked at Powers, and calmly said, "Now, Jack, if you want me to hold off on Alton, I will. But let's work together to finish this job, then you pay me. Okay?"

"Yeah," Powers said, relieved the crisis was over.

Grimes extended his hand, and Powers, though stunned by the abrupt mood change, returned the handshake.

They each ordered another scotch, and Grimes began to extol the virtues of Australia. Powers was amazed that ten minutes earlier, Grimes was ready to put a bullet into his brain, and now he was casually talking about Australia. It was as if nothing had happened. He allowed Grimes to ramble on. At various intervals, he considered informing Grimes that dark-skinned aboriginal people were the native population of Australia, somewhat similar to the situation in Hawaii, but decided against it.

Powers had experienced firsthand, nearly with deadly consequences, the one thing he feared in his relationship with Grimes, controlling the man's violent side. At some point, violence would be necessary in the quest for annexation, and Grimes was perfect for that aspect. In fact, as commander of the Honolulu Rifles, he was indispensable. Powers then recalled the King's signing of the Constitution of 1887, the Bayonet Constitution, which abolished his absolute power.

At the time, the king was under immense political pressure because of his irresponsible behavior and corruption. There were calls for his resignation. He might have signed the new constitution anyhow as a compromise to retain his position on the throne, but reportedly, it was Colonel Ralph Grimes who held a rifle with fixed bayonet to the King's head to make sure.

Powers needed a man like Grimes, at least until the annexation process was complete, but he needed to figure out how to control him. He vowed simply to tread softly.

Eventually, sailors poured into Tiger Lilly's, packing the place. Powers and Grimes conversed until closing. As they stood outside in the cool late-night darkness, Powers turned to Grimes. "What about my Derringer?"

"You'll get it back at the armory on Saturday." Grimes grinned. "Most likely."

THE COUNTRY OF HAWAII maintained no standing army, so in 1854, a volunteer militia called the Honolulu Rifle Company, more commonly known as 'the Rifles,' was formed to deal with internal conflict. Originally a loosely organized outfit, it evolved over the years, and, in the last five years, under the command of Colonel Ralph Grimes, had become an efficient paramilitary force of about two hundred men, all Caucasian, all sharing Grimes' political ideology, and all fiercely loyal to him.

Twice a month, they met at the large armory building at the corner of Punchbowl and Beretania Streets, where they drilled and honed their shooting skills at the firing range. The armory was the largest building, in terms of floor space, in Honolulu. In addition to the spacious covered area used primarily for conventions and large gatherings, there was a sizeable open-air firing range behind the building. A ten-foot high earthen barrier enclosed the grassy range area to keep errant shots from dangerously straying.

David Coe arrived at the armory to meet Jack Powers, as he did almost every Saturday morning. Powers, though not a member of the Rifles as far as Coe knew, got permission to use the firing range on Saturday mornings. Powers was a serious marksman, owned an extensive gun collection, and fired all the guns expertly.

Coe arrived about fifteen minutes early, and Powers was already at the range. As Coe approached from behind, he observed that Powers had five rifles standing upright in a rack next to him and one in his hands. When Powers turned and saw Coe, he smiled. "David, good morning. Come here. I want to show you something."

He extended the rifle in his hands to Coe. "You're now holding the Whitworth rifle, the most accurate sharpshooting rifle in the world and, I believe, the only one in Hawaii."

"It feels heavier than the other rifles I've fired," Coe responded, looking down at the rifle in his hands.

"You're right. It is heavier than the others. It weighs twenty-two pounds, partly because the barrel is longer, thirty-six inches, but it's beautifully balanced, so it shoulders comfortably."

Coe shouldered the rifle and immediately understood what Powers meant when he said it was beautifully balanced. He looked through the sighting scope at the target, a wooden square with alternating red and white concentric circular bands and a red bull's eye in the center, eight hundred yards away.

"Go ahead and fire it. It's already loaded," Powers said.

Coe sighted the target and squeezed the trigger. The gun fired with a resounding boom and strong recoil. The shot hit the bull's eye, striking close to the center.

"Wow!" he exclaimed, seeing the result. "This is one magnificent rifle! Can I fire it again, this time from a thousand yards?"

"Sure," Powers replied and handed the ramrod to Coe so he could load a .45 caliber round down the muzzle. Powers then handed him a round. Coe froze and stared at the bullet, his mind in a daze. Powers smiled as he misinterpreted Coe's reaction to be amazement.

"It's hexagonally shaped," Powers said. "Six flat sides. The rifle barrel, too. That's what makes it so accurate. It was invented by Joseph Whitworth, a brilliant engineer. He applied his 'flat plane' engineering knowledge to rifles. Since flat planes can be machined precisely, the flat planes on the bullet fully engage the flat planes on the barrel, so there's no slippage as the bullet moves down the barrel."

As Powers spoke, Coe continued staring at the hexagonal bullet in his hand, oblivious to Powers' words. It was precisely like the bullet Reb showed him during the visit on Doc's boat, the bullet Doc extracted from his body after an attempt to kill him. Coe's heart pulsated almost through his chest, and beads of sweat formed on his forehead. His mind raced as he attempted to assimilate the facts.

Just a few minutes earlier, Powers said this rifle was the only Whitworth rifle in Hawaii, so Coe's initial thought was that Powers pulled the trigger; however, he dispelled the notion, recalling on the day Reb was shot, Powers was still at the office when he left to board the trolley. In addition, he remembered the DO NOT DISTURB sign on the door; then again, he didn't actually see Powers. In any event, Powers was somehow involved in Reb's shooting, at least as an accomplice for supplying the rifle to the shooter.

Coe's thought process was broken when Powers prompted him. "Come on, David, load and shoot."

Coe looked at him, then lifted the rifle and picked up the ramrod. When he began pushing the ramrod down the rifle barrel, it became stuck, as if something were blocking its path. As he continued to struggle, he became fearful of drawing suspicious attention. His hands began to tremble. Finally, Coe cleared the barrel and loaded the round. He shouldered the rifle and sighted the target.

His focus became sharp, and his hands steady as he imagined it was Powers standing one thousand yards away in the sighting scope. He aimed at the red circular bull's eye, imagined it was Powers' heart, and fired. The shot ruptured Powers' heart. He was dead. For a split second, he wondered if he could actually kill Jack Powers. At that moment, he felt enough hatred to consider it.

The sound of a single pair of clapping hands behind him grabbed his attention. Coe turned around and froze. He immediately recognized the shaved head and the robust handlebar mustache tightly waxed at the tips, and he could never forget the steely blue eyes and the icy, penetrating, evil look. But, apparently, the large, muscular man didn't remember him as he approached Coe and extended his hand. "Colonel Ralph Grimes."

Powers and Grimes also exchanged greetings.

"You're a good shot," Grimes said, returning to Coe.

Coe looked at Grimes as Reb's possible shooter but knew now was not the time to make an issue. He forced out a "Thank you."

"Yeah, the Whitworth is an accurate rifle, but it's hard to clean and reload. I saw you struggling with it, and on the battlefield, that will get you killed, so it wasn't widely used in battle. But for one shot from long range, you can't beat the Whitworth rifle."

Coe felt relieved when Grimes said clearing the barrel was a common problem.

Grimes continued, "In fact, in 1864, during the Battle of Spotsylvania, a Confederate sharpshooter shot and killed Union General John Sedgwick with a rifle just like this one. One shot to the head from twelve hundred yards!"

"Is that right?" Powers said.

"Absolutely."

Grimes continued with a sly grin. "You know, when I sight a target, I always imagine it's a Hawaiian before I pull the trigger."

"Same here," Powers interjected. "Sometimes I imagine I'm on top of a building looking down, like a sniper."

Powers and Grimes both laughed. Coe became filled with equal parts anger and fear; anger toward Powers and Grimes for their probable involvement in the murder plot, fear because he was now alone with two armed men capable of murder. He tried to maintain his composure.

Grimes said, "You know, David, you're young, in good physical condition, and a good shot. We're looking for men like you in the Rifles. Did you ever consider joining?"

Powers interrupted, "David's a lawyer, not a soldier."

"We take lawyers, too. Think about it, David."

"Yeah, I will," Coe said, but he was repulsed by the thought of joining an organization led by a man like Grimes.

Powers turned to Coe and joked, "Now that you're a sharpshooter, David, please don't run off and join the army. We're counting on you at the firm."

Powers and Grimes laughed, but Coe could manage only a subdued, artificial smile.

Coe left Powers and Grimes at the armory as quickly as possible and recalled chapter three, verse twenty-five from the Book of Colossians, "For the wrongdoer will be paid back for the wrong he has done, and there is no partiality."

CHAPTER 17

The next few weeks were busy at the firm as Jack Powers prepared for his trip to Washington, D.C. He participated in numerous meetings with the American minister and members of the provisional government. Powers and Andrew Blackburn planned to travel by steamship to San Francisco, where they would meet with Franz Schmidt, who was already there attending to business with his refineries. Powers and Blackburn would then continue by train to Washington, D.C. They expected to be gone for about two months.

Powers' departure couldn't come soon enough to suit David Coe. Still reeling from his experience with Powers and Grimes at the armory, he questioned whether he wanted to continue working at the firm, whether it was worth working for such an evil man, one involved in murder.

Coe did his best to avoid Jack Powers. It helped that Powers was frequently out of the office during the hectic period prior to his departure. Coe needed time away from him. He hoped the two months with Powers gone would clear his mind and provide an opportunity to evaluate his future in a peaceful, stress-free environment.

He stayed in his office, door closed, as much as possible and immersed himself in his work. During idle moments, he thought about Malia. He hadn't seen her in a couple of weeks. Every night, when he returned home after work, he hoped she would be there, but thus far, every night, he was disappointed.

In the late afternoon on the day before Powers' departure, Coe prepared to leave the office for the day. Certain he had escaped any encounters with Powers, the tension flowed from his body. He began to relax. A knock on the door disquieted him. When the door opened, and Sara entered, he calmly exhaled, then she said, "Mr. Powers wants to see you in his office."

Coe's gut reaction was to have Sara tell Powers he had already gone, but it was unprofessional. Besides, Sara was loyal to Powers and probably wouldn't do it.

"Thank you, Sara," he said as he left his office and headed down the hall. Coe was uncertain what to expect. Powers had given him a long list of action items to complete while he was away. Coe hoped he wanted to discuss the work.

He knocked on Powers' door, then opened it just enough to stick his head in.

"You wanted to see me?"

"Yes, David, come in, please."

Coe entered, leaving the door wide open behind him. Interruptions would be welcomed.

"Close the door," Powers said as he rose from behind his desk and circled around to meet Coe at the conference table.

When they were seated, Powers said, "I need your help."

"What's the problem?"

"It's about Ellen."

"Mrs. Powers? Is she alright?"

"Yes, yes, she's fine. It's nothing like that. You see, Ellen despises me going away. Every time I go, she overreacts. She threatens to leave me. We had a big argument last night," Powers said in a meek, subdued tone.

Coe had never seen him so tame. Powers had always displayed such confidence and bravado but, at this moment, seemed almost embarrassed to continue.

"Why does she threaten to leave you?"

"That's not important. The point is that she left once before and, after last night, I think she'll do it this time, maybe for good. I've never seen her this upset."

"I'm sorry to hear it, but how can I help?"

"I'd appreciate you stopping by about once a week just to visit with Ellen. She always liked you, and your visits will keep her spirits up. And, while you're there, I'd like you to tell her that I'm a good boss and a good person, that I treat you and the others well. I want you to get her thinking fondly of me again."

"I'd like to help, but I don't know Mrs. Powers very well. I'd feel awkward just stopping by, out of the blue, for no reason. Wouldn't she consider it strange?"

"I've taken care of that. I told her you'd be delivering some important files to the house, files I don't want to be kept at the office while I'm gone, and you'd have to access the files periodically."

Powers paused, then leaned over the table toward Coe. "Look, David, my marriage is in trouble, and I want to save it. I need your help. Please, will you help me?"

Coe deliberated for a few moments, still uneasy about Powers' request, but Powers seemed genuinely concerned, and Coe couldn't turn him down. "Of course, I'll help you."

Powers instantly regained his self-assurance and pointed to a stack at the opposite end of the conference table. "Good. There are the files. Wait at least a week after my departure before you deliver them, then go back about once a week to review them. Remember to speak well of me during each visit, then I'd like you to send me a letter about six weeks after my departure. I want to be certain I receive it before leaving Washington to return home." Powers handed Coe a piece of paper. "Here's the address."

Coe looked at the paper while Powers continued to talk. The address was the Washington D.C. office of Senator John James from Massachusetts.

"In the letter, I want you to tell me about Ellen. What does she do? Does she seem content? Is she seeing anyone while I'm gone? How does she feel about me? Does she talk about leaving me? Bottom line, I want her to be here when I return."

"You're asking me to spy on Mrs. Powers."

"Not at all. I'm simply asking you to visit with Ellen periodically while I'm gone. She'll appreciate it. Then I'm asking you to tell me how she is doing. That's it."

"I don't know, Jack."

"David, I'm depending on you to save my marriage, and while I'm gone, you can use my carriage to get up to the house. That'll make it easier for you. And instead of riding the trolley, use the carriage to get back and forth to work. While you're at the office, leave it at the stables on Hotel Street. I have an arrangement with them. Use it whenever you want, and keep it at your place in the evening. There's a stable at the mission houses where you can keep the horse for a couple of months, right?"

"Yes, there is."

Coe was bowled over by Powers' offer. He relished having a horse and carriage at his disposal for a couple of months. All the wealthy men owned at least one, and he envied them for it. It was a sign of affluence. He envisioned a horse and carriage in his future and was elated that a 'trial period' had come this soon.

Powers rose from his seat and extended his hand. The two shook.

"Thank you, David. I appreciate your help. Now, I've got a lot of work to finish prior to my departure tomorrow, so I'm sure you'll excuse me."

Powers walked Coe to the door and opened it. One more handshake and another "thank you," and Powers closed the door. Coe stood in the hallway outside the office, files in hand, his mind awash with several different emotions; confusion over the entire situation, curiosity about the underlying cause, awkwardness, and even anger for agreeing to spy on Ellen Powers and report his findings to Jack Powers, relief that he wouldn't have to deal with

Powers for two months, and absolute joy to have unlimited use of a horse and carriage for a couple of months.

REB SAT ON THE BED in his dingy room in a Chinatown flophouse. Having just returned from an opium den down the hall, he felt relaxed and confident. He held a Sharps breech-loading rifle in his hands. It was loaded and ready to fire. A cockroach emerged from under the bed and streaked across the room, finding safety in a crack in the floorboards in the far corner. Normally, he would chase it and stamp it out. He hated the roaches.

Today he had something bigger on his mind, and now was the perfect time, the evening before Jack Powers was to board his ship for San Francisco en route to Washington, D.C. There would be no time for the mission boys to reorganize if he did it tonight. It would be like an army losing its general moments before a critical battle. He would kill Jack Powers tonight.

He wrapped the rifle in one of the bed sheets and held it close to his side as he descended the steps and exited through the back door into an alley. It was about six-thirty, and the sun had nearly set. He felt hazy and light-headed as he moved. He climbed a fire escape ladder to the roof of a two-story wooden building across Fort Street from the Powers Building and unwrapped the rifle. It was an easy shot, maybe a hundred yards. The Queen would be grateful. The other Royalists would respect him again.

Jack Powers would soon leave his office, departing through the front door. He knew Powers was a workaholic, always working until after dark; then, a disconcerting thought came to him. What if Jack Powers left the office early on this final day before his departure? What if he had last-minute details at home and was already gone? After about fifteen minutes, his concern was erased when a light went on in Powers' corner office, then he saw Powers pass by the window.

He looked up and down Fort Street as he waited. The glow from the street lights seemed to be dancing, like tiny stars flickering in the wind. He became dizzy, so he shook his head hard several times, trying to break out of the daze. The light went out in Powers' office, and Reb tried to steady himself for the shot. Soon Jack Powers exited into the street. Reb stood and raised the rifle to aim but wobbled and lost his balance, falling to the floor. He rose and tried again as Powers walked up the street. Again, he felt dizzy and was unable to aim. Powers passed out of sight before he could make another attempt.

Reb knew Powers was heading to the stables on Hotel Street, where his carriage awaited. He would kill Powers as he left the stables. Hurrying to the fire escape ladder, he began to descend, but felt light-headed, then nauseated, symptoms of a first-time opium user, not an experienced one like himself. Maybe it was the combination of alcohol and opium creating the unexpected effect.

After stumbling to the bottom of the ladder, he vomited in the alley. He knelt briefly, then rose and stood still for a few moments, trying to regain his balance. As he entered Fort Street, the street lights were still dancing. He became dizzy again but made his way forward, running wildly up Fort, rifle flinging in his hand. Pedestrians gawked from the sidewalks in front of the buildings.

Stables on Hotel Street – c. 1890 *(Hawaii State Archives)*

He arrived at the stables, a white-washed, two-story wooden building with a large sliding door through which the carriages passed and two smaller doors, one in front next to the sliding door and one in the back of the building. First, he tried to enter through the back door, but it was locked, then he ran around to the front door which was locked. The large sliding door was also locked. Realizing the building was closed for the day, he banged his fists on the sliding door, then slumped to the ground and sat leaning against the outside of the building, totally disgusted. He had missed his chance.

Reb returned to his room and lit an oil lamp. Sitting on the edge of the bed, he caught a reflection of himself in the small mirror on the nightstand. The mirror perfectly framed his face. His cheeks were drawn and hollow, his eyes tired and bloodshot, his complexion ashen. The image disgusted him. The drugs and alcohol had taken their toll. He lay back on the bed and reminisced about earlier days when he was handsome and dashing. Women were enchanted by his exotic good looks. He vividly recalled his time with an Italian beauty named Franchesca during his brief educational experience in Italy, then most recently with Audrey Powers.

As he sat up again, the reflection stared back at him. If either woman saw him like this, she wouldn't give him a second look. He stood, clenched his teeth, and kicked a nearby wicker basket, sending it flying across the room. Staring into the mirror, he made a personal promise to himself. He would change. He would stop using drugs, get a job, change his diet, exercise, and take more interest in his personal grooming. He would regain the respect of others, especially the Queen, and become a productive member of society.

It was getting late. He figured there was no point in starting such a vast undertaking this evening. It could all wait until the next day. He left his room and headed for the opium den one last time. As for Jack Powers, there would be opportunities when he returned from Washington, D.C.

CHAPTER 18

David Coe stood on the pier at Honolulu Harbor and watched the steamship pull away. The provisional government had chartered the steamer so Jack Powers and the American minister could hurry to Washington, D.C., annexation treaty in hand. The Queen and her entourage were denied passage on the same steamer. The mission boys made sure of it. They felt it was a significant advantage to get to Washington first. Powers and the American minister stood on the main deck and waved to Coe as the ship sailed toward the horizon.

When the ship was out of sight, Coe breathed the fresh air and smiled. It was as if a violent storm had just moved from the area, replaced by clear skies that would remain for two months. He strolled back down the pier to the hitching post where Powers' horse and carriage were tied. Earlier in the morning, he'd driven the carriage bringing Powers and Andrew Blackburn to the pier. He was certain Powers was testing him to see if he could handle the horse well enough.

He looked at the black stallion with pride as if it were his own. Then, approaching the horse, he pulled an apple from his pocket, placed it on his flattened palm, and offered it to Titus. Powers told him the horse was named after his father. Titus eagerly gobbled down the offering. Coe patted the horse on the neck. "Okay, Titus, let's get going. Two months together, just you and me, boy."

Coe climbed into the carriage and snapped the reins. Powers had left him with plenty of action items to occupy his time for the next two months, and he was determined to complete them all, but when he stopped at the Hotel Street stables, he didn't feel like leaving the carriage and trudging into the office. After considering the situation for a few minutes, he decided on an alternative plan.

Just prior to boarding the ship, Jack Powers reminded him of the promise to visit his wife, and even though Powers told him to wait at least a week before delivering the files and making his first visit, Coe decided today was a perfect time. After all, he was his own boss for the next wo months. Besides, it was a glorious day, and he was still enthralled with the horse and carriage.

He first stopped by the office to pick up the files. While loading the files into the carriage, he briefly perused them. As he suspected, they were old cases already settled, unimportant files that could have remained at the office while Powers was gone. Powers had given them to him for the sole purpose of providing an excuse to check on his wife.

After loading the files, he took off for Powers' residence, feeling like a king, majestic and powerful. Reaching the top of the hill to Manoa, he pulled on the reins to stop the carriage, then got out and looked back at the magnificent panorama.

In the foreground was downtown Honolulu. Iolani Palace and Kawaiahao Church were readily identifiable. He looked for his house, but it was obscured by coconut trees. Farther away was picturesque Diamond Head; in the background, the grand Pacific Ocean and clear blue skies. After reveling in the splendor for several minutes, he turned to Titus and affectionately patted the horse, then boarded the carriage. As they left, Coe tilted his face toward the sun and smiled.

COE PULLED THE CARRIAGE up to the front of Powers' house, a large white wooden structure, not as expansive as Franz Schmidt's mansion, but with several architecturally appealing angles. The grounds were professionally landscaped with neatly trimmed native shrubs. The lawn was finely manicured. He imagined someday driving his own carriage to his own house, a house just like the one before him. After gathering the files, he walked up the front steps and knocked on the door. He waited a few minutes with no answer, then knocked again. Again no answer, so he turned to descend the steps, intending to check the backyard. The front door cracked open just then, and a female voice offered a meek "Good morning" through the narrow opening.

"Good morning, Mrs. Powers, I'm David Coe, and I'm here to deliver some files at your husband's request. He said you'd be expecting me."

"Yes, David, come in," Ellen Powers returned as she opened the door while turning away. Coe entered and followed several steps behind as Ellen hastened down the main hallway. When she passed a doorway on the left, she pointed without turning around. "That's Jack's office. You can put the files in there."

He stopped at the office doorway and watched as Ellen continued down the hall and into the room at the end of the hall. He sensed something was wrong. Her gait appeared unsteady, and he was puzzled because she never turned around to talk to him. "Is everything alright, Mrs. Powers?" he called out.

"Yes, David, and please call me Ellen," her voice responded from the room at the end of the hall.

"Are you sure everything is alright, Ellen?"

No answer.

He entered the office and placed the files on a beautiful koa wood desk, the feature piece of furniture in the room. The entire office was paneled in rich, dark wood. Floor-to-ceiling shelves on two walls were filled with scores of books. A large window in the wall opposite the door looked out into the yard. Planting boxes with blooming azaleas were mounted outside the window.

He placed the files on the desk and turned his attention to Ellen. Jack Powers had asked him to talk to his wife, to keep her in a positive mood and speak well of him in his absence, so he left the office to seek her. He walked to the end of the hall, entered the kitchen, and saw her sitting at the kitchen table, head down, peering at a crystal drinking glass containing amber liquid.

"Ellen," he said softly.

Surprised by his presence, she looked up.

He was shocked when he saw her face. "My God, what happened?" he exclaimed as his brain registered a snapshot of her facial bruises before she quickly turned away.

"Nothing, David, just go. Please just go," she exclaimed as she began to cry.

Coe turned to go but realized he couldn't, in good conscience, leave her in this much distress. He approached the table, pulled up a chair, and sat in front of her. "Are you alright?" he asked.

She didn't answer or look up.

"Is there anything I can do?"

Ellen paused with her head down for a few seconds until her tears subsided, then sat up and stared at him.

"Can you stay for a while?"

"Yes, of course."

He could now clearly see the swelling and bruises under each eye and on her left cheek. Coe had met Ellen Powers a few times, mostly at office functions. She was an attractive, energetic woman, always impeccably dressed, well-spoken, and confident.

This morning, she looked completely different. In addition to the facial bruises, her blonde hair was uncombed and messy, her eyes were bloodshot, and she looked tired. Ellen rose from her seat and ambled to the counter. She poured another drink for herself and, without asking if he wanted it, one for Coe. She returned to the table and handed his drink to him.

"I'm sorry to burden you with my problems, but I just have to talk to someone." She took a sip.

"It's okay. Please continue."

"I'm in a bad position and don't know what to do, and I feel I'm partly to blame. My family lives in Massachusetts, and I was at Radcliffe when Jack was studying law at Harvard. We met, and I fell in love. He convinced me to marry him and move to Hawaii.

My parents were staunchly against it, but Jack can be very persuasive. So, I gave up a promising career on Wall Street, and here I am, five thousand miles away from my family with a man who beats me."

Coe thought of his father. He would say exactly the right thing to soothe Ellen. Coe had no clue what to say and sat awkwardly silent until Ellen continued.

"My marriage is a wreck. I want to leave Jack. I just can't take any more abuse, but he threatened to kill me if I leave. All these bruises you see? Yeah, Jack did this. He was drunk, of course, and I guess he wanted to give me a preview of what would happen if I left him."

Coe recalled a moment earlier in the day when Jack Powers, just before boarding the ship, told him to wait at least a week before visiting Ellen. Now he realized the significance of that request. Powers wanted the bruises to be healed by the time he visited so he wouldn't see them.

He returned to Ellen and fumbled for words. "But why? Why did you want to leave him? I mean, I understand now after he beat you, but why before this beating? Did he beat you before?"

"He slapped me before, but not like this. This time he did a thorough job. Don't you think?"

She looked at him and smiled for an instant.

"This was just the breaking point. Since we've been married, I've suspected Jack was involved with other women. A wife can sense these things. He always denied everything and told me I was paranoid, and I always believed him because, I guess, I just wanted to believe he was faithful. I wanted our marriage to continue."

"Ellen, you said you sensed Jack was cheating, but how can you be sure? I'm not taking his side, but just asking if it's possible it was all a big misunderstanding."

Immediately after finishing his question, guilt ran through him. He was beginning to defend Jack Powers. The bruises on Ellen's face weren't a misunderstanding, and, for that reason, Jack Powers deserved no defense.

He was about to apologize when Ellen continued, "You're right. At first, I considered it might all be a misunderstanding. It started with rumors, some from pretty good sources, but still just rumors. But as the rumors multiplied, I became more and more suspicious. One of them came from a good friend, the wife of a man who accompanied Jack on a previous trip to Washington, D.C. Her husband told her about Jack's lascivious behavior in Washington.

When this trip came up, I confronted Jack about it. At first, he denied it, but I persisted. That's when he became enraged and started hitting me, then he admitted his affairs. Lots of them, he said. Threw it in my face how they were all younger and prettier than I am; how I should be thankful he even spends time with an 'old broad' like me. He even tried to justify his behavior by saying the affairs were part of successful deal-making and, since I benefited from his success, I should be grateful."

Coe felt her pain. He wanted to say something to calm her, but no adequate words came.

"I'm sorry," was all he could muster. He took the first sip of his drink, then instantly drew back and coughed in reaction to the sharp taste of Scotch whiskey.

Ellen chuckled, then said, "I'm sorry. I guess I assumed you were a scotch drinker because you spend so much time with Jack. It's definitely an acquired taste."

"Apparently so."

"Here, let me get you something else."

"No, but thank you. I'm Jack's protégé. I guess this will just be part of my learning process."

Ellen smiled a warm, genuine smile. Coe was delighted and returned the smile. Lighter, more casual conversation followed. He told her about his father and his time in Massachusetts, and Ellen talked about her daughter. She refilled her drink glass, and they talked for another hour before it was time for him to leave. Ellen picked an apple from a fruit basket on the counter and walked him to the carriage. As he climbed into the carriage, Ellen approached the horse, then smiled as Titus devoured the apple she offered. She kissed him on the forehead and patted him.

"Thanks for stopping by, David. It really helped."

"Jack asked me to visit about once a week, so I'll see you next week if that's not too soon."

"Come by as often as you like," she returned.

During the trip home, Coe carried a feeling of contentment, pleased he could help Ellen Powers during a stressful period. Jack Powers had asked him to visit Ellen and support him during his absence, but after today's visit, he only wanted to help Ellen.

COE ARRIVED AT THE MISSION STABLES and unhitched Titus from the carriage.

"Nice horse; carriage, too," came a soft voice from one of the other stalls.

"Good evening, Reverend Wilson. I didn't see you there. I wanted to talk to you about this. Can I please board this horse, Titus is his name, for a while? It belongs to my boss, Jack Powers, and he's out of town for a couple of months."

"A couple of months!"

"Yes, but don't worry, Reverend, I'll take care of him, pay for the hay, everything."

"Well, I don't know," the Reverend returned with his customary scowl.

Since Coe's father became ill and left the mission, Simon Wilson was in charge. He was an honest man and a good Christian but often crotchety and stubborn.

"I can even help with the two mission horses if you want, Reverend."

"You say the horse belongs to Jack Powers."

"Yes, Reverend."

"Well, I'll tell you what. You can board the horse here under two conditions; first, you take care of the horse, and, second when Jack Powers returns, you tell him we sure could use an occasional donation here. Powers and all those plantation owners are former missionaries themselves, but they seem to have forgotten all about us. Now, they have plenty of money, and we sure could use some. So you tell him, David. Deal?"

"Deal. Thank you, Reverend Wilson," Coe returned as the two shook hands.

As Coe turned his back to leave, the Reverend said, "One more thing, David. I saw a young woman milling around your house earlier this evening. I don't know what that's all about, but I expect you to live an honorable life, especially while you're living here. You're not a missionary. By rights, you shouldn't be here. I'm only permitting you to stay because of the situation with your father. Do you understand me?"

"Yes, of course, Reverend Wilson." Internally, Coe was bursting with anticipation, hoping it was Malia.

"Remember, David, 'For this is the will of God, your sanctification that you abstain from sexual immorality'."

"Yes, I remember, Reverend Wilson, the first Book of Thessalonians, chapter four, verse three."

When Coe left the stables, he went to his house but saw no one. He walked around the mission property, including Kawaiahao Church; still no one. Somewhat dejected, he returned home, hoping it was Malia whom Reverend Wilson saw and further hoping she would return.

As he entered the house, one of the oil lamps in the living room suddenly lit up. The glow revealed a pleasant surprise. Malia was sitting in the rocking chair next to the lamp, wearing her fullest smile. She got up from the chair, ran to him, threw her arms around his neck, and kissed him. He wrapped his arms around her and pulled her close, savoring her warmth.

"I hope you don't mind I came into your house uninvited, but I was waiting outside for quite a while. I thought your neighbors might think I was a burglar, so I came in. The door was unlocked."

"No. No. It's alright. In fact, in the future, if I'm not here, just come in and make yourself at home. It's really good to see you again."

After they separated, she returned to the rocking chair, and he sat on the sofa. "So, Davey, how have you been since I last saw you?"

"I'm feeling on top of the world and anticipate continuing that feeling for a couple of months."

"That's great."

"Yeah, Jack Powers and the American minister left for Washington, D.C., this morning. The Queen will follow them in a few days. They'll be gone for a couple of months. While they're in Washington fighting about the fate of Hawaii, it should be peaceful here. I'm looking forward to the tranquility. And then you show up, icing on the cake. And, believe it or not, there's even more good news."

"I can't wait."

"I'll show you. Let's go." He rose from the couch and headed toward the door, then suddenly stopped. Thinking about the possibility of running into Reverend Wilson en route to the stables, he paused, then turned back toward the couch.

"On second thought, I think it's better if I show you some other time."

Malia didn't seem overly curious.

"Davey, I may have some good news as well."

"Please continue."

"Well, I don't want to impose, but if you like, I can stay here with you for two months."

His eyes brightened. "Of course, you can stay here. What's the deal?"

"Mr. Schmidt will be in San Francisco checking on his refineries while your people are in Washington. They're going to meet in San Francisco on the way back and return to Hawaii together."

"And you can stay here the whole time?"

"Yes, if you want me to."

"Are you kidding? That would be great," Coe said before considering Reverend Wilson's warning; however, the sheer joy of having Malia in the house for two months was overwhelming, so he dismissed the Reverend's message for the time being.

They sat and talked for a few hours, then retired for the evening. Again, Coe recalled Reverend Wilson's recitation from the first Book of Thessalonians, but he hadn't seen Malia for quite a while and couldn't resist her lead into the bedroom.

CHAPTER 19

The next two months were the most enjoyable in Coe's entire life. The atmosphere at the office was relaxed and serene. The other partner, Alexander Thatcher, was still there daily but he was more of a background person. He, like Powers and Coe, was a Harvard man, well-respected and hard-working but stayed away from the political situations Jack Powers enjoyed and invited, and although the other young associates were present, Coe didn't work closely with any of them. Therefore, he could to choose his schedule, which included not only self-imposed long hours and taking work home but also personal freedom and the opportunity to work without interruption. Under such conditions, he felt most productive and efficient.

The situation was just as good at home, especially after the first week. During that first week, Coe wrestled with the dilemma of dealing with Reverend Wilson once the Reverend discovered Malia was living with him. He knew it would happen eventually. There was no chance the two months would pass without him finding out. In the worst case, the Reverend might be so angry he would force Coe to leave mission housing. About the time Coe considered exploring housing alternatives, just in case, the issue was resolved.

It was on the fifth day of Malia's stay. Coe rode the trolley home after a long day at the office, eagerly looking forward to one of her specially prepared dinners. She was an excellent cook, quick-frying fresh fish or meat with vegetables and oriental spices, such as ginger and hot peppers, in a Chinese wok over an open fire. Before Malia, he had never tasted stir-fried food. Now he savored the gratifying sensory experiences, the sizzle of the meat and vegetables on the hot wok, the aroma of the spices, and finally, the mouth-watering taste.

When he arrived home and opened the door, Reverend Wilson sat alone at the kitchen table, drinking tea. Coe was stunned and, at first, thought the man might be there to evict him, but he didn't appear angry. In fact, he smiled slightly, a facial expression the Reverend rarely displayed.

"If you're looking for Malia, she forgot the onions. She'll be back soon."

Another slight smile was followed by a sip of tea. Coe was bewildered, then the door opened, and Malia came in. She kissed him on the cheek.

"I invited Reverend Wilson to stay for dinner. I hope you don't mind."

"No, no, of course not," he uttered, still with no understanding of the situation at hand.

The three sat down to a delicious meal. Coe remained silent and in total amazement through almost the entire dinner while the Reverend and Malia talked about the garden, the chicken coop, and other mission-related topics. It was as if they had been best friends for years, even though they had met only a few days before.

He gathered from their conversation the following; they met when Malia saw the Reverend tending the garden, which covered over an acre, and offered to help. While working together in the garden, the Reverend told her about his arthritic joints. Malia offered to make ginger tea, an ancient Chinese remedy, to ease the pain. The tea worked so well that he now drank several cups every day and felt twenty years younger. Coe had never seen the Reverend so bubbly and animated. He even exhibited a sense of humor. Coe was amazed at the effects of Malia's charm.

When the meal and conversation were over, the Reverend got up to leave. Malia hugged him, and they said goodbye. He then turned to Coe and, with a straight face, said, "You take good care of her."

After that evening, whenever they met on the mission grounds, the Reverend approached Coe as he always had in the past, with a terse greeting from a straight face. He never showed the exuberance he did that one evening, but he never once mentioned anything about Malia living with him.

Over the next several weeks, Coe and Malia lived like other married couples. Malia cooked, cleaned, and performed other necessary household duties. She maintained a friendly relationship with Reverend Wilson, and he continued to allow her access to the mission garden and chicken coop. In return, Malia cleaned the coop, fed the chickens, and worked in the garden. She often went to the fish market in Chinatown and always returned with fresh fish for the Reverend, which he appreciated.

Coe was the breadwinner, working in the office. After two days of taking the carriage to work, he stopped doing it. Hitching and unhitching the horse, both coming and going, was too time-consuming, so he resumed taking the trolley. From that point on, Titus was used strictly for recreation.

Coe and Malia would ride out to the Pearl Lochs on some weekends. The road to the lochs was quite scenic, with groves of coconut trees and royal palms on both sides and the ocean in the background. Once there, they would relax and picnic while watching the large yachts sailing in and out of the lochs. Occasionally, they would enjoy boat races.

Sometimes, they would go to Reymond Grove near Pearl City, where there was a large dance pavilion. While Coe was inexperienced and clumsy on the dance floor, Malia was graceful and accomplished, but she was eager to teach him, and he was just as eager to learn. They even practiced their dance steps at home. As he became a better dancer, they went to the dance pavilion more often. Eventually, they began competing in amateur dance contests, once taking third place.

On weekday evenings, they often took a short ride into Waikiki and sat on the beach. They grew together by enjoying each other's company.

ABOUT A WEEK BEFORE Jack Powers and the American minister were scheduled to arrive back in Honolulu, David Coe steered Titus and the carriage up to Manoa for his final visit with Ellen Powers. It had been about two weeks since his last visit. He didn't go every week as he'd initially promised, primarily because of his unanticipated involvement with Malia, but Ellen didn't seem to mind. She appeared happy to see him every time he stopped by, and he was pleased she felt much better. Moreover, he observed, from one visit to the next, both her physical and mental condition had improved.

When Coe knocked on the door, Ellen greeted him with her customary smile and gracious manner. By this point, all the facial bruises had healed, and she appeared as he remembered her from the office functions some time ago; congenial, physically attractive for her age, and well-dressed. They sat in soft, comfortable chairs across from each other in the living room, and Ellen, remembering his distaste for scotch, served red wine, a Bordeaux from France.

During previous visits, Coe and Ellen had developed a casual friendship. Their conversations often involved various aspects of each other's lives, so Ellen knew quite a bit about Malia.

"So, how are you and Malia these days?"

"We're both well." He paused, then murmured, "More or less."

"Oh, is something wrong?"

"I'll tell you later, but first, I wanted to talk about you and Jack. This is the last time I'll see you before he gets back, and I want to know if you decided what you're going to do."

"Yes, I have. I'll stay here until the day Jack's ship arrives. Then on that morning, before the ship arrives, I'm going to move into a little bungalow in Waikiki, at least for a while. I'm not ready to give up on my marriage yet, but I know Jack and I need some time apart."

"Are you concerned he might come after you?"

"I'm certain he'll come after me. My concern is what he'll do when he finds me."

"Yeah, that's my concern, too. Look, Ellen, since my first visit, I've been trying to devise a plan to prevent him from hurting you again," he said, vividly recalling Ellen's bruised and battered face from the first visit.

"Thank you, David. That's sweet of you, but this is my problem, and I'll just have to deal with it."

"Well, I have something that may help you." Coe pulled from his pocket a small bundle covered in a dirty white cloth. He unwrapped it.

Ellen gasped. "Oh, my, it's a gun. Where did you get that?"

"It belongs to my father. I never saw him use it, and I don't know where he got it. I just came across it once, a few years ago, when I was searching for something else. I think you should take it."

He rose and walked over to her, extending his arm with the single-shot, muzzle-loaded, six-inch-long pistol in his hand. She hesitantly took the gun, held it gingerly in both hands and stared at it.

"David, a gun; I mean, whatever made you think of a gun?"

"Well, actually, Malia gave me the idea."

"Malia?"

"Yeah, last night, I told her I would see you today, and she became a little miffed. I tried to explain your situation with Jack, how I visited you before, and that I was just trying to help. She blurted out, 'Why don't you just get her a gun?' and then left, slamming the door behind her. But her statement gave me an idea, and, while she was gone I looked for my father's pistol. When I found it, it was a little rusty, but I cleaned it and fired it once this morning. It's ready to go."

"David, I'm sorry if I was in any way responsible for creating a problem between you and Malia."

"Oh, no, it's not you, Ellen. She was caught a little off guard when I told her about our visits. I don't know. I guess the thought of another woman may have made her a little jealous. That's all. She'll come back, and everything will be fine." He paused. "I hope."

Coe turned their attention back to the gun. "So, what do you think of the idea?"

"Well, I guess it can't hurt to have it, but I've never shot anybody or anything. I don't even know how to use it."

"No problem. I'll show you. Let's go out to the backyard." He stood and headed for the door.

"Now. You want to show me now."

"It has to be now. I won't see you again before you have to use it."

Her face turned blank as the stark statement registered. Could she shoot her own husband, even under dire circumstances? Then, after a brief pause, she followed him out the door.

Once in the backyard, they moved to within about six feet of a tree.

"It's already loaded and ready to fire, but remember, you have to be close to your target, like six feet or less."

He then pointed to the tree. "Shoot it. Aim for the torso."

Without hesitation, Ellen raised the gun and fired.

She blinked and flinched at the popping sound as a wisp of smoke and the smell of burnt gunpowder wafted back to them. "Wow! That was great," she exclaimed.

The round hit the tree at about the torso level of a man.

"Good shot. Now let me show you how to load it." He taught her to tamp a ball and percussion cap down the muzzle.

"There. It's ready to fire."

She took the gun in her hand and looked down at it. "It seems really small. If I need it, are you sure it can do the job?"

Coe pointed down at the gun. "That is a .44-caliber Derringer pistol. It's exactly like the gun John Wilkes Booth used to kill Lincoln."

Her jaw dropped, and her eyes widened as she jerked her head up to stare at him.

As Coe directed Titus back from Manoa, he thought about his visits with Ellen Powers. The final one was now over. He enjoyed her company and would miss her. But, mostly, he hoped Jack Powers would realize what a good wife he had and treat her with the respect she deserved.

As he got closer to home, his focus turned to Malia. When he arrived home, Malia had returned, and everything seemed back to normal. He was ready to explain the visits with Ellen in more detail and planned to apologize, but Malia acted as if nothing had happened, and they moved on.

ON THE DAY before Powers, Schmidt, and the American minister were to return from Washington, D.C., Coe took time off from work. After hitching Titus to the carriage, he and Malia headed for the Manoa Valley, where they planned to hike to the waterfall for a picnic. She had never been to the Manoa Valley, and he wanted to share the beauty of the locale on their final day together.

It was a magnificent day for a long ride in an open-air carriage. The sun was out in full force in a clear blue sky punctuated by an occasional puffy, cumulous cloud. The temperature was in the low eighties. A mild breeze tempered the heat.

He looked over at her as they passed through the edge of Honolulu and entered the bucolic countryside. Her hair blew back wildly in the breeze, and the sun shined brightly on her smiling face. She turned to him and blew a kiss in his direction.

Proceeding farther into the valley, the path narrowed until it became impossible to continue with the carriage. They unhitched the carriage and walked the rest of the way with Titus. Both Coe and Malia were entranced by the giant ferns and moss-covered trees bordering both sides of the path, creating a Jurassic, prehistoric look. Large bamboo trees, reaching for the sky, surrounded them. As they approached a clearing, the roar of water striking water intensified.

They emerged from the forest onto the shores of a crystal-clear pool of water. On the far side of the pool, about fifty yards away, a ten-foot wide ribbon of water plunged a hundred feet from a narrow ravine in the black volcanic rock wall and crashed into the pool. Sunlight passing through the mist of water droplets created by the pounding of the waterfall painted a rainbow.

Malia was overwhelmed to tears by the sheer physical beauty of the panorama before them. She turned to him, threw her arms around his neck, and kissed him passionately. They spent the rest of the afternoon picnicking, frolicking naked in the pool, and making love. It was the perfect end to their two-month relationship.

About an hour before sunset, they began the trip back. During the previous two months, Coe felt they had developed a deep understanding of each other. Their relationship had grown from a casual friendship with intense physical moments to a husband-and-wife relationship with mutual love and respect.

Somberness increased as they traveled. Both sat in silence, realizing their time together was ending.

Malia broke the ice. "Have you thought about Jack Powers?"

"That's exactly what I was thinking about."

"And?"

"I'm going to meet him at the pier tomorrow when his ship arrives and turn over the horse and carriage."

He looked at her and smiled. "Boy, we certainly did enjoy having Titus and the carriage."

She leaned over and kissed him on the cheek. "Yeah, we sure did."

"I'll just see how Powers acts. The two months with him away have cleaned the air. Hopefully, things have changed; hopefully, he's changed."

"I think it's naïve to expect Jack Powers will be any different."

"You're probably right."

"And, Davey, he's an evil man."

"Yeah, I know. I think about how he beat Ellen. I can still see her bruised face the first time we met. And his role in Reb's shooting. And just the way he treats people in general."

"So, what are you going to do?"

"A lot depends on the outcome of Powers' trip to Washington. If he got President Harrison and Congress to sign the annexation treaty into law and Hawaii is now a United States territory, I'll have only two options: continue working for Powers or leave Hawaii to build my career. And I don't know if I can work for Powers any longer. In the meantime, I'll keep positive and see what happens. That's all I can do right now."

Coe stopped the carriage about a mile from the Schmidt plantation house. He and Malia agreed it was best to avoid creating a stir by driving to the house. They disembarked, met at the rear of the carriage, stood face to face, and gazed into each other's eyes. Her eyes became glassy as she threw her arms around his neck, pulled herself close, and hugged him. He wrapped his arms around her, not knowing when he would again share her closeness. After several minutes, they pulled back and kissed. Malia smiled and said, "I love you."

The three words produced an awkward feeling for Coe. His strict Calvinist upbringing, for the most part, excluded the expression of emotion. Never before had he said those words to anyone.

"I hope to see you soon," he said.

With a smile and a twinkle in her eye, she kissed him again, then turned and ran toward the plantation house. He boarded the carriage and headed home.

COE REACHED THE MISSION STABLES and unhitched Titus for the last time. As he patted the horse on the forehead, he leaned his head against the side of Titus' jaw. Not only was he losing the convenience of having a horse and carriage, but he was also saying goodbye to a friend.

When he entered the house, the heavy, damp air, which seemed to disappear while Malia lived there, had returned with asphyxiating force. He dropped into the rocking chair as the emptiness overwhelmed him. His two months of blissful existence with Malia were over. She wasn't there, and he didn't know when she would return.

CHAPTER 20

At about five o'clock on a Tuesday afternoon, the steamship *S.S. Charleston* rounded Diamond Head on its way into Honolulu Harbor. Jack Powers stood on the ship's main deck, telescope in hand, and gazed in to shore. Travel between Hawaii and Washington, D.C., in the late 1800s was an arduous journey; around seven days on a steamship between Honolulu and San Francisco; another seven on a train between San Francisco and the East Coast. He'd been gone for more than two months.

The sky was overcast, and a light drizzle fell. The weather reflected the mood on the ship. Powers and Andrew Blackburn had failed to accomplish their primary objective, to execute the annexation treaty that would have made Hawaii a territory of the United States.

They had arrived in Washington, D.C., in the final days of President Benjamin Harrison's term. After meeting with Powers and Blackburn, Harrison, an avowed annexationist, tried to ram the annexation treaty through Congress before to the inauguration of President-elect Grover Cleveland. However, before the treaty could be ratified, the Queen of Hawaii arrived in Washington, and Grover Cleveland was inaugurated as President of the United States.

Cleveland, more open-minded than Harrison, held meetings with both sides and concluded that he wanted more information before rendering a decision. So, he retracted the treaty and sent a special investigator to Hawaii to assess the situation. This turn of events forced Powers and Blackburn to discuss a new plan during the return journey. But, first, they had to convince the special investigator to Hawaii that annexation was the most advantageous alternative, not just for the sugar plantation owners but for the majority of the people of Hawaii.

At present, Jack Powers wasn't thinking of the work ahead. Standing on the deck as the ship approached Honolulu harbor, his only concern was if his wife would be waiting for him. Powers made the journey to Washington, D.C., about once every five years, and after every previous trip, his wife awaited him on the pier, but this time was different for two reasons.

First, his wife now knew with certainty he'd cheated on her in the past. He admitted it to her in a fit of rage. The second reason, one more disconcerting than the first, was that he'd physically beaten his wife and threatened her verbally and physically if she left him. If Ellen didn't show, he was sure it would be because of the second reason.

As the ship moved closer, he raised a telescope to his eye and scanned the sizeable awaiting crowd on the pier. He didn't see Ellen. The thought she wouldn't show entered his mind. Despite his despicable behavior, he still loved her. They had been married for more than twenty-five years and had a daughter together. His wife was an integral part of his life. He hoped to see her on the pier.

Honolulu Harbor – c. 1890 *(Hawaii State Archives)*

THE SHIP BERTHED along one of the piers, and the passengers began to disembark. Powers had almost reached the bottom of the gangway when he heard not his wife but a male voice, "Jack. Jack. Over here."

The voice belonged to David Coe.

Coe smiled and asked, "So, how was your trip?"

"Where's Ellen?" Powers said, eyes glaring.

Coe's smile disappeared. "I don't know."

"Is she at home?"

"I don't know where she is, Jack," Coe answered, even though he knew Ellen Powers had moved into an inauspicious Waikiki beach house earlier that day.

Powers slammed his travel bag onto the pier. "Damn bitch. After all I've done for her, she leaves me. Unbelievable."

As Powers' profanity-laced outburst continued, passersby turned to look at him. One of the passing people, a tall silver-haired man, paused and patted Powers on the shoulder.

"Don't worry, Jack. She'll come back. They always come back," said Andrew Blackburn.

"Yeah. Yeah," Powers returned without looking.

Powers took a deep breath, exhaled, then turned his consternation to Coe. "You were supposed to have her meet me here. What the hell happened? And I never received the letter you were supposed to send."

"I don't know what happened to the letter. I sent it as you instructed," Coe lied again. After getting to know Ellen, he had decided it best not to report on her. Mail service at the time was unreliable, and he figured it believable that the letter was lost en route. Coe realized he'd become a pretty good liar. It wasn't a characteristic he coveted but one that seemed helpful in his profession.

Powers glared at Coe.

"Jack, I did my best."

"Jesus Christ, so this was your best? I hope to hell your work at the office was better than this."

Coe wanted to fire back at Powers that, after treating his wife so severely, he deserved to lose her, but, certain it would worsen the situation, he remained silent.

"I need a drink. Let's go," Powers snapped.

Coe preferred not to join him but couldn't come up with a viable excuse to escape. The two boarded the carriage Coe brought to the pier. Powers snapped the reins to get the black stallion moving quickly. Powers was still fuming as they headed up Bishop Street and approached King Street. They turned right on King, heading toward Waikiki. They had just passed by Iolani Palace on the left and Ali'iolani Hale on the right when Powers suddenly pulled up on the reins to bring the carriage to an abrupt halt. He leaned out of the carriage, looked around the horse, and yelled, "Get moving, you lazy bastard."

An elderly Chinese man passed in front of the carriage when Powers stood and yelled again, "Come on. Get moving, old man."

The old man waved politely in return. After the man cleared the carriage path, Powers prompted the horse to resume and muttered, "I should have just run him over."

Coe exhaled in disgust and realized his two months of tranquility were over. All the issues he faced prior to Powers' departure; Powers questioning his loyalty, Powers' involvement in attempted murder, issues pushed to a subconscious level during the two months with Malia, suddenly exploded into the present. He cringed at the thought of spending more time with the man.

They passed by Kawaiahao Church on the right side. Begun in 1838 and completed five years later, the church was a magnificent structure built from fourteen thousand giant slabs of coral, each weighing more than a thousand pounds, each individually hand-chiseled from an off-shore reef in ten to twenty feet of water by native Hawaiian divers. After the slabs were raised to the surface and transported to shore, strong men teamed up to haul them to their final destination.

Kawaiahao Church

Coe gazed up at the church clock tower. The clock was manufactured in Boston by the Howard & Davis Clock Makers and arrived in Honolulu in 1850, along with trained mechanics to install it. King Kamehameha III himself supervised the installation.

Coe's and Powers' ancestors, as part of a wave of missionaries coming from New England to Hawaii earlier in the century, helped finish the church.

After passing the church, they came upon a group of wooden Cape Cod-style houses where Coe lived. He wanted to go home.

"By the way, Reverend Wilson wants to talk with you. We can stop and see him now if you want, Jack."

"What does he want to talk about?"

"I think he wants to ask you for a small donation to help the mission."

"The Reverend knew what he was getting into when he decided to continue missionary work. If he wanted more money, he should have gone into business or law."

When Powers showed no indication of stopping to see the Reverend, Coe said, "Look, Jack, I'm tired, and I don't feel like going into Waikiki. Please stop the carriage and let me off."

"If you want to be a partner in the firm, you have to go the extra mile. I've been away from the office for over two months, and I want you to bring me up to speed."

Once the carriage passed the houses, Coe resigned himself to spending the next few hours with an angry, arrogant man about to begin drinking. He figured they were headed to the San Souci, an up-scale hotel and lounge in Waikiki. It was a favorite watering hole for wealthy businessmen, Hawaiian royalty, and visiting dignitaries.

POWERS PULLED THE CARRIAGE TO A STOP in front of a large, open-air building roofed with coconut palm fronds. A short Asian man wearing a white shirt, black bow tie, and black pants approached the carriage on Powers' side. When the man extended a hand to help Powers disembark, he shooed the man away.

Coe and Powers entered the building, where another short Asian man dressed like the one outside greeted them. Coe thought the two could pass as brothers. "Mr. Powers. Good afternoon. Let me show you to your table, Sir."

Coe had never been to the San Souci, but his first impression was favorable. He liked the casual décor; catamaran oars, surfboards, and other nautical paraphernalia mounted on the thatched walls and suspended from the ceiling.

About half the tables were occupied. All the customers were well-dressed Caucasian men. Powers exchanged brief greetings with a couple of men they passed as he and Coe were led to a table near the beach. Coe admired the beauty of the sand and the clear, turquoise ocean. When the waiter came, Powers ordered, "Scotch, Glenfiddich."

He turned to Coe. "What will you have, Sir?"

"Draught beer."

"Sorry, Sir, but we don't have draught beer," the waiter responded.

"Then just water for me."

"Nonsense," Powers snapped, then looked at the waiter. "He'll have scotch as well, Glenfiddich."

When the waiter left, he turned to Coe. "Lawyers don't drink water. We drink scotch."

When the drinks arrived, Powers guzzled his and ordered another. Coe took a small, repulsive sip and was reminded of his experience with Ellen Powers. He remembered her saying scotch was an acquired taste and realized, at this point, he still hadn't acquired it.

"Tell me about Ellen. Why wasn't she at the pier?" Powers snapped.

"I'm not sure. You'll have to ask her."

"Did you visit her like I asked you to? I left you Titus and the carriage to make it easier. Did you do it?"

"Yes, I did. I made five or six visits."

"Then you know what she was thinking. Tell me. Why wasn't she at the pier? Where is she?"

Coe paused and took a deep breath. "I visited Ellen for the first time on the day you departed."

Powers' expression went blank. "I told you to wait at least a week."

"Yes, you did, and when I saw Ellen, I knew why. But, Jack, that's why she left. Nobody wants to be treated like that."

Powers raised his empty glass and glared at the waiter, who immediately hustled to the bar for another scotch, then Powers returned his attention to Coe.

"Did you tell her that I'm a good boss to you and the others at the firm, that I'm a kind person? That's what I asked you to do."

"How you treat others is irrelevant when you mistreat her."

"You were supposed to get her thinking favorably of me. You were supposed to help save my marriage. That was the whole purpose of your visits. Now tell me, damn it. Why didn't you do it?" Powers yelled as he slammed his hand on the table.

Coe scanned the room to see the other customers turned toward the commotion. He paused to gather himself, then cleared his throat, leaned forward, and said, "Jack, when I saw Ellen's bruised and battered face, I wanted to help her, not you. I know you're my boss, and I respect you and support you at the firm, but what you did to her was wrong. And I don't understand it. Ellen is such a good woman. We had several long conversations. I got to know her fairly well. Anyone else would consider themselves blessed to be married to a woman like that, and here you have her and treat her like dirt. I don't understand it."

Coe expected an outburst, but it never came. Instead, Powers simmered down as he digested Coe's words, which had obviously touched a sensitive chord inside.

Powers' drink arrived, and he took a sip. "So, where do I stand with Ellen?"

"She said she isn't ready to give up on the marriage but she needs some time apart."

"So I still have a chance."

"Yeah, I think so. She doesn't hate you. She just wants to be respected. We all need that."

Powers tilted his head back and looked away as he slowly nodded. "You're right about that. You're absolutely right about that," he said, his voice trailing off as he finished the statement.

Silence fell over the table as Powers continued slamming the scotches while looking blankly into space. Coe gazed out at the ocean and thought about Malia. Powers obviously cared for Ellen but couldn't properly direct his feelings, and while Coe never physically abused Malia, he wondered if he had adequately shown that he loved her. He never told her so.

Both he and Powers were raised in Calvinist missionary families. As a result, they probably shared some common behavioral characteristics. Coe didn't want Powers' spousal behavior to become one of those shared characteristics.

After the fourth or fifth drink, Powers looked at Coe and, in a mellow tone, said, "David, we're fortunate to have you at the firm."

Coe leaned forward as Powers continued, "As you know, we have a lot of work, and, for a while, there were only three of us. Thatcher is in his early sixties, and I'm just over fifty. John James returned to his home state of Massachusetts to serve a term as senator.

We all realized if we wanted the law firm of Powers, Thatcher, and James to continue, and we all did, we had to get some young blood into the firm, but we didn't want just anyone. We're all Harvard Law School grads, and we wanted another top-flight prospect.

We'd been trying for several years to get a Harvard man, but they all want to work in New York, Boston, or Washington, D.C., someplace big, not Hawaii. So we hired a few young lawyers to handle the increasing workload, but none are qualified to eventually take over the reins of the firm. And then you came along, a local boy, a Harvard grad, and not just any Harvard grad, but number one in your class, and you wanted to practice law in Hawaii. You were the answer to our prayers."

Coe was flabbergasted by Powers' words. He'd been at the firm almost four years, had worked hard, and was respected and praised by other attorneys, but rarely received a verbal compliment from Powers. When he did get one, it was brief and subdued.

To hear Powers refer to him as 'the answer to our prayers' was overwhelming. He knew alcohol played a part in the praise but figured the scotch affected only Powers' verbalization of the feeling, not the feeling itself. Coe took the second sip of his first scotch. It tasted a little better.

After a few more drinks and more shop talk, Powers was ready to leave. Coe had almost finished his first drink. It was dark outside. Powers staggered as he rose from the table. Coe supported him as they moved to the carriage. Coe thought about offering to drive the carriage but didn't want to take the chance the suggestion would upset the positive feelings. They left Waikiki and arrived at the mission houses without incident.

When Coe disembarked, Powers leaned toward him from the carriage and extended his hand. "Thank you, David. It was good talking to you."

Coe completed the handshake, then watched the carriage disappear into the night. He stood for a few minutes under the dim street light and laughed at the incongruity of the evening. He had spent most of the day feeling disgusted with Powers' rage, first over his wife, then over the elderly pedestrian, then over his wife again at the San Souci.

Powers' excessive drinking exacerbated the situation; then, just when Coe felt he couldn't take anymore, Powers surprised him with that effusive praise. Coe still questioned whether he could stomach Powers' arrogance and ruthlessness over the long haul, but, at the moment, everything was fine. He even felt at ease when thinking of Ellen. He knew Jack Powers would find her but was certain he would treat her respectfully, at least in the short term.

As he strolled the unlit paths between the mission houses to get home, Coe heard a soft voice, "Good evening, David. Out late, I see?"

"Oh, good evening, Reverend Wilson. I just had an informal meeting in Waikiki with my boss."

"Jack Powers?"

"Yes."

"I hear Jack Powers is a heavy drinker. Don't let him influence you to follow in his footsteps, David."

"Oh, no, Reverend Wilson, I had one drink all night and only drank about half of it."

"Just remember, wine is a mocker, strong drink a brawler; and whoever is led astray by it is not wise."

Coe added, "Yes, Reverend Wilson, the Book of Proverbs, chapter twenty, verse one. I fully agree."

"By the way, David, have you asked Jack Powers about making a donation? That was part of the deal for using the stables, you remember."

"Yes, I did ask him."

"And?"

"He didn't commit one way or the other."

"Well, keep after him, David. We can use the help."

"Okay, Reverend."

The two men parted in opposite directions, Coe realizing he lied to Reverend Wilson.

THE COOL NIGHT AIR helped sober Powers during his ride home. He thought about his wife. He needed her. During his stay in Washington, D.C., he took a side trip to Boston to visit his daughter, Audrey. She had left Hawaii with bitter feelings toward her father because of his disapproval of Robert Alton. While at college, she received news that Alton was shot and her father was involved. She broke off communications.

He desperately wanted to mend the relationship, but the surprise visit was disastrous. She greeted him with a volley of profanity before storming off. It was the last he saw of her. He wanted ensure the fracture in his relationship with Ellen didn't reach that stage. He couldn't bear to lose both his daughter and his wife.

At home, he turned a light on, poured a glass of Glenfiddich from a crystal decanter, and sat in a comfortable living room rocking chair. As he raised the glass to his mouth, he suddenly froze as a thought raced through his mind. Alcohol had played a significant part in his mistreatment of Ellen. If he truly wanted to make amends, he would have to change. He paused, the smooth taste he savored just inches from his lips, then rose from the chair and poured the scotch back into the decanter before turning out the light and going upstairs to bed.

CHAPTER 21

The following evening wasn't a busy time at the Rialto, at least not when Coe arrived around seven o'clock. Two customers, native Hawaiians, were sitting at the end of the bar closest to the door, fraternizing with Julie. Two young Caucasians, probably sailors from one of the ships in port, were playing pool in the back of the room. David Coe sat alone at the end of the bar, farthest away from the door, staring at his beer.

Earlier in the day, during a closed meeting with the plantation owners, Jack Powers had reported the results of his trip to Washington, D.C. The whole island anxiously awaited the public announcement of Powers' report. They wanted to know if Hawaii would soon be a territory of the United States or if it would continue to exist as an independent country.

Within fifteen minutes of Coe's arrival, the bar population doubled. It doubled again within the next fifteen minutes, then again and again. Soon the establishment was packed. Rumors circulated that the mission boys had failed. Many asked each other if it was true, seeking confirmation, hoping for it.

Kimo came from his office in the back, stood behind the bar opposite Coe, leaned over, and asked, "Hey, bruddah, tell me. Is it true?"

Coe nodded as he said, "Yes, it's true. I was at the meeting with the plantation owners this morning when Powers made the announcement. They failed to pass the annexation treaty into law. So Hawaii will remain an independent country, at least for now."

Kimo smiled. "Thanks, bruddah."

He stood on the bar, looked over the room, and shouted above the crowd, "Listen. everybody, listen."

The patrons quieted. "I just hear from a reliable source that it's true; the mission boys failed. We still a free country. *Ua mau ke ea o ka aina i ka pono.*"

Most of the crowd responded in unison, "*Ua mau ke ea o ka aina i ka pono.*"

Kimo repeated the phrase three more times. The responses grew progressively louder. When Kimo got down from the bar, Coe said, "Look, Kimo, this is a small victory, but it's not the end. The mission boys aren't going to give up. They're going to keep trying until they succeed."

"Yeah, Davey, I know, but it buy us some time. If the mission boys successful in Washington, that would be the end."

Kimo then flashed his broad smile. "So be happy, bruddah."

"I am happy, bruddah."

They both raised their glasses of beer in a toast.

Kimo then turned his attention away from Coe. "Look what the cat drag in."

Coe felt a slap on his back and recognized Reb's voice. "Davey, boy."

"I see this not your first stop," Kimo said after observing Reb's staggering gait.

"No, it's not. Tonight, I've got two reasons for celebration, and I'm making the most of it."

"What's the second reason?" Kimo asked.

"Well, the first reason is that the mission boys failed."

"Yeah, I already know that one. That's why everybody here celebrating. What's the second reason?"

"That I didn't kill Jack Powers."

Coe and Kimo blinked, then raised their eyebrows, eyes opening wide.

"Repeat that second reason," Kimo said.

"Yeah, the night before Powers left for Washington, D.C. I was going to shoot him. I was perched on the roof across the street from his office in perfect position. He came out. I lined him up in the scope. Easy shot. Then I just decided not to do it. Good move on my part. I didn't need to kill him. He failed anyhow. Powers may never realize how lucky he is to be alive."

Kimo and Coe looked at each other expressionless, then at Reb.

"Well, I'm heading back to Chinatown. Big party down there." Reb left after a quick handshake with both guys.

"Kimo, that guy scares me sometimes."

"Yeah, he crazy when he using drugs."

"You think it's true?"

"Who knows? He talk crazy, but I know he hate Jack Powers. He blame Powers for shooting him."

Coe didn't respond to Kimo's comment, but knowing Powers was somehow involved in the attempted murder, he figured, gave Reb some justification.

"Kimo, can we talk in your office for a few minutes?"

"Sure, Davey."

Once in Kimo's office with the door locked, Coe began, "At the meeting this morning, Powers said the outgoing President had already submitted the treaty of annexation to Congress. When the Queen arrived, she convinced the President-elect, Grover Cleveland, to withdraw the treaty."

"Cleveland will send a special investigator to Hawaii to assess the situation. Reportedly, he'll rely heavily on the investigator's report to decide whether to re-submit the treaty of annexation. I'm sure the mission boys will try to influence the special investigator's decision. I thought you should know that."

"Thanks, Davey. I'll tell Victor Kalia."

AS USUAL, A LARGE CROWD gathered on the pier at Honolulu Harbor, awaiting the arrival of a passenger ship from San Francisco. Jack Powers, Franz Schmidt, and Roy Matthews stood at the head of the pier, first in line to greet Mr. James Hunt. President Cleveland had dispatched special commissioner Hunt, former chairman of the House Committee on Foreign Affairs, to Honolulu. Hunt's job was to investigate the circumstances of the revolution, the role Minister Blackburn and the American troops played in it, and to determine the feelings of the people of Hawaii toward the provisional government.

"What does Hunt look like, Jack?" Schmidt asked Powers.

"I have no idea. We'll just have to screen the passengers one at a time until we find him."

Danny, the young Filipino from the stables, had accompanied the Powers group. As the ship moored pier side and the passengers began to disembark, Danny lifted a small sign that read JAMES HUNT.

The first passenger to exit was a tall, well-dressed, stately-looking, middle-aged man accompanied by a younger, attractive, blonde woman.

"I'll bet that's him," Matthews said.

"You're on, Roy. A drink at the San Souci," Powers responded.

"I'm with Roy on this one, Jack. I also think the first guy off the ship is Hunt," Schmidt said.

"Okay. I'll take your bet as well, Franz."

After the man had descended the gangway and stepped onto the pier, Powers said, "Danny, ask that man if he's James Hunt."

The young Filipino approached and asked. The man sneered and said, "Get out of my way."

Danny turned to Powers and said, "I don't think that's him."

The other three men laughed.

They continued to scan the disembarking passengers. Each well-dressed man was a candidate, but none responded to Danny's sign. As the final people, all looking like second and third-class passengers, entered the gangway off the ship, the three began wondering if James Hunt was aboard. Perhaps he missed his ship or was delayed somewhere along the line.

A high-pitched, squeaky voice from the crowd said to Danny, "Good afternoon, Sir. I'm James Hunt."

Powers, Schmidt, and Matthews turned their attention from the gangway to a short, bald, frumpy man dressed in a wrinkled white shirt and equally wrinkled brown pants that were too short.

"You're James Hunt, the special investigator representing the President of the United States?" Powers asked, somewhat in disbelief.

"Yes, Sir, I am," the man responded as he fumbled through wrinkled papers he pulled from his back pocket to produce identification with the Presidential seal.

Powers showed the papers to Matthews and Schmidt, then returned to Hunt and extended his hand. "Aloha, Mr. Hunt, and welcome to Hawaii."

Hunt returned a weak, limp handshake.

Powers introduced himself and the other two, then said, "I'm sure you're thirsty after that long trip, Mr. Hunt. Let's go to the San Souci. It's right on Waikiki Beach. We can have a couple of drinks and get acquainted."

"I don't drink, Mr. Powers."

"Then you can have lunch," Franz Schmidt interjected. "The San Souci has excellent food."

"Thank you, Mr. Schmidt, but I prefer to go directly to the hotel. I'm staying at . . .," Hunt paused as he fumbled through his papers for the name of his hotel.

"We've upgraded you to the Hawaiian, the finest hotel in Honolulu. You'll be much more comfortable there," Powers said.

"Well, I'll be here for three or four months, and I want to be comfortable. I guess it's okay if I accept your offer. Thank you very much, Mr. Powers."

After Danny hauled Hunt's luggage from the ship and loaded it onto Powers' carriage, the four men began the short ride to the Hawaiian Hotel. Once settled into the carriage, Hunt opened a hard-bound black notebook and started writing, interrupting himself only to provide terse responses to questions from the other three men.

The Hawaiian Hotel, an elegant, two-story structure, sprawled across several acres of lush landscape near downtown Honolulu. Powers steered the carriage down the entrance road, adorned by neatly trimmed, blossoming bushes and evenly spaced coconut trees on both sides. He stopped at the lobby entrance. Porters unloaded Hunt's luggage and carried it to his room while the four men entered the open-air lobby. A gentle breeze carried a floral scent from the abundance of flowers through the lobby.

A tall, impeccably dressed man approached Hunt and introduced himself. "Aloha, Mr. Hunt. I'm Justin Thorton, the hotel manager. Welcome to Hawaii. We've got you in a corner suite, one of our finest rooms. If you need anything, contact me personally. Enjoy your stay in Hawaii."

"Thank you, Mr. Thorton."

Thorton exchanged greetings and shook hands with the other three, then departed.

"Well, Mr. Hunt, we'll leave you here to freshen up, maybe take a nap. Is it convenient for you if we stop back around six o'clock and take you out for dinner? Hawaii has many outstanding restaurants and some of the freshest seafood in the world. I'm sure you'll enjoy it."

"Look, Mr. Powers, I appreciate your hospitality. I really do. But my mission here requires that I maintain impartiality. In that light, I prefer to avoid any fraternization. It's nothing personal. I hope you understand."

Powers smiled through Hunt's rejection. "Certainly, we understand. You just want to relax. You'll be in Hawaii for quite a while. We'll have plenty of time to talk later."

OVER THE NEXT FOUR MONTHS, Hunt collected a vast amount of information from interviews, letters, newspaper articles, and other documents. He visited businesses and homes and talked to people on the street, always carrying his notebook and annotating while he interviewed. Available to all who wished to speak with him, he cordially and impartially heard a steady stream of opinions from people on both sides.

As the people of Hawaii became aware of the significance of Hunt's mission, his popularity and familiarity expanded. Soon he became the second most recognizable face in Hawaii. Only the Queen was better known. Individuals approached him on the street just to shake his hand. A few requested autographs. Interviewees often engaged him in casual conversation. Some questioned and even badgered him, trying to get an idea which way he was leaning, but Hunt was an experienced professional and took all the distractions in stride, circumventing all probing inquiries diplomatically.

Hunt turned down all offers from the newspaper to interview him. He also resisted attempts by Powers and his associates to get better acquainted in an informal setting. He went to dinner with them twice, and both times conducted informal interviews during the meal, and, of course, he annotated in his notebook while he talked and ate.

ON A SUNNY THURSDAY MORNING, David Coe sat in his office with the door closed, working at his desk. A knock on the door interrupted his focus. When he looked up, Jack Powers led a short, bald, middle-aged man into the office. Coe recognized him immediately.

"David, this is James Hunt, the special investigator from Washington, D.C. He wants to ask you a few questions," Powers said.

Coe rose from his desk and extended his hand.

"Pleased to meet you, Mr. Coe," Hunt offered in his high-pitched, nasal voice as the two shook hands.

"I was assigned by President Grover Cleveland to investigate the events leading up to the installation of the provisional government. I'd like to ask you a few questions."

"Sure. Please have a seat, Mr. Hunt."

Powers sat in a chair next to Hunt in front of Coe's desk, and Coe returned to his seat behind the desk. Hunt turned to Powers. "Mr. Powers, I'd like to speak with Mr. Coe privately."

Powers' face went blank as he snapped his head toward Coe. Coe immediately recognized Powers' line of thought. He was focused on the aftermath of the overthrow when Coe expressed sentiment toward the Queen. Coe knew Powers didn't want him to offer negative comments and said, "I don't mind if he stays, Mr. Hunt. In fact, I'd prefer it."

Hunt hesitated. "Well, okay, but Mr. Coe, I expect you to answer honestly, and Mr. Powers, please do not speak, or I'll have to insist that you leave."

"Of course," Powers said.

Hunt opened his log book and readied his pen. "Mr. Coe, in your opinion, was the removal of the Queen and the subsequent installation of the provisional government justified?"

"Yes, Mr. Hunt, in my opinion, it was."

"Why do you think so?"

"It was the Queen's decision to abdicate the throne. She wasn't forced to leave. She simply considered the circumstances and made what she thought to be the best decision based on the information at hand. That's how I make decisions in my work, and it's probably the same for you, Mr. Hunt."

"After the Queen vacated the throne, some governmental structure was needed. The provisional government provided that structure."

After annotating in his log book, Hunt looked up. "You don't feel she vacated the throne because she was threatened by the United States troops and did it to avoid bloodshed?"

"I can't speak for the Queen, but, in my opinion, bloodshed wasn't a certainty. Queen assumed it was and made her decision based on that assumption. I don't know. But, in any event, it was the Queen's decision to leave."

Hunt continued to question Coe for about an hour. There were questions about his family background, education, and general political views, as well as detailed questions about the overthrow. Hunt wrote continuously, only occasionally looking up to make eye contact. Powers sat for the entire period without speaking.

Hunt then raised his head and looked Coe in the eye. "I have one final question, Mr. Coe. Would you favor a popular vote to determine whether power should be restored to the Queen?"

"Yes, I would," Coe answered, then observed a disdainful look on Jack Powers' face. "In fact, I would strongly advocate that a special election be held so the registered voters of this country can determine the outcome."

Coe noticed the change in Powers' expression from disapproval to contentment when he used the words 'registered voters' in his answer.

Hunt said, "I don't mean an election by just the registered voters. I mean an election with a vote from all the people on the island, including the native Hawaiians, the former contract laborers from the plantations, and any others who are not permitted to register to vote. Would you advocate that type of election?"

"Mr. Hunt, those groups you mentioned are not qualified to vote."

"Yes, I realize that, but if they were, would you favor an election?"

"But they're not."

"Mr. Coe, I just want to know if you think that most of the people on the island favor returning power to the Queen, whether those people are registered to vote or not."

"Mr. Hunt, the constitution specifies who is qualified to vote. I'm not in favor of permitting unqualified people to participate in an election. It would be a violation of the constitution."

Hunt looked toward the ceiling, then, in total exasperation, responded, "Alright, I think that's it. Thank you very much, Mr. Coe."

As Hunt finished his annotations, Jack Powers rose and headed toward the door, then Hunt stood, and Coe rose from his chair. When Powers turned his back to the other two to open the door, Coe quickly approached Hunt from behind and, with his right hand, stuffed a note into Hunt's jacket pocket. The action startled Hunt, and he turned to face Coe. Coe extended his hand. "Thank you for allowing me to assist in your investigation."

While still shaking hands, Coe lowered his eyes to Hunt's jacket pocket, then continued, "If you need any additional information from me, please don't hesitate to ask."

Hunt gave a discreet nod to indicate he understood the transpiration, then left Coe's office with Powers, who was oblivious to the situation.

HUNT DEPARTED THE POWERS BUILDING and, on the way back to his hotel, reached into his coat pocket, removed the note, and paused to read it. *Rialto on Nuuanu tonight at 9*

He looked around before stuffing the note back into his pocket and continuing on.

AT ABOUT FIVE-THIRTY that same day, Jack Powers left the office and steered his carriage to the lounge at the San Souci. When he arrived, Roy Matthews was already seated at a table close to the beach, drink in one hand, cigarette in the other. He'd ordered a drink for Powers, and it was sitting on the table at the seat across from him. Powers could tell by the large chunks of ice in his drink that Matthews had arrived not long before him on this warm day.

"Thanks, Roy, but I've stopped drinking," Powers said as he pushed the drink across the table.

Matthews chuckled. "You're kidding?"

"Nope. I promised Ellen I'd quit if she came back."

Matthews rolled his eyes and shook his head, then blew a big puff of smoke into the air and said, "Well, Jack, Hunt's leaving tomorrow. What do you think?"

"I'll tell you, Roy, I can't get a firm read on him. I don't know what he's going to report. We've talked to him a couple of times in a strictly social environment but could never get him to confide in us. He stayed at a distance and maintained professionalism his entire four months."

"So you have no idea where he stands, if he's going to support us or the Queen?"

"Not really. We had him followed during his entire stay, and basically, he just meandered around town, interviewing dozens of people and writing in his notebook. He stayed around the hotel at night except on the nights we took him to dinner. Nothing suspicious."

"I'd like to get a look at that notebook," Matthews said.

"Yeah, me, too, but he always carried it with him; probably slept with it," Powers responded. "We had his room searched on three or four occasions while he was out conducting interviews, hoping he left some notes behind. Found nothing."

"Do you think taking him out to dinner will help us? After all, those were some pretty lavish dinners."

"No, I don't. He used most of the time to interview us, so I don't think that will favor us at all."

"So, if you were forced to give an opinion, do you think he favors us or the Queen in his report to President Cleveland."

"My gut feeling is that he favors the Queen."

"Why is that?"

"Well, he interviewed far more native Hawaiians, laborers, shop owners, and other working people, and they're all Royalists. They all support the Queen."

"Then his investigation isn't fair."

"There are far more of them than there are of us. It stands to reason he would interview more of them."

"Yeah, I guess."

"It's more than that. If Hunt rules against us and power is restored to the Queen, all those Royalists may become registered voters under the Queen's new constitution. Then you plantation owners would be in serious trouble. All your political supporters would be voted out of office, and the favorable legislation my office prepared and enacted for you would be reversed."

"Is there anything we can do while he's still here?"

"Like what? He doesn't drink. He doesn't patronize the prostitutes. We tried that. So we can't blackmail him. He won't take a bribe, and we can't kill him. For heaven's sake, the man reports directly to the President of the United States. Let's just wait and see what happens. Besides, it's only my opinion. I could be wrong."

"I hope so, Jack. I really hope so."

AT ABOUT EIGHT-THIRTY IN THE EVENING, James Hunt made his way down King Street en route to the Rialto. Approaching Nu'uanu Avenue, he stopped and looked around, strangely feeling that someone was following him. Nothing looked suspicious, but Hunt wasn't sure he would recognize a tail if there were one. He did become aware there wasn't another Caucasian in sight, then a soft voice from behind said, "Mr. Hunt."

Hunt turned to face a huge Hawaiian man he didn't know. The man continued, "You Mr. Hunt?"

"Ah, yes, I'm James Hunt. And who are you?"

"You looking for Davey Coe?"

"Well, yes."

"Follow me." The Hawaiian then turned away from Hunt, crossed Nu'uanu Avenue, and continued down King Street. Hunt was puzzled. He'd made a trial run in the afternoon to be sure he could find the Rialto at night. He knew he should make a right turn from King Street onto Nu'uanu Avenue to get there, but the Hawaiian man walked quickly down King Street, away from Nu'uanu. Hunt needed to decide whether to follow or simply ignore the Hawaiian and proceed directly to the Rialto.

He chose the former, crossed Nu'uanu Avenue, and hustled to catch up. For two blocks, he followed about ten paces behind, then the Hawaiian opened a door to his right and entered a large building without looking back. Hunt followed. The building was divided into several small booths that housed individually operated produce markets.

Although the markets appeared closed for the day, vendors were still scurrying about. The ambient smell indicated a fish market was also in the building. The Hawaiian exited through the back of the building and turned right into a deserted alley. Hunt became apprehensive but continued to follow.

They crossed a few busy streets, and Hunt wondered if the last one was Nu'uanu Avenue. After all, they had made two right turns off King Street after passing Nu'uanu. If his sense of direction was correct, they were then heading back toward Nu'uanu. The Hawaiian continued into the alley on the other side of the busy street, then turned right again down an unlit pathway.

Hunt stopped cold as he turned to face the darkness. A few seconds later, a door opened on the right side of the pathway, and the light from inside the building provided sufficient illumination for Hunt to see the Hawaiian about thirty feet away. "We here, Mr. Hunt," the Hawaiian said, holding the door open. Hunt made his way down the path and into the building. The Hawaiian closed the door behind them.

Hunt noticed a short hallway straight ahead, almost entirely blocked by the girth of the Hawaiian and another door on his left. The Hawaiian knocked three times on the door, then opened it and extended his arm for Hunt to enter. Hunt entered the cramped office, and a young man rose from a seat behind the desk. "Good evening, Mr. Hunt. I'm glad you could make it."

The Hawaiian closed the door without entering.

"Good evening, Mr. Coe." Hunt smiled. "I enjoyed the little tour."

"Yeah, they did that in case you were being tailed. I can't take any chances. I trust you'll keep our conversation here a secret. I can't have my name attached to anything I tell you, or my career is over. You do understand that, right?"

"Yes, I understand and assure you that what you say here will be kept in strict confidence."

"Good. First, Mr. Hunt, I feel somewhat like a traitor talking to you here. Jack Powers is a good lawyer and an astute businessman; I've learned a lot from him. Although I have issues with him personally, he's gone out of his way to help me professionally. However, what he, the American minister, and the other mission boys did to the Hawaiian people is just wrong; illegal, too."

"Kimo, the guy who owns this establishment, is my best friend. He and his family are native Hawaiians and like family to me. I've known them my whole life. I just can't stand by and let this happen. I have to do something."

"I understand, Mr. Coe. Please continue."

"First of all, there's a principle of international law called *pacta sunt servanda*. Literally, it means 'pacts must be respected.' Legally, it means treaties must be obeyed. For example, the United States and Hawaii shared a treaty of friendship, commerce, and navigation establishing good relations between the two sovereign states. This treaty was violated when American troops were landed to overthrow the Queen and install a provisional government."

"Wait a minute. Wait a minute," Hunt exclaimed as he opened his notebook and began to write. "So, you're saying international laws were violated."

"I am."

"Please continue."

"They also violated the United States Constitution, which states that treaties are the supreme law of the land. That means the invasion and overthrow of the Hawaiian government was a violation of both international law and the United States Constitution."

Hunt continued to write feverishly.

"Furthermore, the American minister abused his power and his duty to protect the lives and property of American citizens when he landed the troops off the *Boston* and stationed them directly across the street from Iolani Palace. I mean, if the troops were landed to protect Americans, they should have been stationed in an area of endangerment. Right?"

Hunt nodded without looking up as Coe continued, "But there was no endangerment area, no threat at all to American citizens. The country was at peace. The troops were landed only to intimidate the Queen and force her to surrender, which she did to avoid bloodshed."

"And notice in her statement that she surrendered not to the provisional government but to the superior forces of the United States. That's significant. It means the United States government, not the provisional government of Hawaii, should execute the conditions of the surrender."

Their conversation continued for over an hour. Coe told Hunt everything he knew, including the attempted assassination of his friend, Robert Alton. At the end of the evening, Hunt thanked Coe. "Your statements are most enlightening, Mr. Coe. They'll weigh heavily in my report."

"Heavily, but anonymously."

"Right," Hunt responded while turning to leave.

The Hawaiian escorted him along a different but equally circuitous route back to a section of King Street and pointed Hunt toward his hotel.

AT TEN O'CLOCK THE NEXT MORNING, Jack Powers and Roy Matthews stood on the dock in Honolulu Harbor and watched as the steamship *S.S. Claudine* departed for San Francisco with James Hunt aboard. They waited to see if Hunt would appear on the main deck for a final farewell wave, but he didn't show. As they turned to leave the pier, Danny, the young Filipino from the stables, ran up to Powers.

"Mr. Powers, we should talk. It's about Hunt."

Both the young man and Powers looked at Matthews.

"What? If it's about Hunt, I want to hear it," Matthews said.

"Okay," Powers returned, and the three men headed back to Jack Powers' office a few blocks away.

"So, Danny, what's the issue?" Powers asked once the men were seated in Powers' office behind closed doors.

"Well, Mr. Powers, I'm not sure if this is important, but last night, at about eight o'clock, Hunt leave his hotel room and walk into town. At the corner of King Street and Nu'uanu Avenue, a large Hawaiian man come up to him. They talk, then the Hawaiian turn away and go down King Street. Hunt follow about ten feet behind. They both turn into a doorway to the marketplace on King."

"I follow them, but when I get inside, another large Hawaiian man block my path and tell me the market closed. I tell him I'm trying to catch up with my friends, but he grab me by the shirt and push me back out the door. I search the streets for Hunt, but couldn't find him. So I go back to the hotel and wait. He come back at nine forty-five."

"Hunt was gone almost two hours!" Matthews exclaimed. "Something fishy is going on there."

"Yeah, but what?" Powers said before turning to Danny. "Did you recognize either of the Hawaiians?"

"Yeah, both of them. I see them around the bars on Fid Street, mostly at the Rialto. They work as bouncers on busy nights."

"Then find them and ask what this is all about. Pay them off if you have to," Matthews interjected.

"The Hawaiians are very close. They not take money to betray each other."

"You're Hawaiian, and you turned on them for money," Matthews returned.

"I'm Filipino, Sir."

"Filipino, Hawaiian; what's the difference?"

Danny turned to Powers. "Mr. Powers, if I offer money, they turn on me."

"Yeah, okay, Danny. Anything else?" Powers answered as he rose from his chair.

"That's all right now, Mr. Powers. If I hear anything, I tell you."

As Danny left the office, Powers pressed a folded bill into his palm and thanked him again. Powers closed the door and returned to his seat.

"What do you make of it, Jack?"

"I don't know, Roy, I just don't know."

"I don't know either, but I do know Hunt wasn't down there sightseeing."

After Matthews departed, Powers leaned back in his chair and put his feet on the desk. He knew the Rialto was owned by David Coe's closest friend, but didn't want to bring it up in front of Matthews and hear him rant again about how he should fire Coe.

If Coe were one of the ordinary young attorneys at the firm, Powers would have fired him months ago, at Matthews' first insistence, but he wasn't ordinary; he was Powers' hand-picked successor to run the law firm, his law firm. Powers wouldn't give up that easily on Coe, but still, he realized there was a problem.

CHAPTER 22

In the weeks after James Hunt's departure, Hawaii settled into an uneasy stability. The American troops on *USS Boston* remained on high alert, ready to come ashore if needed. Every person in Hawaii anxiously awaited word from Washington. Would power be restored to the Queen, or would the United States annex Hawaii as one of its territories? Everyone knew Hunt's report played a large part in answering the question.

Rumors were rampant. A few individuals said Hunt had confided in them one way or another. Others claimed to have actually seen the contents of the black, hard-bound notebook Hunt always carried with him like another appendage. The rumors that had Hunt favoring the Queen and those with him favoring the mission boys seemed about evenly divided.

On a sunny Monday afternoon, about two months after Hunt's departure, Benjamin Tate arrived in Honolulu unannounced. He disembarked from the ship, walked from the pier in Honolulu Harbor to the Hawaiian Hotel, and checked in. His luggage would be delivered.

Tate carried two items with him. First, he brought copies of James Hunt's final report for distribution to the Queen and the officers of the provisional government. The second item was a letter from the President of the United States ordering the dismissal of Andrew Blackburn as American minister to Hawaii and designating him, Benjamin Tate, as the replacement.

THE NEXT DAY at about eleven o'clock in the morning, Jack Powers sat behind the desk in his office, reading Hunt's report. The report stated that an overwhelming majority of people in Hawaii favored the Queen and opposed the provisional government and annexation. The report further noted, *There is not an annexationist in the Islands, so far as I have been able to observe, who would be willing to submit the question of annexation to a popular vote. (www.hawaii-nation.org)*

Andrew Blackburn had stopped by about two hours earlier in a state of shock. He informed Powers that a tall, well-dressed, cocky young man with authority from the President of the United States had come to his office first thing in the morning to relieve him of his duties. Blackburn said he would soon leave Hawaii and return to Washington, D.C., for reprimand. He also said Benjamin Tate was disrespectful and accusatory and warned Powers he should expect trouble. Before leaving Powers' office, Blackburn left behind a copy of Hunt's report.

Powers was surprised by Blackburn's abrupt dismissal, although he had anticipated Hunt's report would likely be unfavorable and there would be repercussions. As for Benjamin Tate, Powers already disliked the man even before meeting him.

Suddenly the office door flung open, and a tall, thin, neatly dressed man in his late thirties entered and strode brashly up to Powers' desk.

Powers, already irritated by the Blackburn situation, was incensed by the intrusion. "Don't you believe in knocking?"

"I'm Benjamin Tate, the American . . ."

"I know who you are." Powers yelled. "What do you want?"

Tate initially appeared startled by Powers' confrontational attitude but cleared his throat and continued. "Earlier this morning, I called on the officers of the provisional government to inform them that the President of the United States will restore power back to the Queen, where it rightfully belongs. They advised me to see you. I brought a copy of James Hunt's final report, but I see you already have one."

Powers glared at Tate but said nothing.

"Did you read it?" Tate asked.

"Why don't *you* tell me what it says, Benjamin?" Powers delayed for a split second before saying 'Benjamin,' contemptuously and emphatically drawing out the enunciation.

"In short, Mr. Powers, the report states that the former American minister, Andrew Blackburn, conspired in the overthrow of the government of Hawaii and that the overthrow wouldn't have taken place without the landing of U.S. troops."

"So what?" Powers snapped.

Tate swallowed hard. "Mr. Powers, the President of the United States has decided that, in the name of justice, he will do everything in his power to reinstate the Queen. I've been appointed by President Cleveland to replace Andrew Blackburn as American minister to Hawaii, and I aim to carry out the President's objective."

"Now you listen to me, Benjamin," Powers stated, pointing his finger at the startled American minister. "Hawaii is an independent country, and the President of the United States has no authority here. And you, you're simply a visitor on foreign soil. Now get out of my office."

Tate stammered to respond.

Powers stood and raised his volume to a roar. "Get the hell out of my office."

Tate scurried from the office.

Powers marched to the door and slammed it shut. He returned to his desk and opened the bottom drawer. It was a moment for Glenfiddich, then he remembered he no longer kept scotch in his desk drawer.

"Women," he muttered as he leaned back in his chair and put his feet on the desk. Then, he returned his attention to Benjamin Tate. Undoubtedly, he had somewhat intimidated the new American minister, but he was sure the young man wouldn't be deterred from his mission. His resolve may even have increased once he gathered himself.

LATER IN THE AFTERNOON, in his first official act as American minister, Benjamin Tate, acting on the President's behalf, ordered the American flags flying over Iolani Palace and Ali'iolani Hale taken down and replaced by the Hawaiian flag. As passersby observed these actions, rumors quickly circulated that power would be returned to the Queen.

A crowd gathered around the Queen's residence at Washington Place as Tate entered. During his meeting with the Queen, he apologized on behalf of President Cleveland for the unauthorized invasion by American troops that forced her to abdicate the throne. He conveyed the President's intention to make amends to her and the Hawaiian people. He also relayed the President's message that, before he would restore power to her, she must grant full amnesty to all American participants, a provision to which the Queen readily agreed.

By the time Tate departed Washington Place, about two hundred people had gathered. When Tate smiled and nodded, the crowd let out a loud cheer. Nearly half the people left for downtown to spread the joyous news. The other half followed Tate as he marched back to Ali'iolani Hale to re-visit the representatives of the provisional government.

He first assured them of the Queen's amnesty, then showed them a letter signed by President Cleveland acknowledging the wrong committed by the United States in the revolution and requesting all officers of the provisional government to resign and cede power back to the Queen. Tate told the officers of the provisional government he would summon the United States troops to remove them by force if they did not willingly comply.

When Tate emerged from Ali'iolani Hale, he was met by a throng of several hundred. He paused at the top of the steps, smiled, gave the thumbs-up signal with both hands, then declared, "Ladies and gentlemen, I have a brief announcement. The officers of the provisional government will resign from their positions, and the Queen will return to the throne. Thank you."

The crowd broke into a roaring cheer that began a week of raucous celebration in Honolulu.

IN THE LATE 1800s, Waikiki consisted of a few oceanfront cottages owned by Hawaiian royalty and wealthy foreigners, and a single hotel, the San Souci, serving tourists and weekenders, but native Hawaiians occupied most of the area. The marshy terrain was perfect for growing taro, a low, large-leafed plant with a bulbous root. The bulb was pounded into a paste called poi, which was a staple in the Hawaiian diet.

David Coe enjoyed surfing in the ocean off Waikiki. Unlike the north shore with its gigantic winter surf, the Waikiki waves were relatively small, but the shallow water and smooth bottom produced long gentle rides. At about three o'clock on a sunny afternoon, Coe straddled his ten-foot-long wooden surfboard a few hundred yards offshore and gazed up at Diamond Head, the extinct volcano jutting skyward behind Kapiolani Park.

Diamond Head supposedly got its name because sailors on passing ships observed sunlight reflecting off minerals in the crater wall, causing them to glisten like diamonds. Coe had viewed Diamond Head at all times of the day and night, in all degrees of sunlight and moonlight, and never saw any resemblance to sparkling diamonds, but he loved Diamond Head just the same. It was Hawaii.

Dropping his view and looking toward shore, he noticed Kimo and another surfer paddling toward him.

"Hey, bruddah!" Kimo yelled. "Look what I found."

Reb flashed a huge smile and, as he reached Coe, sat up on his board and leaned over to deliver a hug. "We won! I knew it would happen. We won!"

"He hugging everybody, Davey. People starting to avoid him," Kimo said.

"I wish you had warned me sooner." Coe laughed.

"Can you believe it's finally over? Man, the whole island is going crazy. Downtown is one continuous party," Reb declared.

"Yeah, the Rialto packed solid for three days now. This the best business we ever have," Kimo added.

"I'll feel a lot better when the mission boys officially return power to the Queen," Coe said.

Reb laughed. "That's just a formality, Davey. What are they going to do, fight the United States military forces?"

"I just wouldn't underestimate Jack Powers."

Reb was ready to respond when the first of a promising set of waves arrived. All three caught the first wave and enjoyed the long ride. After surfing for several hours, they paddled in to shore and sat on the beach, peering out at the waves, reflecting on the beauty of the experience. Surfing always created an aura of spiritualism they couldn't explain nor cared to. It just felt good.

A horse-drawn carriage stopped on the road just above the beach. Five fully dressed men stepped out and strode onto the beach directly toward Coe, Reb, and Kimo. One carried a long slender bundle wrapped in a blanket and slung over his shoulder.

The three young surfers looked at each other apprehensively, uncertain about the contents of the bundle. But, judging by the shape, it could contain rifles. As the men approached, the one carrying the bundle stopped and said, "Looks like we're in for a beautiful sunset today."

He then unwrapped the bundle, exposing not rifles but a camera and tripod. As he set up the tripod, then mounted and focused the camera, the other four took off their shoes and socks and ran to the ocean. The three surfers looked at each other and laughed, then they became solemn, each silently realizing that, despite the current jubilation, unresolved tension lay just beneath the surface.

JACK POWERS ARRIVED at Tiger Lilly's at about six-thirty in the evening. The place wasn't crowded at that hour, just as Powers preferred. He ordered two scotches from the bartender, then moved to a secluded table where he could see the front door.

Grimes arrived about fifteen minutes later and scanned the room for Powers. When he noticed a waving arm in the back shadows, he turned to Powers' table.

"Why are you sitting back here?"

"Don't want any eavesdroppers."

Grimes nodded, then sat and grabbed the glass of scotch in front of him. They lifted their drinks in a toast, then Grimes downed his in one gulp and rose to get another.

"Ralph," Powers said, looking up at Grimes as he lowered his glass to the table and pushed it across. "I'm trying to quit."

"Maybe I'll try that someday. Maybe not." Grimes smiled as he sat. "So, what can I do for you, Jack?"

Powers already had a plan but was curious about Grimes' always unique train of thought.

"What do *you* think we should do, Ralph?"

"About the new American minister?"

"Yeah."

"Kill him," Grimes responded without hesitation.

"The American minister?"

"Yeah, the American minister. It'll be months before they clean up the mess and send a replacement."

Powers would have been shocked by such an idea from anyone else, but from Grimes, he expected something violent.

"And when the replacement arrives?"

"If he's not with us, kill him, too."

Powers grinned at the radical plan but, in a strange way, understood Grimes' reasoning. As long as there was no American minister, the current situation wouldn't change. The mission boys would remain in charge, and Grimes' plan was to continue killing the American ministers until they got either a corruptible minister to work with them or annexation.

"I understand your suggestion, but after the second or third assassination, the United States government would become outraged and come after us."

"Not if we made the killings look like an accident."

"An accident?"

"Yeah, an accident. You know, one has an overdose, the next one drowns, next one has a heart attack in bed with a prostitute, next one falls out of a coconut tree."

They both laughed after the coconut tree scenario.

"There's a million different accidents," Grimes said.

Powers felt like testing the plan on Benjamin Tate.

"That's an imaginative idea, Ralph. I'll keep it in mind, but I believe we have the law on our side. I want to first try something legal, and I may need the support of the Honolulu Rifles."

"You got it, Jack. That's why you're paying me ten thousand dollars."

Powers froze as he recalled the last time they discussed the ten-thousand-dollar payment. It was right there in Tiger Lilly's, and Grimes threatened to kill him. Powers was cautious to avoid a similar response.

"Suppose you had to fight the United States troops to earn the money?" Powers asked, then braced for Grimes' reaction.

"If that's what it takes, we'll do it." Grimes' nonchalant demeanor surprised Powers.

"The Honolulu Rifles will take on the military forces of the United States of America?"

"Yeah."

"You think you can beat the United States military?"

"We can't beat them in a direct confrontation using conventional military tactics, but we can beat them."

"Honestly?" Powers said, his level of astonishment skyrocketing.

"Well, Jack, if they were to send their entire army to Hawaii, we can't win, but we can win against the troops off the *Boston*, and I like our chances even if they send another shipload of soldiers as reinforcements."

Powers was amazed by Grimes' statement. "How can you possibly win?"

Grimes downed his scotch in one gulp and leaned across the table. "Did you ever hear of guerilla warfare?"

"Guerilla warfare?"

"Yeah. Guerilla warfare tactics have been used successfully throughout history. It was only a few decades ago, during the Peninsular War in Spain, small groups of Spanish freedom fighters defeated Napoleon's highly superior French army using guerilla warfare tactics."

"They hit small groups of French soldiers with quick surprise attacks, then disappeared, went home, and blended in. They hit the French supply lines and ammo depots the same way. As the fight dragged on and on, Napoleon became frustrated and discouraged. Eventually, he withdrew his troops and went home to France."

"And you think it'll work here?"

"Hell yeah. The strategy is ideal for a small country defending its homeland against a superior foreign invader. The way I see it, that's the situation here. The American troops are five thousand miles from home. If they were to get involved in a long, drawn-out war against an enemy they can't find, they'd eventually get frustrated and go home. It's not like they're defending their homeland. The United States doesn't care much about Hawaii, just like Napoleon didn't care much about Spain."

"Interesting."

"Yeah, Jack. Think of us guerillas as mosquitoes. If we continuously swarm a man in his own home, he won't leave. He's home. He's going to stay and fight. But if he's away somewhere and we continuously swarm him, at some point, he'll get frustrated and go home."

Powers was inspired by Grimes' confidence. He never envisioned having a viable military response if Benjamin Tate summoned the American troops.

SUGAR PLANTATION OWNERS from all over the Hawaiian Islands, including all five members of the 'big five,' gathered in the large conference room at Powers, Thatcher, and James law offices. Collectively, they were unsettled, some even panicked, by the recent chain of events. Andrew Stevens, the supportive American minister, had been abruptly dismissed. He was currently on his way back to Washington, D.C., for reprimand.

The incoming American minister supported President Grover Cleveland's orders to return power to the Queen of Hawaii. He personally shared the President's view that the overthrow of the Queen was illegal. The mission boys were in a dire situation. Jack Powers informed them that he had developed a plan of action, and they were all eager to hear it.

With everyone was seated, Jack Powers stood at the podium in the front of the room and announced, "Quite simply, our only option is to refuse to yield power back to the Queen and put the burden to make the next move back on the United States government."

The room broke out in an uproar. Daniel Mitchell stood. "Jack, we can't stand up to the United States government and their military forces."

Powers considered bringing up Grimes' plan to fight the American troops but decided to refrain unless necessary. The mention of war might jolt the plantation owners away from his ideas.

"Daniel, you have no choice. If you decide to cede power to the Queen, you'll never get it back. With the Queen on the throne, having the support of the American minister and the U.S. troops, there's no practical way for you to re-establish control if you were to lose it. Once it's gone, it's gone forever."

"No, Daniel, this is it, and if you lose control, the Queen will exact vengeance on you. She'll reverse the political gains you've made over the years. The Reciprocity Treaty will be gone. Your sugar will lose its tax-free advantage. You won't be able to compete with other global suppliers. You'll be finished. Your decision today is for all the marbles. Think hard about it."

The plantation owners turned to each other in a clamor of discussion. After allowing the talks to continue for a couple of minutes, Powers injected. "Also, think about this. Hawaii is an independent country. Our sovereignty is recognized by many other nations. The United States has no legal right to interfere in the internal affairs of a foreign country. They're out of line with their directives to cede power to the deposed Queen just as it would be out of line for our government to issue a similar directive to the United States."

Mitchell, still standing, asked, "What if they use military force?"

Again, Powers was tempted to bring up Grimes' plan but refrained.

"As long as we don't voluntarily give up control, the United States would be considered the aggressor. Their attack would constitute an act of war. It would cast a huge negative shadow on President Cleveland if a world power like the United States were to attack a small defenseless country like Hawaii. It may be a gamble, but I feel certain they won't do it."

Roy Matthews stood and added, "I agree with Jack. The United States won't start a war over this. Besides, if they land military troops and force us to give up power, we'll be no worse off than if we had just given up in the first place."

Powers continued, "If you read Hunt's final report, he concludes that the former American minister conspired to overthrow the Hawaiian government and that the landing of American troops forced the Queen to leave the throne. Those are acts of the United States government, not our Hawaiian government."

"From a strictly legal standpoint, President Cleveland is certainly within his jurisdiction to discipline those American officials, but he has no legal authority to interfere in the domestic affairs of the Hawaiian government."

Powers was flushed with confidence as he stood silently and observed the plantation owners discussing the situation among themselves. He knew he had hit the right buttons. Their body language, gestures, and tone of voice told him they were rallying around his plan.

After ten minutes, Roy Matthews stood and faced the podium. "We're in, Jack. Let's hold our position and force them to make the next move.

BENJAMIN TATE WAS SHOCKED when he received word the provisional government of Hawaii wouldn't yield to President Cleveland's orders to cede power back to the Queen. Official notification came in the form of a formal letter from the law offices of Powers, Thatcher, and James, legal representatives of the provisional government. In the letter, the provisional government renounced the right of the American president to interfere in their domestic affairs. In addition, the letter stated that if the American minister and the American military forces illegally assisted the revolution, the provisional government wasn't responsible. Sitting at his desk, Tate read the letter for the third time, still in disbelief. Finally, after mulling over the situation, he rose from his desk and stormed out.

JACK POWERS SAT IN HIS OFFICE, feet up on the desk, when Benjamin Tate barged in without knocking. Powers expected the visit.

"I demand an explanation," Tate exclaimed, shaking the letter at Powers.

Powers calmly responded with a condescending grin, "It's all right there, Benjamin. I assume you can read."

"I swear, Powers, I'll call in the troops," Tate shouted.

Powers removed his feet from the desk and stood, meeting Tate eye to eye. "Calling in the troops constitutes an official act of war. Only the President of the United States has the authority to declare war on a foreign country. Be careful, Benjamin. You're way out of your league."

Tate stuttered and fumbled briefly before muttering, "We'll see about this."

When Tate left the office, Powers sat, lifted his feet onto the desk, and smiled. He knew no scotch was in his desk drawer but didn't care.

SHAKEN BY POWERS' STATEMENT that summoning the troops would constitute an act of war, Tate took no action. He didn't want to risk usurping the power of the President of the United States. He simply forwarded the official notification letter to Washington, D.C.

ON DECEMBER 18, 1893, Grover Cleveland, President of the United States, made an eloquent speech to Congress (Reference: www.hawaii-nation.org) addressing the Hawaiian situation.

"This military demonstration upon the soil of Honolulu was of itself an act of war; unless made either with the consent of the government of Hawai`i or for the bona fide purpose of protecting the imperiled lives and property of citizens of the United States. But there is no pretense of any such consent on the part of the government of the queen ... the existing government, instead of requesting the presence of an armed force, protested against it. There is as little basis for the pretense that forces were landed for the security of American life and property. If so, they would have been stationed in the vicinity of such property and so as to protect it, instead of at a distance and so as to command the Hawaiian Government Building and palace. ... When these armed men were landed, the city of Honolulu was in its customary orderly and peaceful condition. ... "

The President continued:

"But for the notorious predilections of the United States minister for annexation, the Committee of Safety, which should have been called the Committee of Annexation, would never have existed.

"But for the landing of the United States forces upon false pretexts respecting the danger to life and property, the committee would never have exposed themselves to the plans and penalties of treason by undertaking the subversion of the queen's government.

"But for the presence of the United States forces in the immediate vicinity and in position to accord all needed protection and support, the committee would not have proclaimed the provisional government from the steps of the Government Building.

"And, finally, but for the lawless occupation of Honolulu under false pretexts by the United States forces, and but for the American Minister's recognition of the provisional government when the

United States forces were its sole support and constituted its only military strength, the queen and her government would never have yielded to the provisional government, even for a time and for the sole purpose of submitting her case to the enlightened justice of the United States. ... "

He further stated,

"... if a feeble but friendly state is in danger of being robbed of its independence and its sovereignty by a misuse of the name and power of the United States, the United States cannot fail to vindicate its honor and its sense of justice by an earnest effort to make all possible reparation."

President Cleveland concluded by placing the matter in the hands of Congress. Congress debated the issue, but couldn't come to resolution. In the end, neither the President of the United States nor Congress acted to either restore the monarchy or annex Hawaii.

WHEN WORD OF THE DEADLOCK in Washington, D.C., reached Hawaii, the leaders of the provisional government decided to form a more permanent form of government while they waited for a more opportune political climate. They formed a republic, drafted a constitution, and declared it law by proclamation, the very act for which they had forced the Queen from her throne. The new constitution required voters to swear allegiance to the republic. Nearly all the native Hawaiians refused out of loyalty to Queen. Foreigners who supported the provisional government were allowed to vote. However, property requirements and other qualifications were so strict that few Hawaiians and no Asians could vote.

Proclamation of the Republic of Hawaii *(Hawaii State Archives)*

On July 4, 1894, Sanford Dole, the chief justice of Hawaii's Supreme Court, announced the official formation of the Republic of Hawaii and was inaugurated as the republic's first president.

CHAPTER 23

David Coe stepped into the Rialto and took a seat at the end of the bar, farthest from the door. The room was crowded, but the place was like a morgue. Everyone was in a somber mood. They knew all the political maneuvering was over, that the Queen had exhausted all avenues of appeal, and that the mission boys had won. They now ran the country, and it was just a matter of time before the United States agreed to annex Hawaii as a territory, the final nail in the coffin. It was a bitter pill to swallow. Like everyone else in the place, Coe realized the alternatives for the Hawaiian people had been narrowed to just one--fight for their country or lose it. Nobody wanted that, but it was all that was left.

From behind the bar, Kimo leaned toward Coe. "Bad day all around, huh?"

"Sure is. Just look at all the faces. Everybody's so down."

"Yeah, but it's not over yet. We going to do something about it."

"I figured that, and I want to help."

"Yeah, Davey, I know you with us."

"I don't mean simply providing moral support. I want to do something. You tell Victor Kalia I want in."

"I don't think that's a good idea, bruddah. I know you on our side. That's enough."

"It's not enough."

"Davey, you have too much to lose. What if Powers find out?"

"I have a backup plan to deal with Powers."

"Not if he kill you."

Coe glared and raised his voice. "Kimo, Hawaii is my country, too. I was born here and lived my whole life here. The mission boys stole my country, and I want to do something about it. So you tell Kalia."

"Okay, Okay. I tell him. Man, you angry."

Coe's face softened, and his devilish half-grin emerged. "Beneath all these layers of education and sophistication, right at the very core, I'm a wild animal."

They both laughed, then Coe said, "Seriously, Kimo, I want in."

"You in, Bruddah," Kimo said before changing directions. "Hey, you ready for the trip to Molokai next Saturday? Chance to see your father."

Coe nodded as he thought about the journey. On the one hand, he was excited about leaving the turmoil on Oahu, even if it was only for a day. The fresh ocean air was always exhilarating, and spending the day on a boat with Kimo and Reb would be an upbeat experience; then he thought about his father.

Coe had last visited him over a year ago. During that visit, his father showed only minor physical symptoms, but Coe was aware that advanced leprosy could result in horrid changes in physical appearance. From previous visits, he vividly recalled images of other leprosy victims showing extensive bleeding ulcerations on their hands and faces, hideous skin nodules, and facial deformation. Those images still haunted him. He could never get them out of his head. Coe knew his father might now exhibit those symptoms and dreaded seeing him in that condition.

Trying to erase the memories, he ordered another beer. It didn't work. He ordered another.

THE NEXT SATURDAY MORNING, Kimo and Coe arrived at the pier in Honolulu Harbor at about the same time. The sun had not yet risen. The air was fresh and cool. Missionaries scurried about stacking supplies, including blankets, clothing, food, and other donated items. The goods would be delivered to the Kalaupapa leper colony on the island of Molokai. The voyaging canoe carrying them to Molokai was berthed at the pier. It was a smaller model of the large double-hulled vessels Polynesian cultures had used for centuries to migrate across the Pacific Ocean. Two narrow V-shaped hulls were spanned by a flat deck and held together with braided lashing, which allowed them to be exceptionally flexible. Two small triangular sails, constructed from plaits of the tough, fibrous leaves of the hala tree, were lashed to two spars, the mast and the boom.

"Reb's not here," Coe said.

"Yeah, I was afraid of this. Let's go."

Kimo marched off the pier in a huff. Coe followed him up Bethel Street to Hotel Street. They turned left on Hotel and headed into Chinatown. The sidewalks were littered with drunks and drug addicts lying about, sleeping off the previous night's high. Two young, scantily dressed Asian women approached Kimo and Coe from the opposite direction. They both passed by Kimo, but one of them stopped and put her arm out in front of Coe. He stopped. The other moved behind him and put her hand on his shoulder. They both smiled through heavy makeup.

"Hey, haole boy. Want to have some fun?"

Coe smiled, intrigued by the attention. The flowery perfume was overpowering but a pleasant break from the ambient neighborhood odors. The moment was broken when Kimo shouted from twenty feet ahead, "C'mon, Davey, we don't have time for that."

Coe hurried to catch up. "It's a different world down here at this time of night, fascinating. I wasn't going to follow up on their suggestions. I was just curious. They were really cute."

"Yeah, they take you to a room, then drug you and rob you. Then you not think they so cute."

They turned into a bar. Kimo looked at the bartender. "You see Reb?"

"Up in his room, Kimo."

Kimo stormed up the steps, taking two at a time, with Coe close behind. They reached the top of the steps, turned left, and approached Reb's room, the second one on the right. The door was wide open, and they entered. The room reeked of vomit, nauseating Coe. He buried his nose and mouth into his shirt. On the floor next to the bed lay a huddled mass completely covered by a dirty yellow blanket. Kimo ripped off the blanket and yelled at the mess that was Reb, "Get up, man. Get up."

He grabbed Reb by the shirt collar and lifted him to his feet. Reb staggered and fell onto his back on the bed, revealing damp, pasty puke on his face and clothing.

"Let's go, Reb. We already late."

"Late? Late for what?"

"We going to Molokai today. Everyone waiting on the pier for you. Let's go."

The mention of the trip brought a modicum of sobriety. "Oh, my God. You're right. This is Saturday, isn't it? But I can't go like this."

"We fix you up on the way." Kimo grabbed Reb under one arm. "Davey, get his other arm."

They picked Reb off the bed and led the staggering man out of his room, down the steps, through the bar, and out into the street. A few heads turned at the sight, but not many.

As they approached the harbor, the sun was rising. They walked partway down the pier, then Kimo stopped and escorted Reb to the side of the dock.

"Deep enough here," Kimo said, then he threw Reb from the pier into the water. The surprised man thrashed about, shouting obscenities from the water to Kimo on the pier.

"Take ten minutes to wash up, then come help load the supplies," Kimo said, then he and Coe walked ahead to help the others.

Reverend Wilson approached Kimo, Reb, and Coe as they were in the loading process. Looking at Reb with his clothes and hair drenched, the astonished Reverend asked, "My gosh, what happened to you, Robert?"

"Got a little too close to the edge of the pier, Reverend."

Reverend Wilson looked puzzled as the other three laughed.

"Well, I just want to thank you boys for helping out with this mission." The Reverend shook each man's hand. He had known all three since they were small children attending the mission school.

"It's a dangerous trip, and I pray for your safety."

REVEREND WILSON WAS RIGHT about the trip being dangerous. The Kaiwi Channel between the islands of Oahu and Molokai was about twenty-six miles wide and one of the most treacherous passages on earth. The weather often changed in an instant, turning calm seas into an ocean of heavy waves, strong currents, and violent head-on trade winds.

The Reverend experienced the tumultuous seas firsthand when he accompanied the crew on the mission's first trip to Kalaupapa a few years before. He became severely seasick during the trip over to Molokai. While the supplies were unloaded, he was too sick to help, so he lay down, trying to recover. Unfortunately, he had no choice but to make the return trip later in the day and again became violently ill. The prolonged vomiting caused severe hydration that nearly killed him. It was his first and only trip to Kalaupapa.

AFTER ALL SUPPLIES WERE LOADED and secured to the deck, the three men shoved off from the pier, waving to Reverend Wilson as he imparted blessings to them by crossing himself and folding his hands in prayer. The sun had barely risen above the horizon, and the seas were calm as they began the six-hour trip with Kimo, the captain directing Reb and Coe to trim the sails. Regarded as one of the best open ocean sailors in Hawaii, Kimo's sailing experience included multiple trips to the outer Hawaiian Islands as well as a trip to his native island of Samoa in a Polynesian voyaging canoe.

After they were well off-shore and the island of Oahu dipped beneath the horizon, Reb curled up and fell asleep in a shaded area on the deck. Coe leaned back against a soft stack of blankets and thought about his father, reliving the awful day he was diagnosed with leprosy.

It was almost three years earlier, a day he would never forget. His father had developed a presumably minor skin irritation that had begun to spread. He went to the doctor. The diagnosis was quick, leprosy. His father was immediately herded onto a boat and sent to Kalaupapa without an opportunity to prepare or say goodbye. Coe was at home when he received word his father was on his way to Molokai and wouldn't return. The immediacy of the events jolted him. In the morning, his father was at home feeling well; by evening, he was gone forever. Coe had never fully recovered from that day. It was the same traumatic experience many families endured during the leprosy epidemic.

Leprosy was first diagnosed in Hawaii in 1848, probably introduced by European visitors. Earlier epidemics of measles, smallpox, cholera, and syphilis had struck Hawaii. While the diseased victims were quarantined, they weren't exiled from the island.

However, the grotesque visual symptoms seen in leprosy victims evoked such a strong visceral reaction among the general public that, in 1865, a law was passed to purchase land in the Kalaupapa Peninsula on Molokai and force leprosy victims into exile on that tract of land. The area was cordoned off from the rest of the island by two-thousand-foot cliffs and accessible only by sea. It was a prison.

Conditions for the first groups were wretched. At the time, leprosy was thought to be highly contagious and incurable. Therefore, many boat captains refused to take their boats close to shore. Exiles were often forced off the boats while at sea and had to swim. Supplies were frequently dumped overboard and dependent on the current to take them to shore.

In Kalaupapa, with no formal government, anarchy reigned. The strong hoarded the meager supplies that were delivered. The weak were forced to scour the landscape for food. With no residential structures, they all lived in caves and other makeshift shelters. Sanitation was poor, and there were no medical facilities. Simply stated, people were transported to Kalaupapa to die.

Coe was thankful Father Damien, a Roman Catholic priest from Belgium, had arrived a few years earlier and significantly improved the living conditions at Kalaupapa. Still, the situation was depressing.

Coe sat on the deck next to Kimo, who was manning the rudder. Reb approached Kimo.

"Kimo, what are we going to do? If we don't fight, the mission boys will just wait until the United States annexes Hawaii. Then it'll be too late."

"Listen. Victor Kalia, captain of the Royal Guard, making plans with the Queen, but they having trouble getting guns."

"What are you talking about, Kimo? There are plenty of places where you can buy guns."

"Not now. They go to all those places. They say the mission boys buy up all the guns before the stores get them."

"Those sons-of-bitches. They bought up all the guns to prevent us from fighting. Now what?"

"Kalia tell me the Queen trying to get guns from California, but it will take time."

Kimo looked toward Coe. "Davey, you quiet today. Everything okay?"

"He's in with the mission boys. Maybe he knows where they hid the guns," Reb interjected.

"You know, Reb, come to think of it, I might know where those guns are." Coe's voice trailed off as a thought filled his mind.

"Seriously?" Kimo said.

"Maybe. Listen. It was quite a while back. I went to Franz Schmidt's house with Jack Powers to discuss some contracts. Schmidt gave us a tour of the plantation, and we ended up in this large building where they hauled all the cane and processed it into sugar. Pretty impressive machinery, by the way."

"What about the guns?" Reb asked.

"Reb, give the man a chance. Go ahead, Davey."

"As I was saying, we were in this building, and I looked to the back of the building and saw this big stack of wooden boxes. It was covered by canvas, but the canvas had fallen off part of the stack, so some boxes were exposed. I asked Schmidt what they were, and he fumbled around, not knowing what to say, then said they were spare parts, but he hurried back to the stack and started to cover them with the canvas."

"One of the workers saw him and ran back to help. After the boxes were covered, Schmidt reprimanded the guy. I'm sure it was for the boxes being uncovered. The whole situation was suspicious. I don't know what was in those boxes, but I'm sure it was something important, something they wanted to keep hidden."

Kimo and Reb maintained their astonished look for several seconds after Coe was finished, then Kimo asked, "How big the boxes?"

"I was a good distance away and only had a quick glance, but I'd say about four or five feet long, two feet wide, and maybe a foot or two high."

Reb looked at Kimo. "Rifles."

"Yeah, rifles," Kimo returned. They both smiled.

"Good, Davey, good," Kimo said.

"Glad to help, but remember, it's been a while since I saw the boxes. They might have been moved by now, and I'm not sure what's inside them."

"Yeah, yeah, I understand. We check, but it's a start."

Soon after, the wind picked up, and the sea became rough. Kimo ordered Coe and Reb to ensure the supplies were secured, then to position themselves to trim the sails as he directed. Finally, after two hours of fighting the seas, Coe was comforted when the island of Molokai appeared on the horizon.

As they approached Molokai, the seas became calmer. Coe stood on the deck, exhausted, looking into shore. A brilliant green patch of land surrounded by a horseshoe-shaped configuration of tall, black, vertical cliffs stood before them. The view was breathtaking. As the boat neared, a group of people assembled on shore. All were lepers.

THEY DROPPED ANCHOR in shallow water and waded to shore to retrieve two wooden rafts from the beach. The three men had built the rafts before the last trip, specifically to facilitate delivery of the supplies. All the while, Coe scanned the crowd looking for his father. He wanted to see him, and he didn't.

Father Damien had died the year before from leprosy, but Father Cyril continued his work. He greeted them with a handshake and an embrace, thanked them, and inquired about Reverend Wilson. Coe wanted to ask about his father but decided to delay until they were finished unloading.

They dropped the supplies from the boat onto one of the rafts and, wading through the shallow water, pushed the raft onto the beach. While the more able residents unloaded the first raft and took the supplies to their village, the three men returned to the boat and loaded the other raft. Coe's father was among this group of 'more able' residents during the last trip. This time he wasn't. In quick succession, he went from feeling apprehensive to fearful. He became light-headed. Right after they dropped the final bundle onto a raft, Coe hurried out of the water and ran up to Father Cyril. He was choked up to the point where he could barely speak.

"Where's my father?"

Father Cyril lowered his head and said, "Follow me, David."

They passed small wooden cottages with spacious vegetable gardens. Two more prominent buildings, one a church, the other a hospital, rose above the houses. All the buildings were painted white. It was the first time Coe had traveled into the community, and he was impressed by the overall pleasantness.

Coe noticed a man sitting in a chair beneath a coconut tree about a hundred yards ahead. The man struggled to stand when he saw them. Coe knew it was his father and began to run toward him. The man labored toward Coe. As they got closer, Coe's worst fears were realized. Large, irregular skin nodules covered his father's face, his jaw bone had deteriorated, resulting in hideous facial distortion, and open sores covered his arms and hands. His appearance was grotesque, but Coe continued running, weeping uncontrollably. When they met, Coe embraced his father.

"David, I'm glad you came. I don't have much longer, and I wanted to see you before I go. I wanted to tell you one final time how proud I am of you," he said in a soft, sickly voice.

"Thanks, Dad," Coe garbled through his tears.

They sat down and settled into a casual conversation, both realizing this was the last time they would be together. They talked not only as father-to-son, but as equals, even laughing when they reminisced about the old times. Then David asked, "Dad, I know you grew up with Jack Powers and knew him well. What did you think of him?"

"We got along well even though we were exact opposites. If he liked you, he'd go out of his way to help you, but if he didn't, my Lord, look out."

"Well, Dad, professionally, he's very talented, and he's gone out of his way to help me, but personally, we have issues."

"How so, son?"

"I don't know if you're aware, but there are serious political problems in Hawaii."

"Yes, I'm aware. We get the newspaper here. It's old news by the time we get it, but I know the mission boys are trying to annex Hawaii to the United States as a territory."

"That's right, and Powers is spearheading the movement. Not long ago, he saw me with Kimo and Reb, and since then, he's questioned my loyalty. There are other things, too. I think he has a lot of evil in him."

"Remember this, David. Jack Powers is very competitive. He always has been. He'll stop at nothing to win, and he can be ruthless if you cross him. So you be careful. Be wary of him at all times."

"I'll remember that, and thanks for the advice, Dad."

"And, son, remember there's always missionary work. It won't make you wealthy or famous, but you'll be rewarded in other ways by helping the needy. Jesus spent his entire life doing missionary work. It's the Lord's work."

Coe always admired his father's contentment with simplicity.

When it came time to leave, both men stood. They hugged long and tearfully, then Coe departed. He knew he would never see his father again and was sad about that, but at the same time, felt a sense of tranquility and closure as he headed toward the boat, the blue sky and the turquoise ocean before him, and the sun kissing his face.

THE RETURN TRIP TO OAHU covered smooth seas for the entire voyage. The sky was clear, and the stars twinkled brightly above. About halfway into the journey, Reb approached Kimo at the rudder. "You know, Kimo, I was thinking about the rifles."

"Yeah, Reb. What about the rifles?"

"I was thinking we'll have to have to take them from Schmidt's plantation."

"Maybe you right, Reb. If the Queen can't get guns from California pretty soon, we might have to take the guns from Schmidt, else the time pass, and the United States annex Hawaii. Then it be too late to fight."

"What's the plan for taking the guns?"

"First, I talk with Victor Kalia and tell him about the boxes. He'll decide what to do, but first, we have to make sure the boxes still there and that guns are in the boxes. You hear Davey. He see boxes, not guns."

"How are we going to find out?"

"I talk to Victor about it, but I think Doc has relatives still working on the plantation. Maybe we check with him. Man, Reb, you have lots of questions. We just find out about the boxes this morning."

"I want to be involved. I could organize a surprise attack on that plantation warehouse to capture the guns."

"Davy, come over here and hold the rudder," Kimo said.

Kimo and Reb stepped away. "Look, Reb, I know you want to help, and we try to find something for you to do, but you not going to lead anything. You addicted to opium. You not reliable. We can't count on you."

"What? To hell with you, Kimo. I'm not addicted. I can stop anytime I want. And besides, I went to military school in Italy. I know more about military strategy than any of you. You need me."

"We don't need a drug addict."

"I told you I can quit whenever I want."

"Then quit, and maybe we take you."

"I don't quit because I enjoy it."

"Then we not take you."

Reb cranked up to begin a tirade when Kimo interrupted him. "I already told you what you have to do, and that's it."

When Reb became angrier, Kimo seized him by the shirt and pulled him closer. "I told you. That's it."

Kimo stepped back to the rudder. "Thanks, Davey. I take over now."

Reb stormed off to the bow and plopped down on the deck, pulling his knees up to his face, bowing his head, and mumbling.

With Reb at the other end of the boat, Kimo said, "Davey, when I tell Victor about the boxes, he probably want to talk to you. You still in?"

"One hundred percent."

Kimo smiled. "Okay, bruddah."

REB SAT ALONE near the bow; his anger now subsided. He thought about what Kimo had said and knew he was right. He had to stop using opium to be a part of the revolt. He recalled the night when he planned to shoot Jack Powers. He re-lived the hallucinations that kept him from pulling the trigger. As Kimo said, he was unreliable and couldn't be counted upon. He demonstrated that characteristic earlier in the day, forcing Kimo and Coe to come for him. At that moment, he once again vowed to clean up his life. This time he'd do it for the Queen.

CHAPTER 24

Reb left his room at the boarding house, descended a flight of stairs, and walked through the bar toward the Hotel Street exit. It was late afternoon, and all eight bar stools were occupied. He looked past the patrons to the mirror behind the bar area and was pleased by the reflection. It was six weeks since his last opium hit. He had transformed his diet and begun a healthier lifestyle, even managing two part-time jobs. His dashing good looks had returned, his black hair combed straight back, his hazel-green eyes alert and focused, his skin tanned from surfing and swimming in the ocean, and his engaging smile. He was proud he could stick to the resolution he made to himself on the boat during the return trip from Molokai.

He exited the building cautiously, still leery of potential assassins, and headed toward Doc's tailor shop. As soon as he entered the alley leading to the rear entrance, he recalled that his last trip down the path was made with a bullet in his belly. He opened the back door and entered. The others were already there, some sitting, others standing. David Coe and Kimo came over and embraced him.

"Good to have you back, Reb," Kimo said.

Victor Kalia was less enthusiastic about Reb's arrival. Kalia, tall, lean, and in his early forties, was an experienced military man, captain of the Royal Guard during the Queen's reign, and in charge of planning the revolt to return the Queen to the throne. He was well-organized, disciplined, and logical; the exact opposite of Reb. He acknowledged Reb only with a straight-faced nod. In addition to Kalia, four other former Royal Guardsmen were there. Like Kalia, they greeted Reb with only a nod.

Kimo looked at Reb from across the room and asked, "First time back here?"

Reb nodded slowly as he looked around the room. He walked over to the couch where he once lay as Doc treated his wound. Two faint red stains, each about a half inch in diameter, were still visible in the couch fabric. It was an eerie feeling to see his own blood.

Doc split the curtains separating the back room from the tailor shop in front. "Good afternoon, gentlemen. Mama watching the front door. Okay to begin."

As the others sat, Victor Kalia stood and said, "Let's get started. We know the mission boys have been intercepting shipments of rifles to Hawaii. They're anticipating a revolt and want to keep us unarmed. Kimo informed me that some time ago, Davey Coe saw a stack of wooden boxes at the Schmidt plantation, which may contain rifles. Since Davey is the only one who's been inside the building and has seen the boxes, I asked him to join us today. We need to find out if the boxes still there, and if so, do they contain guns?"

Doc said from his seat, "The boxes at Schmidt's plantation still in the same place as Davey Coe say. My nephew, Yao, work on the plantation, and he say there's a big stack covered by canvas in back of main processing plant."

"So he didn't actually see the boxes?" Kalia asked.

"No, he say all workers forbidden to go near the canvas, but he hear from others there are boxes under the canvas."

"And the boxes are filled with rifles?" Kalia asked.

"He say he doesn't know what's in the boxes, but there's talk it's rifles."

"Doc, can your nephew or someone else can check the boxes more closely? Before considering a move, we need to know what's in those boxes."

"I'll ask, but he say all workers forbidden from going near the boxes."

Kalia turned to Kimo. "You think there's any chance the mission boys are trying to set us up by planting a decoy?"

"There's always a chance, Victor, but I don't think so. When Davey tell the story, he say Franz Schmidt very upset that the boxes uncovered. I figure something important inside."

Kalia turned to Coe. "What about it, Davey?"

"Yeah, Schmidt said the boxes contained spare parts, but he was genuinely angry when he saw the canvas was off the stack. I don't know what's in those boxes, but I bet it isn't something as mundane as spare parts."

"Yeah, but are there guns inside? That's what we have to find out. It could be several things in those boxes; some sort of industrial secret, something illegal, even spare parts, as Schmidt told Davey. Could be a decoy, too. There are numerous possibilities. We must be certain boxes contain rifles before taking action."

Doc spoke, "You know, Victor, Yao is my brother's son. My brother hate the mission boys as much as I do. If you going to take the boxes, you might need help from someone who work at the plantation. My brother tell me Yao has friends who are willing to help."

"Thanks, Doc."

"Your brother, Lee, who runs the laundry where I work. That's Yao's father?" Reb asked.

"Yes, Lee is Yao's father. After Lee finish work on the plantation, he take American name, name of Robert E. Lee. By the way, Reb, he tell me that you hard worker. He like you. You like working at the laundry?"

"It's hard work, Doc, but I'm thankful you recommended me to him and that he gave me a chance."

"We all happy you stop using drugs and get your life back. You look much better."

"And I feel much better, too. Thanks again, Doc."

Kimo asked, "So, Victor, what's the next step?"

"Before we formulate any specific plans, we have to know what's in those boxes. If we can't get that information, we'll have to wait to see if the Queen gets guns from her source in San Francisco."

Kalia turned to Coe. "Davey, you're the only one who's been in the building and seen the boxes. Do you have any ideas on how we might get a look inside those boxes?"

"I was only in the building for about twenty minutes, and, during the entire time, we were in the front of the building where Franz Schmidt explained the operation of the sugar processing machinery to Jack Powers and me."

"Were you near the boxes?"

"No, they were in the rear of the building, quite a distance from us."

"So, when the processing machinery is running, the workers are far away from the boxes."

"I can't say with certainty since no workers were running the machinery when I was there, but your assumption seems reasonable to me."

"Do you think it's possible to approach the boxes from the rear while the workers run the machinery in the front?"

"Possibly, if there is a rear door. The stack of boxes blocked my view of the back of the building, but if there's a rear door and it's not guarded, you could probably get to the stacks from behind."

"How tall are the stacks?"

"I'd estimate about six feet. When Schmidt and the plantation worker were behind the stacks, I couldn't see them."

"Anything else?"

"Yes. The building had electric lights, but the boxes were close to the back of the building. So, I don't think the bulbs will provide any light behind the stack. I think it'll be pitch black back there, especially at night. Plan for that if you go at night."

"Thank you, Davey."

The men talked for another half hour or so, then departed one at a time through the rear door.

REB WAS FIRST to leave. When David Coe departed, he found Reb waiting in the alley.

"I need to talk to you, Davey. Follow me back to my room." Reb then started walking. They wound through back alleys and narrow passages Reb seemed to know well but which were completely foreign to Coe. They entered through the back door of a dilapidated wooden building, climbed a set of stairs, strode halfway down the hall, and entered a room. Once inside, Reb locked the door, threw both hands into the air, and exalted with a smile. "Home, sweet home."

"Nice," Coe said sarcastically as he scanned the dingy surroundings. "I especially like the window shades."

Strips of tattered, faded, dark blue fabric, each strip about two inches wide and five feet long, were hung from a horizontal metal bar fastened to the ceiling above the window. Those fifteen to twenty strips of thick fabric hanging next to each other across the window's width, each extending the length of the window, provided shade for the room.

They laughed, and Reb said, "After I get a full-time job and save up a little money, I'll move to a nicer place, but right now, this will have to do."

"So, what's up? Why do you want to see me?"

"I need you to tell me about Schmidt's plantation."

"I already told you everything I know; there are a bunch of boxes out there, but I don't know what's in them."

"Yeah, yeah, I got that, but tell me more details about the plantation, the layout of the building where the boxes are, the entrances, what else is in the building, everything."

Coe recognized the twinkle in Reb's eyes. He'd seen it often during their long friendship, and it always meant trouble.

"You're planning to go out there, aren't you?"

"Yeah, Davey, let's go. Just you and me. We'll dress as plantation workers, enter through the back door, open a couple of boxes to see if they contain rifles, then leave. It'll be a snap."

Coe laughed. "Reb, I'm too tall and too white to pass for a plantation worker. I might as well carry a big sign that says, "Haole.""

Reb snickered. "Yeah. Maybe you're right. I guess I'll go alone. What do you think?"

"It's risky. What if there is no rear door? What if there is one, and it's guarded?"

"You know me, Davey. I'm a risk taker. If an unexpected problem comes up, I'll fix it on the fly. So, will you help me?"

"Yeah, I'll help you."

"But don't tell the others."

"I won't, and, by the way, I think it's a gutsy move on your part. The information is vital."

Reb beamed. "Thanks, Davey."

AS THE SUN WAS SETTING, Reb and Lee rode in an old buckboard Lee had borrowed. They were heading out to the Schmidt plantation to meet Yao. In the distance, black smoke from burning cane fields billowed into the blue Hawaiian sky. Lee said, "I think we here at the right time."

The buckboard pulled up near a dirt roadway at the edge of the Schmidt plantation property, and Reb hopped out. "Okay, Lee, I'm to follow the path to the building where the Chinese workers live, and Yao will meet me when it gets dark."

"Yes, just stay on the path," Lee said. "It's the third house. Yao will meet you behind the house. If he not there, it mean he can't get away from work, so wait for him. I see you here."

Lee reached into his pants pocket and pulled out a small jumble of metal that reminded Reb of cheap jewelry.

"One more thing," Lee said as he extended the narrow chain strung with a small metal disk over Reb's head and onto his neck, like a necklace. Reb lifted the tarnished, bronze, inch-and-a-half diameter disk in his hand and stared at it. Stamped into the thin metal were the letters PAC. SUG. CO. in a straight line across the top of the disk. Underneath the letters, in larger characters, was the number 88.

"What is it?"

"Bango. All plantation workers get one. Must wear it all the time."

"Bango? What's it for?"

"It tell the plantation owners who you are. To the mission boys, we not a name, we a number. At Pacific Sugar Company, I was number eighty-eight."

As Reb studied the metal disk in his hand, Lee pointed to the bango and added, "That bango bring you good luck. Eight is lucky number for Chinese, and you have two eights."

Reb smiled and said, "But, Lee, I'm not Chinese. Will it still work for me?"

Lee returned the smile. "That bango belong to Chinese man. It bring good luck to anyone who wear it."

"Thanks, Lee."

After the two shook hands, Lee pulled the buckboard away, and Reb headed down the path. He wanted to reach the house before dark. The path was bounded on the right side by sugar cane fields. Sugar cane consisted of a tall stalk about ten feet high with long narrow leaves growing off the stalk. Reb had walked for about fifteen minutes of the one-hour trip when suddenly he froze in his tracks. The sound of horse hooves clopping on the hard-pan roadway indicated that someone was approaching from around the bend ahead.

He ducked into the cane field before the horses were in sight. While hunched down behind the dense cane overgrowth, he heard voices from the path. Looking through the maze of thin branches and leaves, he saw two Caucasian men on horseback. As they passed, he noticed both carrying a rifle tucked in a saddle sleeve. His pulse quickened. He knew they'd kill him if he were recognized, and this time he had provided a legitimate excuse by trespassing.

Reb waited about ten minutes after they passed, counting slowly to six hundred while lying still in the underbrush. Darkness was approaching as he emerged from the cane field. He quickened his pace but hugged the cane line on the right side of the path in case he had to make another fast escape.

He was dressed like a cane field worker, wearing a long-sleeved white shirt, long white pants, and a broad-brimmed hat. All his clothing, borrowed from Lee, had been yellowed by age and sweat, but the light color still stood out like a beacon in the approaching darkness. He made a mental note that if they returned at night to get the guns, they should wear a dark cover-up over the white clothing they needed to blend in with the other field workers.

He passed the first house, a long, one-story wooden structure on the left side. Plantation laborers resided there. The process of harvesting sugar cane was labor-intensive. As the sugar industry expanded, the dwindling population of native Hawaiians resulted in a labor shortage.

To satisfy the increasing demand for workers, plantation owners created a contract labor system, importing laborers first from China, then from the South Seas Islands, Japan, and finally

Portuguese laborers from the Azores and Madeira Islands. The laborers signed a contract to work for several years, receiving pay, housing, and medical care. They were segregated into housing based on their country of origin. Reb wasn't sure which group of laborers resided in the house on his left. He was looking for the third building, the one housing the Chinese workers.

In ten minutes, he arrived at the second house, which looked identical to the first. In another ten minutes, the third house stood before him. He left the path and crept to the back of the house. No one was there. The plan was for him to wait behind the house for Yao, but a full moon low in the sky shone brightly on the back of the building. Reb removed his clothing and sat naked against the house, his brown skin and black hair providing better camouflage. He kept the metal pry bar he would use to open the boxes nearby in case he needed a weapon.

While waiting, he reviewed the information he had received from David Coe. Coe told him the boxes were at the rear of the building, far removed from the processing equipment. He hoped he could make his way back to them, open a couple of boxes by working from behind the stack, then exit through a rear door. Coe didn't mention a rear door, but Reb thought there was a good chance such a large building would have one.

Reb suddenly became alerted to the sound of footsteps in the gravel path along the side of the building. He slowly rose and tiptoed to the corner of the building. As the footsteps came closer, he raised the pry bar above his head, then three short whistles came from around the corner of the building. Reb returned the three whistles, lowered the pry bar, and reached for his clothes. Yao rounded the corner just in time to see Reb pulling on his pants. When Reb explained, Yao laughed.

Yao said, "When we get to the fields, it best if you not talk."

The two young men then headed into the cane fields to blend in with the other workers. The smell of smoldering foliage became stronger as they progressed. Sugar cane was harvested by first setting the cane field afire. The leaves burned completely, but the stalk, with its tough outer skin and high moisture content, was charred only on the outside. After the fire burned out, laborers trampled through the razor-sharp debris to chop down the cane stalks, drag them out of the fields, and load them onto carts waiting on crude service roads.

Workers in cane field – c. 1890 *(Hawaii State Archives)*

They approached an area of charred cane where several workers were busy chopping the stalks. Two looked up as Yao and Reb approached. Yao nodded to them, and they both nodded back. Reb watched as Yao drew his machete and began to chop the tall stalks. Reb used his pry bar to hack at the stalks. He wasn't effective but only had to carry out the charade for a brief time. Soon Yao signaled to him to help load the cut stalks onto a cart. When the cart was loaded, Yao nodded to the two others who helped with the loading. Those two swapped positions with Reb and Yao. They returned to the field to chop cane while Reb and Yao guided the cart to the processing plant.

As the cart approached the large building housing the processing equipment, far more people were around. Reb assumed most weren't involved in Yao's plan, and some were enemies of the Royalist cause. He pulled his hat down just a bit and lowered his head. He slouched when he noticed he was a couple inches taller than the other workers. He thought about David Coe, who was three inches taller than he, then smiled while continuously looking around for anyone carrying a gun.

The main processing plant was a long, rectangular building, and as the cart approached the narrower front to unload, Reb noticed a doorway about halfway back on the right side of the building. The door was open. Based on David Coe's description, he figured it must be the door through which he, Powers, and Schmidt entered the building. As they waited for a cart in front of theirs to unload, Reb studied the layout.

He could barely see the canvas-covered stack in the back of the building. No one appeared around the stack, and the area seemed poorly lit. Although the stack was Reb's primary interest, all the others seemed to completely ignore it. Also, he didn't see anyone enter or exit the side door during the five or ten minutes they waited. He came up with a plan.

After the wagon in front had completed unloading and had moved, Yao and Reb pushed their cart forward. Just ahead, two gigantic stone rollers, positioned horizontally, crushed the cane to extract the juice. Beyond the rollers were other pieces of machinery. All machinery appeared to be operating at capacity. The sound was deafening as they fed their cane to the rollers.

When they were done unloading, they turned and pulled their cart to the right so the one behind them could approach the rollers.

Reb was on the left side of his cart, closest to the right side of the building. As their cart moved from the light of the building, Reb dashed to the outside of the building and squatted against it while inhaling a couple of deep breaths to calm himself.

He looked down the side of the building. It was pitch black except for the light from the open side door. He rose and slinked in a crouched position to the door. Then, peering around the corner and seeing no one looking in his direction, he darted past the opening and continued to the back of the building. As he suspected, there was a rear door. He cracked the door open and entered after seeing no one inside. Now directly behind the stacks and hidden from the operations at the front of the building, he approached the stacks and lifted the canvas. Heavy dust slid off the canvas when he lifted it. He let the canvas fall over his head as he knelt beside the boxes. He reached into his pocket for matches and lit one.

He smiled when he saw the stencil painted on one of the boxes, WINCHESTER MODEL 1886 RIFLES, 10 COUNT. There were two stacks of four boxes. These two stacks were placed end-to-end across the width of the building. Behind them were two stacks of four boxes; these stacks also placed end-to-end. Another two stacks of five boxes sat behind them, closest to the front of the building. Twenty-six boxes, each containing ten rifles; two hundred and sixty rifles. Additionally, there were several smaller boxes with the stencil AMMUNITION. All the boxes were nailed shut.

Reb figured they could empty all the boxes in the four-box stacks, a total of sixteen, but had to leave the two five-box stacks untouched. The five-box stacks would maintain the shape of the canvas, so that, from the front of the building, no movement would be apparent.

The match went out. Reb retrieved his pry bar and another match and lit the match. He pried open the lid of the top box from the rear-most stack. The wood creaked as he lifted, but he was sure the sound would be drowned out by the roar from the machinery in the front of the building. A rack containing five rifles spanned the width of the box. Another rack of five rifles lay beneath the top rack.

The match went out. As he reached for another, he felt an irresistible urge to remove one of the rifles. Besides, he might need it for protection on the way out, so he lit another match and lifted the lid enough to remove a single rifle. He closed the box by pressing the wooden cover back down. Then, using the flat edge of the pry bar, he tried as best he could to push the nails back down into the wood. He chose not to use the pry bar to hammer the nails back down, fearing the metal-on-metal clanging might be heard even through the roar of the machinery up front. After opening one of the ammunition boxes and removing a small box of shells, he pressed the lid back down and exited through the back door.

Once outside, he attempted to load the rifle but discovered this model of rifle was unfamiliar, so he hurried off without loading it. He stumbled upon a service road like the one he and Yao used to take the cart to the processing plant. It seemed to run parallel to the other road but was a few hundred yards away and unoccupied since it traversed an area of cane not currently harvested.

Reb followed the service road back toward the house using the full moon as his directional compass. As he hustled along the cane line on the shady side of the road, he reasoned that the plantation probably contained several parallel service roads so the carts could be used to transport cane from all areas of the plantation back to the processing plant. He reached the house without incident and ran down the dirt roadway to leave the plantation.

The buckboard was parked at the pre-arranged meeting spot. Lee was asleep in the back. Reb tapped on the side of the buckboard with the rifle, and Lee arose. Reb proudly lifted the rifle and exclaimed, "There are rifles in those boxes."

"Oh no, Reb, you shouldn't have taken one. Now they know someone has been there."

"Don't worry. It's not a problem. Nobody has been under that canvas for months."

"I hope you right, Reb. I hope you right," Lee said as they drove off.

CHAPTER 25

On a warm, breezy Hawaiian evening, Victor Kalia, Kimo, Reb, and David Coe were among the ten men sitting in the back room of the Queen's beach house in Waikiki. The Queen resided in her Washington Place home.

Victor Kalia stood and said, "We're all here. Let's begin."

Kalia then turned to Reb. "Reb, if you intend to be part of this movement, it's imperative that you coordinate your actions with the rest of the group. It's good we now know the boxes at Schmidt's plantation contain rifles, but you jeopardized the whole operation by taking one. Now the mission boys may know someone was there."

"No one will know, Victor. The canvas covering the stack of boxes was really dusty. No one has looked under that cover for months."

"You can't be sure," Kalia shot back, raising his voice. "You were working by match light from under the canvas. Your range of visibility was limited. Outside the canvas, it was pitch black. Suppose they routinely check the boxes by lifting the canvas from the front and the dust from the front slid back. You wouldn't be able to see that. You screwed up, Reb, and I knew this would happen. I only asked you here because the Queen insisted. She thinks including you in our plan will help keep your recovery on track, but I knew better. I knew you would screw things up sooner or later, and you surely did."

"To hell with you, Victor. I risked my life to get valuable information."

"What good is it now?"

"What good is it? It lets us know with absolute certainty there are rifles in those boxes."

"Yeah, but the knowledge is useless because of your idiocy."

"Does that mean you're not going after the rifles?"

"Damn straight. That's exactly what it means. My men are all members of the Queen's Royal Guard. They're good soldiers. They know the dangers and accept them, but I won't risk casting them into a deadly trap, and that's exactly what will happen if the mission boys know we're coming after those rifles."

Both men sat back and exhaled. Then, Kimo said, "Davey Coe says the rifles at the Schmidt plantation really good."

Kalia then looked at Coe. "Davey, thanks for coming to this meeting. We've never seen a rifle like this, but Kimo says you're familiar with them."

"Yes, that's the Winchester Model 1886 rifle," Coe said, pointing at the rifle in Kalia's hands. "I've fired them on several occasions at the armory."

"Show us, please," Kalia said as he extended the rifle to Coe.

Coe accepted the rifle and a handful of bullets. "The big advantage is that this is a repeating rifle. You can fire up to nine rounds without reloading. You load the rounds here," Coe said as he used the nose of a bullet to press the loading gate down, then pushed the bullet into the tube magazine.

After loading eight more rounds, he said, "Loaded and ready to fire."

Coe stood, lifted the rifle, aimed toward the ocean, and pulled the trigger. Then, quickly, he cocked the lever to eject the spent shell and automatically load another bullet into the firing chamber, then fired again. He repeated the process three more times, firing a total of five rounds in rapid succession, then turned to the others and said, "I can fire four more rounds just like that before reloading."

"Impressive," Kalia stated. "Most of our rifles are muzzle-loaded. We have a few Sharps breech-loading rifles, but they're all single-shot."

"Those Sharps rifles are from the Civil War," Coe said.

"Yeah, I know. But, unfortunately, advancements in technology are slow to come to Hawaii."

"Apparently not for the mission boys," Reb retorted.

Kalia snapped his head toward Reb and glared.

Reb said, "So it would be advantageous for us to have rifles like this."

"Yes, it would, but I've already told you I won't risk my men under these circumstances," Kalia said as he continued his stern gaze at Reb.

Reb turned to Coe. "So, Davey, what do you think?"

"Well, no doubt you increased the risk by taking that rifle. I agree with Victor. You shouldn't go. It's too risky."

Reb waved his hand at Coe, turning his head away and said, "What do you know?"

Coe smiled as he shook his head.

Kimo asked, "Victor, how is it going with getting guns from the Queen's connection in San Francisco?"

"There's been no progress as far as I know."

"They repeating rifles like this one?"

"I don't know."

Reb interjected, "If you won't send your men, Victor, I know some guys who'll help me get those rifles."

"Kimo?" Kalia asked.

"Victor, I'm with Reb. You say there's too much risk, but there's even more risk by waiting. What if the guns never come from San Francisco? By then, if the mission boys know we looking at the rifles, maybe they move them."

Kimo became more intense. "Then we can't get guns anywhere. We can't fight. The mission boys just take Hawaii and annex it to the United States. I can't live with the thought of losing my country without a fight."

Kalia appeared surprised by Kimo's response. After consideration, he said, "Even though I discourage you from going, I wish you the best of luck if you decide to do so. Tell us, Reb, exactly how you plan to get those rifles out?"

"I'm taking a buckboard in the same route I came out. Take the dirt roadway across the back of the plantation, then that vacant service road to the back of the building. Move the boxes out the back door. Load them onto the buckboard, then get out."

"Are the roads patrolled?" Kalia asked.

"I saw two men on horseback on my way in; nobody on the way out."

"If the mission boys know you're after the rifles, there may be more guards."

"We'll take care of it."

"How do you plan to take care of it?"

"We'll figure something out."

"You realize you'll have to subdue them without a shot being fired by either you or them. Otherwise, everyone on the whole plantation will be alerted."

"Yeah, yeah. I know."

Kalia paused, then said, "Reb, frankly, I don't think you've thought this through."

"Yeah, Reb, I agree with Victor," Kimo added.

"If you guys have a better plan, let's hear it." Reb snapped.

"Consider this," Kalia said. "Eliminate the wagon and carry the rifles out by hand. You carried one out yourself. Get enough guys to carry out all the rifles in one trip. That way, you can use the cane fields for cover if you run into trouble."

Kimo's face lit up. "Yeah, that's a better plan. Davey, hand me that rifle, please."

Kimo considered the weight of the rifle. "Each man carry two, one in each hand."

"If you're going to take a hundred and sixty rifles, you need eighty men," Kalia said. "Can you get eighty men?"

"Can get a thousand men by tomorrow when I tell them they saving Hawaii," Kimo said.

"Yeah, it's perfect," Reb added. "We go at night dressed in black and use the cane fields for cover. I'll go into the building and open the boxes. The men can hide in the cane field near the building, come in one at a time, get their two guns, then leave. We park a buckboard off the plantation, and the men take the rifles to the wagon, unload them, then simply go home."

"Good idea," Kimo said, then turned to Kalia. "What do you think, Victor?"

"I still advise you not to do it, but if you're determined, I think it's a better plan."

Coe said, "If you leave the boxes empty, the mission boys will soon discover the rifles are gone by the weight change in the boxes. They'll come after the rifles. So it might be better to weigh the boxes down and close them back up. Then they probably wouldn't know the rifles were missing until they decided to open the boxes. It would buy some time, maybe a lot of time."

"Weigh them down with what?" Reb asked.

"Each man will be carrying two rifles out. Each rifle weighs about nine pounds. Have every man bring two rocks into the plantation, each rock weighing approximately nine pounds. It doesn't have to be exact. Surely each one can find a couple of rocks somewhere. If a man can carry two nine-pound rifles out, he should be able to carry two nine-pound rocks in. It's the same thing, right?"

"Clever idea," Kalia said. "I think you should do that. It might keep the mission boys off our backs looking for the rifles."

Kimo turned to Coe and smiled. "Davey, you so smart."

"One more thing," Kalia said. "If you decide to proceed with the plan, you should do it as soon as possible before anything changes."

Reb responded, "You're right. We have to do it before they set fire to the adjoining cane field. After that, we won't have cover."

Kimo said, "We go in two days. Tomorrow we get the men. Next day we meet and go over the plan. That night we get the rifles."

"I strongly advise you not to go," Kalia said, then turned to Kimo. "Kimo, those eighty men you get, they're all Hawaiians, just like us. They're our brothers. They're from Hawaiian families. Please don't jeopardize their lives. I'm telling you, there's just too much risk. Once Reb opened that box and took that one rifle, it potentially informed the mission boys of your intention. If they know, they'll set up a trap. You'll all be killed."

"I know you concerned, Victor. I'll tell all the men about the risk and let them decide, but we have to do something now, or we lose our country. Simple as that."

AFTER THE MEETING, David Coe stopped at the Rialto to see Kimo, but he wasn't there. Coe assumed he was already out recruiting. He ordered a beer. After two hours and a few more beers, Kimo still had yet to show.

"Hey, Julie," Coe yelled to the other end of the bar. "Is Kimo coming in tonight?"

"I thought he'd be here by now, Davey. Maybe he'll be in for closing, but I'm not sure."

"Thank you."

Coe desperately wanted to talk to Kimo but decided not to wait any longer, especially since Julie wasn't certain Kimo would show.

He arrived home quite inebriated. His immediate goal was to avoid Reverend Wilson. He wasn't in the mood for another lecture about the evils of alcohol. Fortunately, the Reverend wasn't patrolling the mission grounds. Coe made it safely into his house. He lit an oil lamp, and his face brightened when he saw Malia sitting on the couch. She rose and ran to him. They hugged.

"I hope you don't mind, but you said when you're not here, I should just come in and make myself at home."

"You're absolutely right. That's exactly what I said. It's great to see you again."

"Davey, you've been drinking."

Coe babbled, "Yeah, I stopped at the Rialto to talk Kimo out of going. Victor Kalia is leading a revolt. They're going to steal guns from Franz Schmidt's plantation. But Kimo wasn't there."

"Davey, slow down. You're not making any sense. Who is Victor Kalia? And what about the guns at Schmidt's plantation? Let's sit down, and you can start from the beginning."

Malia listened intently as Coe explained the plan to get the guns, then asked, "You're not going out there with them, are you?"

"No, I'm not, and I wish Kimo, Reb, and the others weren't going either. It's too risky. Victor Kalia tried to talk them out of it, but they wouldn't listen. I wish I could do something to stop them. I'm very concerned."

"You've done all you can. Now I think you should just leave it alone."

"What do you mean I've done all I can? I haven't done anything."

"How can you say you haven't done anything? You've done a lot. You swayed that special investigator, Hunt. Because of your input, his report strongly supported the Queen, and now the President of the United States advocates restoring her power."

"I don't know if my information affected Hunt's position at all."

"But it helped. It was a strong opinion from a voice he respected."

"Regardless. The Queen never returned to the throne."

"But, Davey, you provided an opportunity. That's all you can do, and it's not settled. Maybe she'll return to power. And you gave them another opportunity when you told them about the rifles at Schmidt's plantation. And then you showed them how to use those rifles. They didn't know. Davey, just think about it. You've given them a great deal of help."

Coe drew a deep breath and blew it out through his mouth. "I'm very uneasy about this whole situation in Hawaii. I have a feeling it's going to end badly for everyone."

"Except maybe for Jack Powers and the mission boys," she said.

Coe smiled without opening his lips, exhaled through his nose, and nodded. "You're probably right, not for Jack Powers and the mission boys."

"Davey, let's just leave Hawaii. We can go to New York or maybe San Francisco and start a new life there. A steamer leaves Honolulu every Thursday. Let's get on the next one and just go. Before it's too late, before everything falls apart and something bad happens to you."

"Malia, I've already thought of leaving. Maybe someday I'll have no choice, and your offer to go with me makes the idea all the more enticing, but you have to understand, Hawaii is my home. My friends are here. I love living here. I won't leave until I see how this all plays out. If the Royalists can get the Queen back on the throne, I'll accept the position as her chief legal advisor."

"Legal advisor to the Queen? Davey, you could become a senior partner in one of the big firms in New York. Why would you settle for less?"

"Working as the chief counsel to the ruler of a country is not settling for less. It's parallel to the United States attorney general, a prestigious position."

"I think you need a change of scenery. All this turmoil is getting to you."

"Look, I don't know what I want right now, but I do know this; the injustice of this whole situation here in Hawaii sickens me. The way it looks now, the Hawaiians will lose their country. I know they won't give up without a fight. Maybe I can help them in some way. I don't know how, but if I have the chance, I want to be here to do it."

Malia ran to him and threw her arms around him. "Davey, you're really scaring me."

COE AWOKE IN THE MIDDLE OF THE NIGHT in a cold sweat. He dressed quietly while Malia slept. As he left the room, the creaking of the wooden floor awakened her.

"Davey, where are you going?"

"There's something important I have to do."

"It's three o'clock in the morning."

"It can't wait."

He closed the door behind him, cutting off her pleas to return to bed. The cool night air refreshed him as he headed toward downtown Honolulu.

The bars on Hotel Street had all closed for the night, but seeing the drunks and prostitutes still cluttering the sidewalks indicated the closings had occurred not long ago. He hoped he wasn't too late.

Coe turned right on Nu'uanu Avenue and arrived at the Rialto. The front door was locked. He banged on the door for several minutes without response, then dropped his arms to his sides, exhaled deeply, and hurried through the alleys to the back door.

Kimo's office was near the alley door, so he would hear the knocks if he was there.

Coe pounded the door, and in a few moments it opened.

Kimo's eyes widened. "Davey, what are you doing here?"

"I have to talk to you."

"Yeah, sure. Come in."

They entered Kimo's office, and both men sat.

"So, what's up?"

"Kimo, I'm troubled by your decision to go to Schmidt's plantation to get the rifles. You shouldn't go. It's too risky."

"Don't worry. Everything going to be okay."

"Maybe. Maybe not. But if the mission boys know you're coming, you'll all be killed. That's for sure. It's not worth the risk. The downside is too high."

"It's too late. I already talk to some of the men. They ready."

"It's not too late until you actually do it. Please, give it more time. At least wait until you get the final word on the Queen's connection in San Francisco."

"Look, Davey, after I talk with Reb, I think we be okay."

"Reb. Really? What did he say that makes you feel so comfortable?"

"I ask Reb about the boxes. Reb tell me there twenty-six boxes. He open just one. The other twenty-five not touched. That box he open, after he take the rifle, he push the nails back into the lid with the pry bar. Box practically look like it never opened. Mission boys only know the rifle missing if they open the box."

"But that's where you're wrong, Kimo. It's not the only way they can know. Reb said there was a lot of dust on the cover, and it fell off when he lifted it. Maybe, in daylight, it's easy to tell the cover was lifted by the pattern in the dust, and, if it was then they can examine the boxes more closely. You said Reb pushed the nails back in with the pry bar. They'll see those nails aren't driven into the wood as if hammered in. They'll know the box was opened, and there are other ways they could know."

"It wouldn't surprise me at all if they mark the ground to show the corners of the boxes, and if the boxes were moved and not replaced precisely on the corner marks, they know the boxes were moved. Don't you see? There are a lot of things they could have done."

"Davey, I think you reaching."

"No, I'm not; not at all. That's exactly how Jack Powers thinks. He's crafty and very meticulous. He'll consider the minutest detail and has a sixth sense about these things. Don't underestimate him."

"Yeah, you better look out for Powers, too. He find out you helping us, he come after you."

"I've already thought about it."

"Yeah?"

"Well, if he finds out, he'll fire me, and it's possible I'll have to leave Hawaii."

"Leave Hawaii? But, Davey, you Hawaiian. Where will you go?"

"The East Coast; probably New York, maybe Boston. I had several lucrative offers from big firms in both cities. I don't want to leave Hawaii, but if I have to, I guess I could be happy there."

Kimo smiled. "Maybe I come with you. Sell the bar here; open one in New York. I be the only Hawaiian bar in New York."

"You're probably right. Also, no coconuts or pineapples in New York. You could get your family to ship them to us. You sell them outside your bar. I'll sell them to the other lawyers. We'll make a fortune."

They both roared. As the laughter wound down into silence, both men leaned back in their chairs.

"Kimo, what happened? It seems not that long ago everyone got along."

"I know. Remember when we kids, we have big luaus at my house. My mother and aunties cook. Everybody come."

"Yeah, I remember. My father loved those outings, and Reverend Wilson always came, crabby as usual."

"Yeah, he so crabby, he funny."

"How about the time Reb tripped and fell into the poi."

"Yeah, his whole face covered. He look like a ghost. Everybody laugh."

"Those were the good old days."

"You right, bruddah. Haoles and Hawaiians eat, drink, laugh together. Everyone love each other."

They basked in the memories for a few moments when the reality of the present struck them simultaneously. They wouldn't share time again until after the mission to Schmidt's plantation. They stood and gazed at each other, both men thinking the same thing. They didn't want it to end.

Coe said, "I know it probably won't make any difference, but I have to tell you one last time. It's too risky. I wish you weren't going. Especially you."

"Thank you, Davey. You very kind. I see you in a couple of days, bruddah."

"You be careful, bruddah. I'll pray for you."

They moved forward and embraced, then Coe turned and departed, tears streaming down his cheeks.

CHAPTER 26

The new moon provided only dim light as Lee pulled the buckboard into a clearing behind a stand of trees about a half mile off Franz Schmidt's plantation. Reb and Kimo, sitting next to Lee, jumped off the front seat. Several others leaped from the buckboard bed. Eighty young men were gathered at the site. Many had walked. All were dressed in dark clothing, and they all brought with them two nine-pound rocks. Reb stood in the bed of the buckboard as the others gathered around. "Listen. We'll go in single file. Follow my lead. Hug the cane line on the right side of the road. No talking. Everyone knows the plan, right?"

The men nodded in agreement. Reb and Kimo turned to Lee.

"We'll see you in a couple of hours," Reb said.

"Good luck."

Reb reached for the bango hanging from his neck, gazed at the two eights, then pulled it to his lips and kissed it. The eighty silently moved out. Briskly striding along the dirt roadway across the back of the plantation, they passed the plantation houses where the workers lived. When they passed the third house, the one housing the Chinese workers, Reb began looking for the vacant access road on his right.

The clopping sound of horse hooves ahead startled him, and he ducked into the cane field. Looking behind as he moved, he saw the others, in a choreographed sequence, leaping into the cane field for cover.

His chest pounded as he and the others crouched among the stalks of sugar cane. The clopping sounds drew near, and he peered through the leaves. Three horsemen, riding side-by-side, slowed, then stopped on the road about twenty feet from him. The rider closest to him carried a rifle in his saddle sleeve. Reb couldn't see the others but assumed they were also armed.

The rider nearest the cane field dismounted. As the man walked toward him, he wondered if the horsemen were alerted by the rustling sounds of his men ducking into the cane underbrush. He clenched the nine-pound rocks in his fists, lifted them chest high, looked to the man crouched next to him, and nodded. The man raised the rocks in his fists and returned an acknowledging nod. Reb looked back to the road.

The horseman paused at the cane line in a location blocked from his view by a localized dense growth of small branches and leaves. His heart raced as he listened. Soon he heard what sounded like a stream of water gently striking the dry leaves a few feet in front of him. He smiled when he realized the horseman was urinating. When the horseman finished, he mounted his horse, and the three continued down the dirt road.

Reb sat back and unwound while awaiting the pre-arranged signal. In a few minutes, he felt a tap from behind on his right shoulder, then stood and stepped out from the cane field onto the dirt road. They had set up a system whereby the last man would wait until the danger had passed and, when safe, tap the man in front of him on the right shoulder. The 'chain of taps' would continue to the other end of the line so every man knew it was safe to move out. Reb looked back to see the others following his lead onto the road.

They turned onto the empty access road and reached the rear of the main processing plant without further incident. Reb, an assistant and the first man to receive two rifles entered the rear door. The others remained outside, squatting in single file behind a row of sugar cane next to the service road.

Inside the building, the roar of the sugar-processing machinery filled the space. The three men removed the section of canvas covering the rear stacks of boxes, careful not to disturb the covering of the forward stacks. Reb pried the lid off the first box, removed all ten rifles, and handed them to his assistant.

After the first man left with his rifles, the next two had come in, one at a time, handed their two nine-pound rocks to Reb, and departed after receiving two rifles from the assistant. The fourth man had just entered the back door and given his nine-pound rocks to Reb. Reb's helper handed the man two rifles as Reb placed the rocks into the rifle box. Thus far, their plan had gone off without a hitch.

Just as the fourth man opened the back door to leave, several shots rang out outside in the cane fields. The three startled men stood and looked blankly at each other as the shots continued. Reb then dashed to the back door and peered out. The sight horrified him. As many as twenty men on horseback were firing their rifles into the cane field where his men were waiting. Many others on the ground were also shooting into the cane field. Reb moved to the side of the stack of boxes, leaned around the corner, and looked toward the front of the building. All the workers were running from the large door in front. With no one looking toward the rear of the building, he dashed to the side door and exited into the darkness. The assistant and the fourth man followed.

OUT IN THE CANE FIELD, mass panic prevailed. Several had already been shot dead. Kimo and the other survivors fled deeper into the cane field, away from the gunmen on the service road. As they ran, the smell of burning leaves became stronger. In a second, they were confronted by a raging inferno racing toward them. The cane field had been set afire, and the trade winds were fanning the flames rapidly in their direction. With no choice, Kimo and the others turned away from the fire and ran back toward the service road. When blood-curdling screams pierced the air, Kimo knew fire has consumed some of the men. As the others ran from the cane field, gunmen were waiting.

Kimo remained in the cane field as long as possible. His heart raced as a salvo of shots fired on the service road. He glanced through the cane stalks to see his Hawaiian brothers falling as they exited the field. Soon the intense heat from the approaching fire bore down on him, leaving no alternative but to leave. He grabbed two nine-pound rocks his men left behind when they fled. Then, when he saw two horsemen turn their horses away from him, he charged from the burning field.

Rushing up to the men from behind, he hurled a rock at one of the horsemen. It struck the man in the head, opening a bloody gash and knocking him unconscious from his saddle. The other horseman turned his rifle toward Kimo. Kimo grabbed the end of the rifle barrel and pushed it away as a shot fired harmlessly. He pulled the horseman closer by yanking on the rifle barrel, then reached up and slammed the other rock into the side of the man's jaw. Blood spewed, and the man screamed as Kimo pulled him to the ground. He straddled the man, lifted the rock above his head, then buried it into the man's skull.

Other shooters turned toward the commotion and raised their rifles. A barrage of shots rang out. Kimo was killed instantly.

REB AND THE OTHER TWO continued running. The road they took was different from the one by which they entered, but fortunately, it led them off the plantation. They ran until they were exhausted, then stopped. Well off the plantation and presumably safe, they looked back. The gunfire had ceased, but a bright hue from the flames was visible against the darkness. They hoped many others had escaped, but feared the worst.

Just then, a horrible thought struck Reb. Victor Kalia may have been right. Clearly, the mission boys knew of their plan and had prepared a deadly ambush. Maybe by taking that one rifle, he had tipped them off. As a result, he might be responsible for dozens of deaths. The thought overwhelmed him with guilt. He became short of breath, then dropped to his knees and bawled.

SEVENTY-SEVEN. Two days after the slaughter at the plantation, Reb sat on the edge of the bed in his room, haunted by that staggering number. He kept the curtains drawn so the room was dark except for the stray beams of light passing around and between the fabric strips. The only survivors besides him were the two men who left with him and Lee. All the others were killed, seventy-seven. Seventy-two were shot to death, five suffered the horrific agony of being consumed by the fire, and he felt responsible for every one of them. He alone had caused unimaginable grief for seventy-seven Hawaiian families. Seventy-seven. He didn't deserve to survive.

The Honolulu newspaper placed the responsibility for the attack on the Queen. They labeled her an anarchist and said she was too unstable to resume governing and that the people of Hawaii were best protected by the republic. Once again, he had disappointed the Queen, this time on a grand scale. He had caused many of the people of Hawaii to now turn against her in favor of the republic. He may have forever doomed the native Hawaiian people to an existence controlled by the mission boys. The independent country of Hawaii may never again belong to the Hawaiian people, and it was his fault. He didn't deserve to survive. Seventy-seven; the number kept returning to him.

Since that night, he hadn't bathed or shaved. He had barely eaten and hadn't shown up at either job. Except for the time he spent in nearby opium dens, he'd stayed in his room, often weeping for hours, thinking of his departed friends, all seventy-seven. Funerals took place all over the island. He felt obligated to attend them all, to apologize to the families of the deceased and ask their forgiveness, but he couldn't bring himself to go to a single one.

On this day, however, there would be a funeral he had to attend. Kimo was being buried. He'd known Kimo his whole life, the family as well. He wasn't sure how he would be received and was afraid, but he had to go. Finally, he mustered the strength to stand. It was a long walk, and he wanted to arrive on time. Being late was an omen of bad luck for the family because it was believed it foreshadowed the death of another household member. He left filled with trepidation.

MORE THAN ONE HUNDRED MOURNERS gathered at Kimo's family house on the day of his funeral. Like many Hawaiian families, Kimo and his family lived in a small house constructed of a wooden frame held together by braided lashing and covered by a thatched roof.

While the family remained inside, near the body, to greet arriving mourners, most people waited outside in the spacious yard. David Coe stood alone at the edge of the property, exhausted and numb from two days of grieving. He had no more tears to shed. The full sun engulfing the yard reminded Coe of his friend's beaming, ever-present smile, a smile that now and forever existed only in his memory. "Goodbye, bruddah."

Hawaiian house - *(Hawaii State Archives)*

Victor Kalia approached Coe. "We all lost a good friend."

"The best of friends."

"And I lost three nephews, too."

"I didn't know, Victor. I'm sorry."

"Yeah, and it's due to Reb's stupidity."

"I'm certain he feels worse about it than anybody."

"He should. It should be his funeral we're attending."

Coe quickly changed the topic. "What's the status of your plan, Victor?"

"We're still awaiting word on the guns from the Queen's connection in San Francisco. When we get guns, we'll make our move."

"If there's anything I can do to help, please let me know."

"You could march with us, Davey."

"You mean actually join you in combat?"

"Exactly. You're young, reliable, in good physical condition, and know how to handle a gun; just the type of person we want."

He was caught off guard by Kalia's offer. When Coe said he would help, he meant in an advisory capacity, like when he met with them to provide information about the Schmidt processing plant where the rifles were hidden or to demonstrate the operation of the Winchester Model 1886 rifle.

He never considered actually fighting, but the idea immediately appealed to him. He admired guys like Kimo, who were willing to fight for something they believed and was honored that the captain of Queen's Royal Guard, a revered career soldier, requested that he join the battle.

Kalia said, "Kimo would smile down from heaven if you joined us."

Without hesitation, Coe returned, "I'm in, Victor."

"Good to have you. I'll keep you informed," Kalia returned while extending his hand. Coe smiled and vigorously returned the handshake.

REB HAD ARRIVED in plenty of time. He stood on the hill above the grass house and looked down. The various shades of green from trees and the grass surrounding the house gleamed in the bright sun. Dozens of people were conversing outside in the yard. He descended the hill and entered through the back door. The place was packed, and all hushed to stare at the dirty, bedraggled man. They parted to create a path as he passed through. Reb spotted Kimo's mother standing next to her son's body. When she looked at him, he ran to her, weeping. They hugged each other, and he cried out, "Forgive me. Please forgive me."

"Robert, of course, I forgive you," she returned as she patted him on the back while continuing to hug him. Kimo's other family members also approached and consoled him, expressing their forgiveness. The other mourners, nearly all of whom knew him, followed with hugs and pats on the back. Reb began to feel some level of consolation until he walked over to Kimo's body. The body had been placed on mats with a wooden pillow beneath the head. The lower part of the body was covered with another mat. When Reb looked down at Kimo's lifeless face, his remorse and depression returned at a higher level. He resumed weeping.

"I'm sorry. I'm so sorry. It should have been me. It should have been me. I don't deserve to live."

BEFORE BURIAL, the body was wrapped in fine mats and tied three times, once toward the head, once toward the middle, and once over the legs. After being blessed, the wrapped body was put on a bier of wood consisting of two long poles with cross pieces and carried through the front door, legs first, so the eyes faced the direction in which the burial party was headed. As soon as the body was out of the house, the white mat that had served as a canopy and the mats on the deathbed were folded and removed, symbolizing the end of the person's life. Folding the mats immediately after the corpse was gone was a way of making a new death in the house unwelcome.

The pallbearers and mourners began chanting as they walked toward the burial site. The chanting continued until the wrapped body was lowered into the grave. The bier was dismantled soon after the burial and left at the burial site to rot. The crowd attending the burial then returned to the house where the body had lain in state to partake in the funeral feast.

With the funeral over, the mood became less solemn. The people exchanged fond remembrances of Kimo and shared a sumptuous meal. Everyone's mood lightened except Reb, who remained depressed, and Victor Kalia, whose mood vacillated between sorrow and anger. Several times Reb glanced at Kalia, sitting on the grass about ten feet away, but each time he met an incensed glare and quickly turned away. Finally, Kalia rose and moved over to Reb. When Reb looked up, Kalia dived on top and pummeled him. Reb recoiled to protect himself. Quickly the others pulled Kalia from Reb.

Kalia looked down while being restrained and cried out, "You killed my family. You killed Kimo. You killed seventy-seven others. It should have been you whom we buried."

Reb would have vociferously fought back at any other time, but not today. He looked up sorrowfully and said nothing. In his mind, Kalia was right. It should have been him, not the seventy-seven others, who was being buried.

When the ceremonies ended, and the people headed home, David Coe and Reb walked out together. "Remember, Reb, the Lord loves you and forgives you. Many passages tell us so."

"Thanks, Davey"

"I know just what you need," Coe said. "A day of surfing. Surfing relaxes the mind. That's what you need right now, to get your mind off this whole situation. What do you say?"

"Yeah, maybe."

"How about tomorrow? We'll meet at the beach in Waikiki tomorrow at ten o'clock."

Reb nodded as the two headed their separate ways.

THE NEXT MORNING, the sun beamed in a clear blue sky. Diamond Head exhibited a lush, velvety green covering, the result of recent rainfall, but Davey Coe sat alone on his surfboard, unable to enjoy the magnificent setting. He recalled the last time he surfed Waikiki. It was during the days of celebration after the new American minister announced that power would be restored to the Queen. Kimo and Reb had joined him. It was a joyous occasion.

The situation had changed drastically since that day. The mission boys had taken firm control of Hawaii, Kimo was dead, and

Reb was at least an hour late. For the first time, Coe hoped Reb had simply passed out from alcohol and opium, but he feared worse.

REB SHOULD HAVE BEEN OUT IN THE OCEAN, surfing with Coe. Instead, he sat on the edge of the bed in his room, buried in deep depression, then he arose and walked toward the window, slowly and deliberately, as if in a trance. After moving a small bench over to the window, he stepped onto the bench, raising his head almost to the ceiling. Grabbing a handful of the fabric strips that hung from the bar above his head, he wrapped them around his neck. After pausing for a moment, he stepped off the bench.

Immediately, he regretted his decision and caught a small break, giving him a chance to survive. The weight of his body, along with the pull of gravity, crushed his esophageal tube, but only partially, and didn't fracture his neck. A small amount of oxygen continued to pass to his brain, allowing him to remain conscious. His survival instincts took over, and in the next few seconds, he made three quick moves, desperately trying to save himself.

The weight of his body had caused the fabric strips to stretch a bit, so the tips of his toes touched the toppled bench beneath him. He struggled to stand tiptoed on the bench, like a ballerina on point, to relieve the pressure on his neck, but his toes weren't trained like a ballerina's, and he couldn't get enough support. Realizing this move would fail, he quickly reached for the fabric straps and tried to loosen them from his neck, but they were tangled and taut, and he wasn't able to do it. Fading from consciousness, he resorted to his final option, clutching the bar above him and using his arms to pull himself up and relieve pressure on his neck.

OVERCOME WITH ANXIETY, Coe paddled into shore without catching a single wave and ran home. After changing clothes, he hurried into Chinatown. He entered the building where

Reb roomed, ran through the bar area and bounded up the stairs and down the hall to Reb's room. Coe hammered on the door and yelled, "Reb, Reb, it's Davey Coe. Open up."

Other boarders, alerted by the noise, opened their doors. A middle-aged Chinese man hustled up the stairs and approached Coe. "What's the problem?"

"It's my friend, Reb. I think he's in trouble."

"Reb often like this. Probably just opium."

"Please, open the door. He needs help."

The Chinese man fumbled through his keys. When he came upon the right one and opened the door, a foul odor rushed from the room. Coe's eyes opened wide in horror as he instinctively covered his nose and mouth with his hands.

They were too late. With insufficient oxygen circulating to his brain, Reb lost consciousness before he attempting the life-saving lift. He'd dropped limply, suspended by the ligatures around his neck. His brain cells had died off and stopped functioning. With the rest of his body being deprived of direction from his brain, his organs had ceased to function. His body had relaxed into a flaccid state; his bladder and bowels had simultaneously evacuated.

Coe silently prayed for him from the first Book of Thessalonians, chapter five, verses nine and ten; 'For God has not destined us for wrath, but to obtain salvation through our Lord Jesus Christ, who died for us so that whether we are awake or asleep we might live with him.'

He turned away from the grisly sight, lowered his head, and wept. Then, as he somberly sauntered down the steps and out into the street, thoughts of Victor Kalia's plan consumed him.

CHAPTER 27

A clicking sound in the evening stillness alerted Jack Powers. He looked up from the documents on his desk, his attention drawn to the doorknob in his office door, and watched the knob slowly rotating back and forth.

"Who's there?" he shouted.

Suddenly, the door flew open, and a young Asian woman charged to his desk.

"You used me. You used me. I quit," Malia screamed.

"What the hell are you doing here?" Powers yelled as he rose from his chair and hurried past Malia to the office door. He stepped outside the office and looked down the hall. At nine o'clock in the evening, the building was deserted. Powers hastened back into the office and locked the door behind him.

"I told you never to come to the office. Did anyone see you come in?" he said as he approached her.

"I don't care. I quit. Get yourself another spy."

He grabbed her by the arm. "I paid you to do a job, and you're going to finish it."

Malia pulled a roll of money from her dress pocket and slammed it onto the desk.

"There. There's all the money you paid me. Count it. It's all there. Now find someone else to spy on Davey Coe. I never felt right about it, but I needed the money, and you said it was to protect him. You said no one would get hurt. Now seventy-seven people are dead. You killed them, but their blood is on my hands, too, for informing you."

Powers then grabbed her by the neck with his left hand and pointed his right index finger in her face. "This isn't a game. You can't quit. There's a lot at stake here, and I'll tell you when you're finished."

"Take your hand off my neck," she shouted while grabbing his left wrist with both hands, trying to break his hold. When Powers tightened his grip, Malia spit in his face. Powers clenched his jaws as rage raced through his body. Still gripping her neck with his left hand, he slapped her face with his right. Malia screamed as the sharp sting inflamed her face, then he lifted her off the floor and threw her across the room. She tumbled into a chair under the conference table, toppling it.

She lay in place on the floor for a few moments, then rolled over and sat up. Through her tears, she yelled, "You can beat me all you want, but I'm done doing your dirty work. I quit."

Powers stood on the opposite side of the room and reflected. Malia had obviously gained David Coe's trust and was able to extract valuable information from him. Moving forward, he considered it vital for the stream of information to continue.

He walked over to Malia and, while standing over her, calmly said, "You know, there's a ship sailing for Shanghai next Tuesday. I think I'll put you on it."

He paused briefly, then, with a wry grin, continued, "And have Mr. Ling meet you when the ship arrives in Shanghai."

Malia's tears stopped, and her face filled with horror as she looked up at Powers. Seeing he got her attention, he said, "That's right. I know all about your past. I know you were a prostitute in Shanghai. You ran away from the brothel and stowed away on a ship bound for Hawaii. I also know Mr. Ling would happily welcome you back."

Malia stared at the floor.

"Well," Powers said from above. "Are you still in, or will you be traveling back to Shanghai?"

Malia began to sob.

Powers nudged her with a kick in her side. "Answer me."

"I'm still in," she muttered.

"Good. Now get the hell out of here, and don't ever come to this office again," Powers said as he reached down, grabbed her arm, and lifted her to her feet. He dragged her toward the storage room in the back of the office. As they passed Powers' desk, Malia scooped the money from the desktop with her free hand. Powers led her back through the storage room, down the stairs, and out the back door into the alley behind the building. Once in the alley, he grabbed her by the throat and warned, "You better not double-cross me."

He then threw her down to the pavement and re-entered the building, closing the door behind him.

MALIA SAT ALONE on the pavement in the alley and cried for several minutes before gathering herself. Then she stood, wiped her eyes, brushed off her clothes, and plodded toward David Coe's house. As her mind calmed, it became clear she had only three options.

First, she wanted to spend the rest of her life with David Coe, but this scenario couldn't occur in Hawaii, not as long as Jack Powers was still alive. After all, she had taken information Coe told her in confidence and essentially sold it to Powers. That information was directly responsible for the death of seventy-seven men, including Coe's best friend, Kimo. In addition, it led to the suicide of another close friend. She pegged Powers as an unscrupulous man who now had heavy leverage on her and would use it over and over again in the future if she stayed in Hawaii.

Additionally, Powers now knew Coe sided with the Royalists and, at some point, would retaliate against him. It meant Coe also had to leave Hawaii, although he was currently unaware of it. She figured he might forgive her for being a prostitute, but he could never forgive her for betraying him as she had. The only way she could share a life of affluence with David Coe was to convince him to leave Hawaii without divulging why it was essential for him to do so.

If she couldn't persuade Coe to leave Hawaii, she had to continue helping Jack Powers. She wouldn't go back to Shanghai under any circumstances. Malia flashed back to her life there. Mr. Ling owned several brothels in Shanghai, including the one where she worked. He vigorously pursued runaways and severely punished those he caught to deter future escapes by others. She remembered one captured runaway at her place.

The girl was chained in a dark basement, underfed and malnourished, denied human companionship, and allowed minimal personal hygiene. She was often raped and sodomized by the staff and their associates. Because of her wretched living conditions, she became physically unattractive and was undesirable to businessmen and other well-heeled clientele who usually treated the girls well. Therefore, she was used for low-class customers who often demanded the most perverse sexual acts and beat her afterward. The girl died within a year. Malia couldn't imagine a more dreaded existence.

Her third option was to kill Jack Powers. There were plenty of people who wanted him dead. Maybe she could find the right person for the job. She mulled over the third option as she walked.

She reached Coe's house and entered through the unlocked front door. It was late, and he was asleep. Once inside, she closed the door and softly called his name.

"Davey. It's me, Malia."

He didn't awaken, so she tiptoed to his bedroom door and called him again. He rolled over and looked at her through the dark shadows. "Malia, are you alright?"

He rose from his bed and went to her. They embraced, and she began to cry.

"What's wrong?" he said, leading her into the living room, then lighting a lamp. The illumination showed her torn and dirty dress and the redness and swelling on her left cheek.

"My God, what happened?"

"Davey, I have to talk to you, and I need your understanding and forgiveness."

"Of course; what is it?"

"I've been keeping a horrible secret from you. I'm sorry, but I thought you would abandon me if you knew."

Coe stared at her without speaking.

"Back in Shanghai, after my father left us and my mother committed suicide, I turned to prostitution to support myself. I had no other choice. A man here in Hawaii somehow discovered my past. Last night, we argued, and he hit me."

Coe's jaw dropped. Malia, seeing his expression, ran to him, weeping. He extended his arms to keep her at a distance.

"I had to do it. I had no other choice," she uttered through the tears.

Coe was raised in a strict, puritanical Calvinist community and still read the Bible often. According to the Bible, not only was prostitution a sin, but his participation was also a sin. The Book of First Corinthians, chapter 6, verse 13, states, "The body is not meant for immorality, but for the Lord, and the Lord for the body."

Verses 15 and 16 from the same book and chapter also applied, "Do you not know that your bodies are members of Christ? Shall I therefore take the members of Christ and make them members of a prostitute? Do you not know that he who joins himself to a prostitute becomes one body with her? For it is written, 'The two shall become one.'"

"Malia, prostitution is a sin, and engaging a prostitute is a sin. You tricked me into committing a sin."

"That was in China. I don't do it here in Hawaii. I didn't trick you. The reason I come here is because I love you."

Coe shook his head and returned, "I don't know what to say. You've given me a lot to think about. It's late. I have to get up for work tomorrow. You can stay on the couch tonight if you want."

He turned and went to the bedroom, shutting the door behind him.

Malia was tempted to leave. She was well aware of his early upbringing and knew he might not want her in his life any longer, but she didn't want to go without trying something, anything, to save the relationship. Another thought suddenly entered her mind, and this one terrified her. What if Coe decided to end their relationship and she could no longer help Jack Powers? Would he blame her and send her back to Shanghai as punishment? She resolved to remain in Coe's house and stay awake until she came up with a plan for the morning. A Bible on a nearby table caught her eye.

COE LAY DOWN IN BED, wide awake, and rehashed the evening's events. He figured he hadn't sinned since he didn't know she was a prostitute, but he loved her and didn't want to stop. In the morning, they would talk. Then, just before falling asleep, he realized he now knew where she had learned so many exotic sexual positions.

AFTER A SURPRISINGLY SOUND SLEEP, David Coe awoke the following day to the aroma of fresh coffee. When he left his bedroom, he found Malia in the kitchen preparing breakfast. She turned to him, flashed a huge smile, and said, "Good morning, Davey. I made fresh coffee and got a few eggs from the coop. Scrambled or sunny side up? I never know because you keep changing."

She poured a cup of coffee, carried it to him, and kissed him on the cheek.

"Thank you. Look, Malia, we have to talk."

"Yes, we do. Scrambled or sunny side up?"

"Scrambled. About last night, tell me what's going on."

After preparing the eggs, Malia plated and served them, then sat at the table across from Coe. "Davey, I've decided I'm going to leave Hawaii. I have to."

"What? Why do you have to leave?"

"As I told you last night, I ran into a man who knew me from Shanghai. He threatened to take me back and turn me in for a reward. He tried to restrain me, but I was able to escape."

"I don't understand. What kind of reward? Who is this guy?"

"In China, prostitutes are owned. I escaped and stowed away on a ship to Hawaii. The brothel owners want to discourage escape, so they offer a reward for the capture of runaways. If I'm returned, the owner will beat me, torture me, then kill me as a deterrent to other girls thinking about escape. I just can't stay here and risk being captured."

"But where will you go? What will you do? "

"I was thinking, why don't we move to San Francisco together? I love you; you love me. Nobody knows us there. We can start out fresh."

"Malia, you may be overreacting. Who is this guy you keep talking about? Is he living permanently in Hawaii or just visiting from Shanghai? If he's just visiting, maybe he'll leave soon, and you'll never see him again."

"Davey, do you love me?"

Coe didn't respond. Even though he did love her, he had never told her so. It felt awkward to say it now.

"Do you love me?" she repeated.

Again, he couldn't pull the trigger.

"Yeah, we've been close for quite a while now. Why do you ask?"

Malia pursed her lips in disgust, then said, "At some point, I want to settle down, get married, have a family."

Her face softened, and her eyes moistened. "Davey, I love you and want to share that life with you. You have to decide if you want to share it with me. I can't stay in Hawaii. I no longer feel safe here. Please, be with me. I love you."

"Malia, you're asking a lot. I need some time. Look, I have to get off to work, or I'll be late. Will you be here when I get back?"

"Do you want me to stay?"

"Yes, I do."

"Oh, Davey," Malia called to him as he was about to open the door. Coe turned to face her. She raised his Bible in her right hand. "Remember the Book of Matthew, chapter six, verses fourteen and fifteen, 'For if you forgive men their trespasses your heavenly Father will also forgive you; but if you do not forgive men their trespasses, neither will your Father forgive your trespasses.'"

Malia smiled. "Please forgive me, and have a great day."

Coe returned the smile, walked back to her, and kissed her. "You've already been forgiven."

He opened the door and left.

THROUGHOUT THE DAY, Coe struggled to concentrate on his work. First, he pondered Malia's offer to leave Hawaii together. Maybe it was time to get a fresh start elsewhere. The Hawaii he knew and loved was slipping away. His two closest friends were dead. He had established closure with his father, and, at work, spending so much time with a wicked man had outweighed the learning benefits.

On top of everything else, he loved Malia. He still couldn't tell her so, but he surely felt it. She was an ideal mate. He enjoyed her company and felt comfortable talking to her about everything, not to mention her extraordinary physical beauty. He smiled when he recalled her reciting biblical passages that morning; such a clever way to ask for forgiveness. He appreciated and admired that she spent time searching through the Bible, a book unfamiliar to her as far as he knew, to find just the right passages to move him.

The smile then left, and his spirits dropped as her revelation about prostitution overtook his conscious thoughts. Forgiving her was easy. Accepting that he was considering marriage to a prostitute was the tricky part. During his maturation into manhood, he realized that his strict Calvinist upbringing had imparted many good qualities; honesty, the value of hard work, and belief in God, but he also learned intolerance and prudishness towards customs that were different. For example, he was taught from childhood that even the hula, the traditional dance of the native Hawaiian people, was lewd.

Going away for his education and working at the law firm with people outside the Calvinist ministry had softened the hardline position he was taught as a youth. But vestiges of those early teachings remained, and marriage to a former prostitute was a big step. Still, if she left Hawaii and he remained, he might forever regret his decision to let her go.

This circular logic haunted him throughout the day. I can't marry her because she was a prostitute, but I can't let her leave because I love her, but I can't marry her because she was a prostitute, but . . . He was unable to come to a resolution.

Coe worked until nine o'clock that evening. Thoughts about Malia and the overall situation in Hawaii consumed him as he rode the trolley home. Approaching the door of his house, he paused, reluctant to enter. For the first time since they met, he wasn't sure he wanted to see her. Coe pushed the door open and entered.

Standing in the living room, Malia looked at him and said, "Sit down, Davey. Tell me what's wrong."

Coe sat in the rocking chair; Malia took the couch.

"Is it me?" she asked.

"It's everything. Right now, I feel like all my roots have been cut, and I'm just drifting aimlessly in the wind with nothing to hold on to. I have to get grounded again."

"Why don't we just leave Hawaii? Let's just go to San Francisco and begin a new life together."

Coe gazed at her, his expression blank, slowly shaking his head. "Malia, our relationship is part of the problem. After what you told me last night, I don't know how I feel about you anymore. I hope you understand."

Malia stiffened. "I *do* understand, but I hope *you* understand that I can't stay in Hawaii. I have my own problems. As I told you before, I don't feel safe here."

"I don't know what I want. I need some time."

Coe rose from his chair and went to the door.

"Where are you going?"

"Out."

"Davey, we need to talk."

"I won't be long."

He closed the door behind him and began aimlessly strolling through the mission grounds. A brisk walk always seemed to clear his mind, and that's exactly what he needed. Just past Kawaiahao Church, he ran into Reverend Wilson.

"Good evening, David," the Reverend said. Coe returned the greeting as the two men passed, then he heard the Reverend's voice from behind. "You know, I saw Malia earlier today."

Coe turned to face Reverend Wilson. A beaming smile spanned his face as he continued, "It was just wonderful talking with her again. I hope you realize you are blessed to have her in your life."

Coe's expression froze as the Reverend's words registered.

"Are you alright, David?"

"Yes. Yes, I'm fine. Thank you, Reverend. Thank you so much," Coe said as he turned and hurried home.

After entering the house and closing the door behind him, he gazed at Malia sitting on the couch. She looked at him, expressionless. Coe smiled. Malia and ran to him. They wrapped their arms around each other, then he picked her up and carried her into the bedroom.

Once they were naked in bed, she moved on top, looked down at him, and smiled. He looked back when suddenly, a stark notion overcame him. He wondered how many customers had been in his position and received that same smile. Confusion and insecurity, not pleasure, overwhelmed him. After changing positions and starting again, she began to moan. He questioned the authenticity. Surely, she had faked orgasms with her customers to enhance the thrill of their experience. Did she do the same with him?

"What's wrong, Davey?" she asked.

They separated and flopped onto their backs beside each other, both gazing at the ceiling.

"It's just been a stressful day."

"I'm sure it's because of me. I'm sorry. Let's just lie here and talk about more pleasant times."

She paused, then said, "Remember the day we hiked up to the waterfall in Manoa?"

The vivid memory of their final day after two months together sparked a sense of happiness. It was a great day, capping one of the most enjoyable periods of his life. In the middle of his memory, they simultaneously turned to each other, seeking verification that someone was knocking on the door, then three unmistakable knocks followed.

"Wonder who that is?" Coe said as he rose from the bed and dressed.

"Yeah, it's late for visitors."

Malia pulled a sheet off the bed and draped it around her chest and under her arms. She peeked around the bedroom door as Coe opened the front door.

"Victor Kalia," Coe said. "I'm surprised to see you. Is there a problem?"

"Sorry to bother you at this late hour, but I want to talk to you," Kalia said.

Coe stepped outside and closed the door behind him. He returned about thirty minutes later, smiling and invigorated. "It's all set. We're going to do it."

"Do what?"

"That was Victor Kalia, and we've got the guns. We're going to do it."

"Davey, what in the world are you talking about?"

"We're going to return Hawaii to the Hawaiian people where it rightfully belongs. After the mission boys refused to cede power back to the Queen, Victor Kalia and some other Royalists began developing a plan. Now we're ready to execute the plan. Next Wednesday night, we're going to occupy Iolani Palace and Ali'iolani Hale, bring the Queen from her Washington Place residence to Iolani Palace, and reinstate her on the throne."

"Not another revolution, Davey. You remember the last one. Several were killed."

"No, no. This time it's much less risky. I don't think there will be any violence at all."

"Then why do you need guns?"

"We need the guns as a show of force to secure the palace and Ali'iolani Hale through the night. Then, when the sun rises the next morning, the Queen will be on the throne, and everything will be in place."

"The Queen's aware of your plan?"

"Yes, the Queen has been involved from the outset. In fact, the guns are being stored at her Waikiki home."

"When you say 'we,' you don't mean you'll be carrying a gun, do you?"

"Yes, I'll carry a gun, and I'm honored to do so. I'm doing it in memory of Kimo. He would have been proud to participate," Coe returned with bravado.

Malia ran from the bed, leaving the sheet behind, and hugged him.

"No, Davey. No. It's too risky. Please don't carry a gun. You can help some other way."

"Don't worry. There won't be any fighting. We just have to get the Queen on the throne and guard the palace and Ali'iolani Hale until morning. That's it. Several members of the Royal Guard who were dismissed when the Queen was overthrown will participate. The former captain of the police force, who was replaced when the Queen was overthrown, will also lead a group of men, and Benjamin Tate, the new American minister, will support us."

Coe felt her hug tighten. He kissed her on top of the head.

"Malia, Benjamin Tate despises Powers and the mission boys. He and President Cleveland were embarrassed when they refused the President's order to return power to the Queen. Tate told the Queen he was so angry that he wanted to land American troops to remove the mission boys from power, but he couldn't make the first move and have the United States be the aggressor."

"However, he said that if she could somehow occupy the throne, he would immediately recognize her sovereignty. Then, if the mission boys tried to overthrow her, he would summon the troops ashore to prevent violence. So, you see, we only have to get the Queen back on the throne and hold the palace and Ali'iolani Hale until morning. After that, the United States military will take over and preserve the Queen's position."

Coe observed that Malia relaxed a little.

"Davey, what do you plan to do after the revolt? You won't be able to stay at your law firm. Jack Powers will fire you after he discovers you moved against him."

"You're right; he would, but I'll leave before that occurs. I'm going to accept the Queen's offer to head her legal staff. I'm ready to leave the firm anyhow. I know Jack Powers tried to kill Reb and wouldn't be surprised if he was somehow behind Kimo's death. I don't want to work for a man like that."

"I don't want to be negative, but what will you do if the revolt fails?"

"It won't fail. We have the support of the President of the United States and most people here in Hawaii. There's a saying that possession is nine-tenths of the law. All we have to do is get the Queen on the throne, and everyone will support the change. The mission boys will be on the outside looking in, and no one will support any plans they may have to re-take Hawaii."

"You said possession was nine-tenths of the law. What if the other tenth prevails and the mission boys remain in charge? What will you do then? It seems unlikely, but it's possible, so you should be prepared."

"I'm sure the plan will work, but yes, I do realize there is that possibility."

"Yeah, and what are your plans in that case?"

"I'll leave Hawaii. I don't want to, but I'd have to. Probably go to New York, maybe back to Boston. I had several lucrative offers from major firms in both cities, but don't worry about that," he said. "It's a good plan, and it's going to work."

"I just wish you weren't carrying a gun. You could honor Kimo afterward as the Queen's legal advisor. Help with the new constitution, something like that. Just don't get involved in the fighting. You know, Davey, it scares me."

"I appreciate your concern but don't worry. Everything is going to be fine."

THE NEXT MORNING, Coe departed early for work. Malia stayed in bed and reminisced about her childhood in Shanghai. She recalled the anguish her mother experienced after her father left them, an anguish so intense it caused her to take her own life, an anguish created entirely by the loss of a deep love. An emptiness overcame her as she imagined herself experiencing such agony. Even though she repeatedly reminded herself it was too early to commit her absolute love to David Coe, she found herself doing exactly that. She tried to redirect her focus away from emotion. Her primary goal was to move from a menial existence as a housekeeper to a life of wealth and prestige, and David Coe was her pathway to that goal.

CHAPTER 28

At three o'clock on a sunny Wednesday afternoon, David Coe stood on King Street, waiting for the trolley. He never left the office so early, but it was his final day of employment at the law firm of Powers, Thatcher, and James. Coe grinned with contentment. His last day had gone well. The first thing in the morning, Sara told him Jack Powers would be out of the office all day.

Relieved that there would be no awkward encounters, Coe could focus on his job. He told no one he was resigning but feverishly worked to tie up all loose ends on his projects to make the transition as smooth as possible.

Coe smiled at the irony. Later that evening, he would avidly participate in the taking back of a country from Jack Powers and the mission boys but, as a conscientious employee, felt obligated to minimize the impact of his departure from Powers' law firm.

He boarded the trolley and immediately felt as if a heavy weight had been lifted from his shoulders. His tenure with Jack Powers was behind him. As the trolley passed by Iolani Palace, he was reminded that he would be there at the palace in about nine hours to help return the Queen to the throne. Tomorrow morning, he would begin a new chapter in his life as her legal counsel. Coe said it out loud, "Chief legal counsel to the Queen of Hawaii."

As the trolley approached his stop, he thought about Malia. "Why not? It's time," he said to himself as he disembarked. He turned a corner and met Reverend Wilson on the walkway. They exchanged greetings while passing, then Coe stopped, turned back to the Reverend, and said, "Reverend Wilson, I'm going to marry Malia. Will you perform the ceremony?"

The Reverend turned around and displayed the widest smile Coe had ever seen from him. "Of course, David. I think you've made the right decision. She's a good woman. When will you two be getting married?"

"We haven't set a date, but soon."

"Just let me know, and congratulations to both of you."

Coe entered the house. Malia had her back turned as she cut vegetables for the evening dinner. He approached her from behind and wrapped his arms around her. She flinched, then turned to face him.

"Will you marry me?" he said.

She smiled as her eyes filled with tears. "Of course I will. I love you." She threw her arms around his neck, moved her cheek against his, and squeezed.

As they hugged, Coe said, "I've been thinking about what you said; that you wanted us to get married, settle down, have a family. That's what I want, too."

"Davey, you've made me so happy."

"I'm happy, too. Tonight, the Queen returns to the throne, and tomorrow, I'll begin my career as her chief legal advisor. Just think, we'll be invited to all the big affairs at Iolani Palace, and we'll travel with the Queen when she goes to Washington. We're going to have a great life together."

Coe felt her body go limp and pulled away while still holding her hands. He observed the joy had drained from her face.

"What's wrong?" he asked.

"No, Davey. Please. We have to leave Hawaii. I told you I don't feel safe here."

"Malia, I think you're making too much of this. You're safe here. That guy probably went back to China by now. You'll never see him again."

"You don't know where he is; neither do I, and neither of us knows if others are working with him."

"You think there's a team here from China for the sole purpose of taking you back? Your imagination is playing tricks on you. Please be realistic."

"I can't live my whole life looking over my shoulder, and that's how I feel, like every stranger could be the one after me. I don't feel safe here, and you said you'd be willing to leave Hawaii if you had to."

"I said I would consider leaving Hawaii if the plan fails tonight. I would have to leave. There would be no other options."

"That's how I feel now. Leaving is my only option. Soon I'll be your wife. Marriage is about understanding. Please try to understand my fears. If you're willing to leave when you face a crisis, you have to be willing to leave when I face one."

"I don't feel this is a crisis for you. If you just give it some time, I think you'll see that."

Malia's expression froze in anger. She raised her voice. "Davey, if you refuse to understand my situation, why do you want to marry me? Is it for the sex?"

Coe's eyes opened wide as his jaw dropped. "What!"

She yelled, "You don't have to marry me for that. I'll continue to provide it, but you'll have to pay for it from now on. It'll be just like in Shanghai."

Malia turned, threw the door open, and left, slamming the door behind her.

Coe inhaled deeply, then shook his head as he slowly let it out. He raised his eyebrows and mumbled, "And the evening started out so well. Just a few minutes ago, we were happy, and she said yes."

IT WAS ABOUT TEN O'CLOCK, two hours before the retaking of Hawaii. Coe had finished dressing in the black clothing the Royalists would wear to provide camouflage and was ready to leave his house. His focus was on the revolution when the door opened, and Malia entered. She had been gone over two hours. He stared at her. They were both uncertain. Simultaneously, as if on cue, they ran to each other and embraced.

"I'm so sorry, Davey."

"I'm sorry, too."

"I've been thinking. I'll try living in Hawaii if that's what you want."

"That's great, Malia. Thank you."

"But I want you to promise me one thing."

Coe held his breath as he awaited the promise.

"I want you to promise you won't participate in the revolution tonight."

Coe pulled away from her. "I can't promise that. You know how important this is to me."

"Please, Davey, I have a bad feeling about tonight. I'm afraid I'll lose you." She leaned into him, her arms around his waist and her head against his chest.

"I'm sorry, but I have to do this, and you won't lose me. It'll all be over in a few hours, and I'll return home. And starting tomorrow, you'll be the future wife of the chief legal advisor to the Queen."

"No, Davey. Please, no. Please don't abandon me. My entire life, everyone I've loved has abandoned me. First, my father, then my mother; now you. I'm begging you. Please don't go. I can't bear the thought of being all alone again."

Coe put his other arm around her and squeezed. "This is important to me. I promised Victor Kalia I would join him, and I want to honor the remembrance of Kimo. I want to do this."

Malia pulled away from him, ran to the couch, curled up, and wept. He paused before opening the door, overcome by a powerful urge to turn around and make another attempt to mend the relationship, but there wasn't time.

As he opened the door, Malia beckoned, "Davey."

He immediately felt a sense of relaxation as he turned to her. Her soothing voice was just what he needed. He smiled, but she stood composed and serious.

"You can always find a reason to do things for other people. You can keep an obligation to Victor Kalia or honor the memory of Kimo, but you can never do anything for me."

She held a small, white piece of paper in her raised right hand. "There's a steamer leaving for San Francisco in the morning. If you leave me tonight, I'll be on that steamer. You'll never see me again."

His jaws tightened as he glared at her. "Look, Malia, this isn't just about Victor Kalia or Kimo. It's about what's important to me. My great-grandfather was one of the first missionaries who came to Hawaii to spread Christianity. My grandfather and father followed him. I was born here and lived my entire life here. I'm rooted here. Hawaii is my home, my country, and the mission boys stole it. Now I have a chance to do something about it, and I'm going to do it. Why can't you understand that?"

Coe turned to the door, paused, then turned back to face Malia and said, "I wish you would stay, but if you feel you have to leave, then go."

He left, closing the door behind him.

COE STRODE DOWN KING Street toward Waikiki. The streets were deserted, and the solitude gave him time to reflect. What if the revolt failed and Malia left Hawaii? He would then have neither his career in Hawaii nor her, the two most valuable things in his life. He briefly considered his father's suggestion to join the missionary movement; no stress and a rich, spiritual life closer to the Lord.

One thing at a time, he thought. First, return Hawaii to the Hawaiians. As he continued down King Street toward Waikiki, the clopping of horse hooves from up ahead alerted him. He retreated back into the shadows and turned his face away. A horse and carriage passed, the horse in a quick trot. Coe briefly glance at the horse, and it looked like Titus, Jack Powers' horse. The carriage looked familiar as well.

After the carriage passed, Coe emerged from the shadows for another look but could see only the rear of the carriage as it quickly rolled into the darkness. He wasn't sure what to make of the situation, then dismissed it. There were many carriages similar to the one Jack Powers owned, and although he would recognize Titus, he only had a momentary glance, and it was dark. It was like people, he told himself. They looked more alike in dim lighting.

Approaching the Queen's Waikiki house, he tiptoed around the perimeter of the backyard, enclosed by a tall fence of white boards fixed close to each other to provide total privacy. Hushed voices rose from the other side of the fence as he searched for the entrance gate. Arriving at the gate, he paused, then stepped back from the gate into the shadows of coconut trees and sat on a rock in the darkness.

He lifted his head to the heavens. "Lord, help me."

Coe rose, walked to the gate, and knocked four times. When a guard opened the gate, Coe said, "Coe to see the Queen."

The guard checked his list and, accepting both the prearranged knock signal and greeting, admitted Coe, directing him through the back entrance to the house where he received a rifle and ammunition. Coe looked at the gun with disappointment. It was a Civil War era Sharps breech-loaded, single-shot rifle. He was familiar with the rifle's operation, but it was an inferior firearm compared to the Winchester Model 1886 Reb retrieved from Schmidt's plantation, the weapon the Honolulu Rifles probably carried.

Coe returned to the yard and was greeted by Victor Kalia. "Good evening, Davey. Thanks for coming. Kimo would be proud."

Kalia observed Coe examining his rifle. "I know you were expecting better. So was I, but it's what we have."

He paused. "I don't think we'll have to use them."

Coe nodded, hoping Kalia was right.

The guard interrupted to inform Kalia that all were present and he had locked the gate. Kalia excused himself, went to the back of the yard, and stepped onto a wooden box. "Everybody listen up. We'll depart here in groups of ten, with about five minutes between departures. Now divide up into your designated group."

The fifty men assembled into their respective, previously assigned groups.

"Each group has a designated leader. Will each group leader raise your hand?"

After the group leaders identified themselves, Kalia said, "If there are questions when you're out there, ask your group leader. Walk with five men on each side of the street. Stay in the shadows as much as possible. Walk fast, but don't run. No talking. We don't want to draw any attention. When you get to Kawaiahao Church, go to the *makai* side, away from the road, and wait for the others. I'll be with the last group. From there, we'll move together to Iolani Palace. Any questions?"

There were no questions, and the first group departed.

Coe was in the last group, led by Kalia. To that point, he was impressed by the organization and efficiency of the operation. After the fourth group departed, Coe realized his group was next. His pulse increased with anticipation.

MALIA SAT ON THE SOFA. She hoped Coe would change his mind and return, but as the minutes passed, she realized it wasn't likely.

Suddenly, a knock on the door caused her spirits to soar. She bounded off the sofa and raced across the room, knowing it was Coe once again playing his childish prank of knocking on the door of his own home just to get her to answer. Malia had tired of the stunt and often didn't even answer when she suspected it was him, but this time she would eagerly welcome him with open arms.

She opened the door with a big smile, but it wasn't David Coe. Her expression drained as she stared at an attractive blonde woman she'd never seen before.

"Hi, I'm Ellen Powers. You must be Malia. Is David home? It's essential that I talk to him immediately."

Malia looked at her and wondered why she had come to Coe's house. What was her relationship with him?

"He's not here," she said.

"Look, Malia, it's vital," Ellen Powers replied as she looked past Malia to scan the house's interior.

Malia closed the door to reduce Ellen's visible access inside and spoke through the narrow opening. "I already told you he's not here."

"Where is he?"

"I don't know."

"Malia, I overheard Jack talking with some men at the house. They left together about an hour ago. The Royalists are planning something tonight. I don't know what it is, but Jack knows about it, and I heard him mention David's name. He's in danger. Please, if you know anything, tell me."

"Try the Rialto on Nu'uanu," Malia said as she slammed the door shut and bolted it.

She turned her back to the door and leaned against it. From outside, Ellen pleaded, "Malia, if you truly love him, you'll help me find him. He's in serious trouble."

Malia slowly sank, back against the door, until she sat on the floor. Tears began to flow.

"OKAY, MEN. LET'S GO," Kalia said. They opened the gate in the fence surrounding the Queen's property and moved out, one at a time. The group strode down King Street, five men, loosely spaced, on each side of the street. It was an ideal night to move. The roads were vacant at the late hour in mid-week. The sky was moonless, the only light coming from the dim, widely spaced, electric street lights. In several areas, overhanging branches provided shade from the street lights. They arrived on the *makai* side of Kawaiahao Church without incident. The other groups were already there, waiting silently.

"Listen up," Kalia said. "Same five groups of ten. My group will go first and enter the palace. Second group of ten, stand guard in front. Third group guards the *ewa* side. Fourth group is on the *mauka* (the Hawaiian word for 'toward the mountains') side. Fifth group on the Diamond Head side. After we secure the building, I'll send two men from my group to Washington Place to bring the Queen down to the palace. Any questions?"

"Let's move out," Kalia said after receiving no questions.

As Coe stood and began moving toward the palace, the reality of his actions struck with full force. He was participating in the overthrow of a government, a legitimate government recognized as such by other countries in the world, and now he wasn't on the periphery providing information about the Schmidt plantation or the Winchester rifle. Instead, he was on the front line carrying a gun. As an attorney, he knew that his actions amounted to treason, a crime punishable by death in any country in the world.

At the same time, he was exhilarated to be part of a noble cause that was coming to a climax. He first recalled chapter six, verse eleven from the Book of Ephesians, "Put on the whole armor of God, that you may be able to stand against the wiles of the devil," then the words of the old Hawaiian man, "The life of the land is preserved in righteousness."

ELLEN POWERS HAD NEVER HEARD of the Rialto. Malia said, 'The Rialto on Nu'uanu,' and that's all she knew. Based on the location, she assumed it was a bar. She first turned left off King Street onto Nu'uanu Avenue and followed it to the water without spotting her target. After retracting the canopy, Ellen slowed the carriage to have a better look as she retraced her route.

The streets were packed with sailors and harbor workers, so there were numerous whistles and catcalls. It seemed every man had focused on her. Her pulse quickened. As she guided the carriage with her left hand, she slipped the right into her purse and clutched the .44 caliber Derringer pistol David Coe had given her. She hadn't fired it since that evening with Coe and debated whether to carry it tonight, but now just having it in her hand created a safer feeling.

As she passed the establishments, all small buildings with either an undistinguished, nearly illegible business sign or no sign at all, she became concerned she might not be able to identify the Rialto and stopped to ask directions. When the inebriated young sailor said he would show her and jumped into the carriage, she instinctively whipped out the pistol and jammed it against his forehead. The sailor threw his hands into the air and froze. "Please don't shoot," he cried out. "It's across King, a half block up on the right."

"Thanks," she said, waving the gun to signal him off the carriage, then snapped the reins and pulled away. A feeling of satisfaction and empowerment filled her.

She crossed King Street to the upper section of Nu'uanu and found the Rialto, identified by a small, hand-painted wooden sign, about a half block up on the right side, just as the sailor said.

After tying her horse, Ellen Powers hustled across the street. The buzz from the throngs of working-class people created an energy she had never experienced. She turned to the Rialto door, opened it, and entered the dim, smoky room. Every customer within fifteen feet of the door suspended activity to stare at the well-dressed, attractive blonde woman. Such women were rare at the Rialto.

After adjusting to the multitude of gawking eyes, she uttered through the silence, "Has anyone seen David Coe?"

Julie yelled to the other bartender, "Frank." She pointed to the bar in front of her, signaling Frank to tend the area, then came around to see Ellen.

MALIA WAS STOOPED behind the bushes in front of Ali'iolani Hale, across King Street from Iolani Palace. The anxiety of staying in the house and awaiting the outcome became unbearable. She was unsure how the evening's events would unfold but knew everything would occur across the street at the palace.

The night was eerily quiet, the chirping of crickets providing the only sound. She'd been waiting about a half hour, plenty of time to think. If the Royalists successfully executed their plan, Coe would be content with his position as chief legal advisor to the Queen and dismiss all thoughts of leaving Hawaii. She told him she'd stay in Hawaii for a trial period but knew she couldn't.

Coe would soon discover she'd betrayed him, then discard her, and she couldn't blame him. Her actions were despicable. Her heart sank at the thought of leaving Hawaii without Coe, but she just couldn't stay. She sadly mused how close she would have been to snagging the man of her dreams only to have to start all over again as a housekeeper in San Francisco.

Her attention turned toward King Street as a large group of men, maybe forty or fifty, all dressed in dark clothing, passed before her and approached the main gate in the wall surrounding Iolani Palace. She knew Coe was among them, having seen him leave the house dressed in black, but it was dark, and all the men looked the same, so it was impossible to identify him from a distance.

AS COE APPROACHED THE MAIN GATE, a horrific thought overcame him, the possibility of shooting another human being. His heart raced, his palms became clammy, and sweat beads formed on his forehead. Unlike many of the others, he wasn't an experienced soldier. Sure, he was a crack shot at the armory range, but those were inanimate targets. It would be completely different killing a man, especially one who did nothing to deserve it, maybe someone's father, son, brother, or even someone he knew. Looking a man in the eyes, then killing him, was appalling. He prayed it wouldn't come to that.

After entering through the gate and striding to the front of the palace with the other men, Coe settled down. The palace grounds were empty and quiet. A sense of tranquility set in. In a few minutes, his group would go into the palace while the others guarded the outside, then Kalia would send two men to Washington Place to escort the Queen. Coe would volunteer for the assignment. He wanted to tell her he was accepting the legal counsel position.

In four hours, all fifty men would be relieved by a group of fifty others led by the former Honolulu police chief. Coe would return home to Malia. He couldn't wait. A few hours later, he would return to the palace to begin his career as the Queen's chief legal advisor. He began to relax.

Coe directed his attention to Victor Kalia, who had turned to face the men. Kalia had just opened his mouth to speak when suddenly his eyes sprung wide open, and blood gushed from a hole in his forehead as the night silence was pierced by the crackle of gunfire. Coe gasped in horror as he watched Kalia's body drop, then snapped his head left and right to see men around him falling to the ground. Several screamed in agony. Others scurried about in disarray. He looked to the top of the palace where several snipers, as many as thirty, stood along the perimeter of the roof, their weapons aimed to the ground, then he heard another round of shots.

ELLEN POWERS LEFT THE RIALTO, her heart pounding through her chest. She ran to the carriage, leaped aboard, and furiously snapped the reins. Titus galloped down King Street, the carriage bouncing behind him. Julie had informed her about the revolution. Ellen knew time was of the essence if she wanted to save David Coe. Each moment of silence, every moment without gunfire, preserved the opportunity. Her hopes buoyed as she approached Iolani Palace, then shots rang out from the direction of the palace.

COE WAS KNOCKED BACKWARD to the ground and felt a searing pain in his chest. He moved his right hand to the wound, then lifted his head to glance down and saw his hand bathed in blood. He gently laid his head back on the ground and looked up at the cloudless night sky. The asterism of Orion's belt drew him to the constellation of the mythological Greek hunter. In a strange way, he appreciated the symbolism of the celestial hunter gazing down on wounded prey. A chill came over his body on this warm night as he bled profusely.

ELLEN POWERS PULLED THE CARRIAGE to an abrupt halt in front of the gate to Iolani Palace and looked in toward the palace. Men with rifles stood on the palace roof. Prone bodies dressed in black were scattered on the dirt roadway just before the front door and on the adjacent grassy area. A few men also dressed in black were running from the palace grounds. She hoped David Coe was among those running, then saw Malia rise from her perched position near the gate. Ellen didn't notice her until she stood and ran into the palace grounds. When Malia dropped next to one of the bodies, Ellen shuddered, lowered her head into her hands, and wept. After a minute or so, realizing she was too late to help, she sat up, exhaled a deep sorrowful breath, then snapped the reins and moved away.

OUT OF NOWHERE, Coe felt warm hands cupping his cheeks. "I'm sorry. I'm so sorry," Malia repeated as she kissed his lips, then placed her arms around his neck, her cheek next to his, and hugged him as her tears flowed. He enjoyed the fragrance of her hair, reminding him of the night they first met. As he closed his eyes and faded from consciousness, glimpses of their special times flashed before him.

A light nudge in his side aroused him enough to look up and see Jack Powers standing tall, Winchester Model 1886 rifle in hand. Coe recalled Powers' words from the armory the day he discovered the hex bullet. 'Sometimes I imagine I'm on top of a building looking down, like a sniper.'

He wondered if it was Powers who shot him.

Powers peered down at Coe, and their eyes met. Coe's eyes showed peace and serenity as he accepted the fate all men must ultimately experience. Powers' eyes moistened as he bowed his head, solemnly moving it from side to side. "David, I'm sorry it had to end like this."

After a few moments, Powers' eyes became hard and cold, his jaw rigid and stern. He looked at Malia, then back at Coe.

"You had such a bright future, but you blew it by putting your trust in her," Powers said thrusting a pointed index finger toward Malia. "You slept with the devil and got burned."

Coe was amused at the irony of Powers calling someone else the devil, but then the pieces fell together so it all made sense. It was Malia who had informed the mission boys about the surprise attack this evening. Malia also had told them about the plan to get guns from the Schmidt plantation. Seventy-seven native Hawaiians, including Kimo, were killed. Reb took his life believing he was to blame. This was a woman he loved. He had confided in her, and she betrayed him.

Coe looked up at Malia's tearful, grieving face. As their eyes met, he recalled the biblical passage she had once quoted to him; chapter six, verses fourteen and fifteen from the Book of Matthew, 'For if you forgive men their trespasses your heavenly Father will also forgive you; but if you do not forgive men their trespasses, neither will your Father forgive your trespasses.'

He forgave her as he gazed into her mournful eyes one last time. "I love you," he said, then exhaled his final breath.

CHAPTER 29

After the failed revolution, the mission boys searched the Queen's Waikiki residence and discovered a cache of rifles and ammunition. The Queen was arrested and charged with misprision of treason (having knowledge of treason and failing to report it), then imprisoned in a corner room on the second floor of Iolani Palace. The entrance to the room was guarded around the clock, and she wasn't permitted visitors. In addition, all the windows in the room were painted over, so she couldn't look out, nor could her loyal followers see her from the palace grounds below.

Soon after her imprisonment, she was presented a declaration of abdication and informed that failure to sign would result in the execution of her treasonous followers. The Queen responded in writing, "For myself, I would have chosen death rather than to have signed it, but it was represented to me that by my signing this paper, all the persons who had been arrested, all my people now in trouble by reason of their love and loyalty toward me, would be immediately released, the stream of blood ready to flow unless it was stayed by my pen."

Despite the signed declaration of abdication, many Royalists received lengthy prison sentences and heavy fines, and a few were sentenced to death. The Queen noted, "Their sentences were passed the same as though my signature had not been obtained. That they were not executed is due solely to a consideration which has been officially stated: 'Word came from the United States that the execution of captive rebels would militate against annexation.'"

From confinement, the Queen penned the Ka Haku Prayer to guide her followers, "Behold not with malevolence the sins of man, but forgive and cleanse . . . And let peace be our portion now and forever more."

Eventually, all the Royalist prisoners, including the Queen, were freed. The Queen traveled to Washington, D.C., carrying petitions signed by thousands of native Hawaiians requesting President Cleveland to restore their Queen, but the political climate was unfavorable. President Cleveland was on his way out, and his successor, William McKinley, was an avowed annexationist.

The outbreak of the Spanish-American War in 1898 resulted in the United States fighting naval battles in the Philippine Islands. The strategic location of Hawaii became even more apparent and heightened the call for annexation. As a result, President McKinley introduced a treaty of annexation, and Congress passed it.

On August 12, 1898, the sovereignty of Hawaii was formally transferred to the United States during ceremonies at Iolani Palace. The Hawaiian anthem, "Hawai`i Pono `I," was played as the Hawaiian flag was lowered. The American flag was raised to the sounds of "The Star-Spangled Banner."

The natives of Hawaii had officially become powerless in their homeland.

Celebration of the annexation of Hawaii *(Hawaii State Archives)*

FOR FIVE DAYS IN JANUARY 1993, thousands of Kanaka Maole came from throughout the Hawaiian Islands to gather on the grounds of Iolani Palace in observance of the centennial anniversary of the overthrow of the Hawaiian monarchy. Representatives from Samoa, Tonga, and other Polynesian islands attended.

After one hundred years, they were a diverse people from all walks of life, but still united as descendants of an ancient civilization that once thrived and prospered in Hawaii, a civilization that, one hundred years earlier, had its future stolen and its right to self-determination denied. They rallied behind their Queen's motto, 'Onipa'a,' which means 'be steadfast, firm, resolute.'

The traditional blowing of the conch shell, precisely at noon on January 13, 1993, opened the ceremonies of the Onipa'a Centennial Observance. Four large bamboo torches were lit and posted on both sides of the Queen Liliuokalani statue between Iolani Palace and the state capitol building.

After the opening ceremonies, the fire of the four bamboo torches was ritually transferred to a site near the King Kamehameha I statue, beginning a one-hundred-hour torch-burning vigil.

John Waihe'e, the first elected governor of Hawaiian ancestry, announced that, during the observance, only the Hawaiian flag would fly above all state facilities encircling Iolani Palace. The Hawaiian flag flew alone for the first time in nearly a hundred years.

In Washington, D.C., United States Senator Daniel Inouye, the first elected United States Senator of Hawaiian ancestry, arranged to have the Hawaiian flag flown at half-staff in the Hall of Flags in Union Station during the Onipa'a Centennial Observance.

After sunset on the first evening of the observance, a multitude gathered at Iolani Palace for a candlelight vigil. The palace was draped in black for the solemn remembrance.

The five-day event consisted of demonstrations of Hawaiian crafts, including quilt making, coconut leaf weaving, and the making of feather leis. There were spiritual offerings at an ahu (altar) on the Iolani Palace grounds. Petitions were signed seeking justice for the historical wrongs. Parades down King Street included a convoy of truckers blowing their horns and thousands of marchers waving Hawaiian flags. Dignitaries offered stirring speeches, clergy offered prayers, and the Royal Hawaiian band played traditional Hawaiian music.

On the final day of the observance, a procession of one hundred torches and thousands of loyal followers marched down King Street to Iolani Palace for a historical reenactment of the Queen's surrender in 1893. The moving event concluded with the Queen addressing her loyal followers from the palace steps in her final moments on the throne.

Candlelight vigil at Iolani Palace, January 1993 *(Hawaii State Archives)*

"Now, my people, hear these words of mine that I say to you in our dark hour. Hold yourselves high and be proud. For each and every one of you has much to be proud of in yourselves and in your people. Hold fast to that pride and love you have for your heritage and your country. YES, *YOUR* COUNTRY. FOR *YOUR* NATION. ONIPA'A. HOLD FAST!"

The crowd proudly roared with deafening applause lasting for several minutes. When the ovation died down all but two of the one hundred torches were extinguished. The final two glowing torches were placed near the statue of the Queen, symbolically illuminating her darkest night.

The crowd then quietly dispersed and went home.

LATER IN 1993, President William Jefferson Clinton visited Hawaii. During a speech on July 11, 1993, on Waikiki Beach, he assured the Hawaiian people, "You will not be forgotten."

ON NOVEMBER 23, 1993, the United States Congress passed, and President Clinton signed into effect United States Public Law 103-150, The Apology Resolution. Section 1, the Acknowledgement and Apology section, states:

Now, therefore, be it

Resolved by the Senate and House of Representatives of the United States of America in Congress assembled,

The Congress
(1) on the occasion of the 100th anniversary of the illegal overthrow of the Kingdom of Hawaii on January 17, 1893, acknowledges the historical significance of this event which resulted in the suppression of the inherent sovereignty of the Native Hawaiian people;
(2) recognizes and commends efforts of reconciliation initiated by the State of Hawaii and the United Church of Christ with Native Hawaiians;
(3) apologizes to Native Hawaiians on behalf of the people of the United States for the overthrow of the Kingdom of Hawaii on January 17, 1893 with the participation of agents and citizens of the United States, and the deprivation of the rights of Native Hawaiians to self-determination;
(4) expresses its commitment to acknowledge the ramifications of the overthrow of the Kingdom of Hawaii, in order to provide a proper foundation for reconciliation between the United States and the Native Hawaiian people; and

(5) urges the President of the United States to also acknowledge the ramifications of the overthrow of the Kingdom of Hawaii and to support reconciliation efforts between the United States and the Native Hawaiian people.

THE NATIVE HAWAIIAN PEOPLE ARE STILL AWAITING THE RECONCILIATION EFFORTS.

THE END

www.ingramcontent.com/pod-product-compliance
Lightning Source LLC
Chambersburg PA
CBHW060949120726
47910CB00002B/559